THE DARKHOUSE

THE DARKHOUSE

BARBARA RADECKI

DCB

The publisher gratefully acknowledges the support of the Canada Council for the Arts
and the Ontario Arts Council for its publishing program. We acknowledge
the financial support of the Government of Canada through the Canada Book Fund (CBF)
for our publishing activities, and the Government of Ontario through the
Ontario Media Development Corporation, an agency of the Ontario Ministry of Culture,
and the Ontario Book Publishing Tax Credit Program.

LIBRARY AND ARCHIVES CANADA CATALOGUING IN PUBLICATION

Radecki, Barbara, author
The darkhouse / Barbara Radecki.

Issued in print and electronic formats.
ISBN 978-1-77086-478-8 (paperback). — ISBN 978-1-77086-483-2 (html)

1. Title.

PS8635.A3365D37 2016   JC813'.6   C2016-904406-8
                                                 C2016-904407-6

United States Library of Congress Control Number: 2016945336

Cover art: Stefanie Ayoub
Interior text design: Tannice Goddard, bookstopress.com

Printed and bound in Canada.
Manufactured by Friesens in Altona, Manitoba, Canada in September, 2016.

This book is printed on 100% post-consumer waste recycled paper.

DANCING CAT BOOKS
An imprint of Cormorant Books Inc.
10 ST. MARY STREET, SUITE 615, TORONTO, ONTARIO, M4Y 1P9
www.dancingcatbooks.com
www.cormorantbooks.com

To my lighthouses
Philippe, Stefanie, Michele

1

Even in the day, the lighthouse light pierces the sky. It finds me at my bedroom window, then flings itself over the ocean. Like it's saying, "Over there, that's the way off the island."

The island is the only place I've ever known. It has a proper name, but everyone just calls it the island, the way you say The Ocean, The World, The Universe. My father hid me here when I was a baby because my mother is crazy. *Crazy, crazy, crazy.* Seagulls in the sky.

He hurt you yesterday. Aidie comes up behind me. She cuddles the stuffed mouse she always carries.

"No, he didn't."

Yes. She points at my wrist. *It still hurts, doesn't it?*

I touch my wrist, smoothing the skin that circles the bones. "Nothing happened." I hide my hand behind my back. "It doesn't hurt."

Aidie taps the nose of her stuffed mouse to my cheek like it's giving me a kiss. It's her favorite toy from when I was little. A ripped-up old thing. A real thing.

The ache of wanting what I can't have throbs like blood.

2

I bundle up against the cold spring wind and climb on my bike.

My father, as always when he's home, is preoccupied in his lab in the backyard. For the first time I notice how small and rundown and ugly the lab is. How it's really just a shed like most people have in their backyards, wood so worn it doesn't have paint left on it, gouges everywhere like a giant wildcat came by and used it as a scratching post to sharpen its nails.

Jonah calls his science "experimental evolution" and his latest experiment the "critical attachment theory." For ten years, he's been working with voles that he collected from around the island. Breeding solitary creatures to pair bond, to rely completely on each other, even to retrieve food as a pair. Ten years of me watching him disappear into his lab to breed and nurture and modify the behavior of tiny rodents. Me modifying too — little girl, older girl, teenager, six, eleven, sixteen. I was never that interesting to him.

I don't give last looks at the house as I pedal away, but feel it at my back, perched in the clearing. A crow on a branch.

The lightkeeper's house has been here for over two hundred years. Built and rebuilt a dozen times for the men who watched over the sea. Two stories, shingled sides, windows mostly shuttered behind someone else's curtains. It can only be reached by a long road from town that runs through a wood so thick the tangled branches press against it like a cage.

Just before Keele's Landing, the road emerges from the wood and opens up onto the Roberts' fields and the whole island spreads out like a map on a table. West Island is the populated side, although people say it's a small population compared to most places: just over a hundred people. East Island is the wild side, nothing on it except Jonah and me, the house we live in, and the lighthouse. When I push my bike down the slope, East Island disappears so smoothly under my wheels it's like the ground is being pulled away.

The island is isolated from the rest of the world, accessible only by ferry and only during the warm months when there's no ice on the strait. It's May now, which means the ferry has started to run again, which means we're only a month or two from the tourists coming.

Jonah doesn't like me talking to the tourists. He says they'll corrupt my way of thinking. I used to talk to them when he wasn't looking or when he was taking the ferry back and forth. But no one warned me that one day I'd hold myself back. That a loneliness would grow around me so powerful it would change who I am. Wanting to be like them, to be like someone, like anyone, and knowing I never will be.

Last summer, a tourist found me sitting on the rocks, sketching in a notepad — a nonsense game I play with myself where I take random words and weave them into drawings. She wasn't much older than me, maybe seventeen or eighteen, and was here with her family. I hid my work from her, but she wasn't looking at me. She'd picked up small flat stones and was trying to skip them across the water.

I imagined what it would be like to be her friend. Both of us teasing each other and laughing like I'd seen her doing with her little brother in front of Peg's Diner. I imagined going to a real school with her. *Hanging out.*

"It's so lonely here," she said after a while.

I flinched, but she didn't notice.

"Only old people," she said. I'd never thought of it before. She was right — everyone on the island is old, except me and Jonah. Retired fishers, farmers, crafters. Any young people — their children — moved away long ago, before I got here. The few shops still left, like the people, are also fading away.

"Pretty soon they'll all be dead," she said. One after the other, her stones skidded on the surface and sank. "What're you going to do? Stay here all alone?" She looked at me, but I couldn't answer.

My life like a katydid: one moment a leaf like any other, the next a predatory insect.

3

I arrive at Peg's Diner. It faces the pier where the MV *Founder's Spirit* is docked. Jonah will arrive soon to take it out. He captains the ferry from the beginning of May until the end of October, four runs a day, one each way in the morning and one each way in the afternoon.

In front of the diner, Peg bangs a doormat against the stoop. Dust spins around her and makes her look like a fairy in a cloud. So delicate and tiny, Peg is the one person on the island I do worry will die.

When she sees me, she drops the mat to wave. I wave back and roll past her to leave my bike near the FoodMart where later I'll pick up groceries for dinner. The FoodMart used to be the island's general store — "a real bustling place," they tell me — but now it's a dull supply depot. A meeting place of goods brought in from the mainland, clean and new during the summer months, then gathering dust over the winter until, one by one, they get bought and taken to our homes. You can make a whole story in your head about the chosen ones, the ones left behind.

"Just getting the place spick and span for tourist season," Peg says when I walk up. Peg's Diner is always perfect as a button, even when there are no tourists. She laces her hands into a bouquet at her waist. "We doing lessons today, dear?"

I've spent almost every day of my life in Peg's Diner, Peg giving me lessons according to Jonah's schedule. Because I'm the only child on the island, there isn't a school. There used to be a schoolhouse that used to be a church, but when the last of the island kids grew up and left, they turned it into a dance hall. No one went to that, either, so now it's boarded up.

Because Jonah is gone so much of each day on the ferry runs, or too busy with his science during the winter months, he asked Peg to teach me. She was required to keep a very strict schedule and teach only courses with factual answers. *Grammar 9:00–10:00 a.m., Math 10:00 a.m.–12:00 p.m., Geography 1:00–2:00 p.m.*

I'm not allowed to read fiction, not allowed to watch TV. Jonah wants my mind diligent and sharp, not dulled by the troubles of imaginary people. He might be alarmed to find so many stories rooted and growing in my head.

I loved learning with Peg. She has an amazing memory and always turned plain facts into adventures and fairy tales. But now she says that, unless I'm interested in medicine, she doesn't have any more to offer me. I wish I were interested in medicine. Or in any of Jonah's hundred books on Darwin or evolution or animal behavior.

Instead, Peg sneaks me musty copies of *Middlemarch*, *Pride and Prejudice*, *Far from the Madding Crowd*, *Moby Dick*, that I read and re-read. Mostly I stare into the sky, up twisting trees, through tumbling fields of hay, out the diner window, across the ocean, and dream of some other life, the one I might've had if things had been different, the one I might have if I were an emperor, an archeologist, a ghost. I love the island and everyone on it, but that doesn't stop me wondering what else is out there. Jonah is right: imagination is distraction.

Peg takes my hand. "C'mon, love, let's have a nice cup of tea." All island problems are solved with a nice cup of tea.

The diner was built a long time ago, during the "busy years." Light shines through the wide windows, even on an overcast day, and reflects off chrome trim and bright turquoise vinyl. When Peg pulls me inside, everyone smiles and waves.

Doris, by the coffeemaker, touches up her lipstick in the back of a spoon. "You look like you could use a nice cup of tea, sweetheart." She blows me a red-rimmed kiss.

Randy tips his cap at me from the grill and keeps scrubbing it for the lunch rush that will come after the truckers arrive from the mainland on the morning ferry and finish their deliveries.

John Woolit waves from one booth, Mr. and Mrs. Roberts from another. They're waiting for the mail to come, for the latest edition newspaper. It's been a long winter without paper news.

Tourists always ask why we don't have computers, Internet, cell service. The islanders answer that our landlines work fine, and if those go down, Mr. O'Reardon has a satellite phone for emergencies. There isn't a house without a shortwave radio. Besides, the telecommunications companies don't consider us worth the expense of their technology. And we say we wouldn't use it anyway.

I can't miss what I never had.

Jonah's van appears on the dock and he parks it and heads to the *Spirit*. There isn't a single vehicle waiting to cross to the mainland this morning. Doris says that the older the islanders get, the less they want to go anywhere. As for me, I'm not allowed to go. Never have been. It's too dangerous when you have a crazy mother on the loose.

A moment later, Hesperos, Jonah's chief mate, ambles up and climbs onto the boat. Even though he's a small man, under five feet, he has the deepest voice of anyone I know. Not a true islander, Hesp spends the winter months on the mainland. I guess he's Jonah's best friend because they spend so much time together on the bridge. I imagine them sharing deep talk as the ferry plows across the ocean, or laughing together at some ridiculous joke, or toasting each other for a job well done. Although there's no sign of that at the end of each workday when they arrive back and go their separate ways.

"We no longer need each other to survive," Jonah says about people. "The tribal bonds have been broken. If we're not diligent, this will be the last genetic marker in human evolution. It means we will die out." That's why he's so fixated on his vole experiment. To prevent us from dying out.

Year after year, he sends his hypothesis to scientific journals. All he wants is to get published. Getting published means he's a real scientist. Respectable. Right. Except the journals keep rejecting him. He doesn't tell me this, but I've seen the letters singe and curl to ash when he burns them in the sink.

I plunk myself into an empty booth by the front window and watch the *Spirit* chug out of the pier and into the sea. Waves crest and froth off the hull. Like it, I start to sail into the distance. Dreaming of other places, other lives. Floating up and away like the burst head of a dandelion.

*B*y the time the *Spirit* returns, I've moved outside to the lower pier. The sun is out and has warmed the day enough to warrant a lazy stretch by the water. I stare into the milky sky. Nothing in it of any significance. How much nothingness can a mind take before it turns into red island rock?

I hardly pay attention as Jonah eases the *Spirit* back home, lulled by its gentle thud against the pier bumpers. The ferry grinds to a stop, and soon after I hear the metal clang of Hesperos coming down the stairs from the bridge. He lowers the ramp that connects the boat to the dock. I count the rumble of four delivery trucks and three cars — fresh supplies from the mainland and a few old friends coming to lend a hand to our lobster catchers.

I don't hear Jonah leaving the bridge. He usually goes back to the house between runs to eat lunch so he can check on his voles and scribble in his journals. I usually stay in Keele's Landing. I prefer Randy's hamburgers or homemade split pea soups or grilled cheeses over our cans of pork and beans or SpaghettiOs.

The *Spirit* pings and purrs into silence. A decent lullaby for an afternoon nap. I blink my eyes closed, half-wondering if the cold air will make me sick like Peg always warns.

But then a different sound alerts me. Like a live wire dropped to my chest, it spins an electrical charge through my whole body.

Jonah says not to believe in premonitions or hunches or omens.

Doris says, "Always trust your instincts." Jonah says there's only one instinct: the instinct to survive.

I sit up to understand it better. It's the echo of footsteps walking the *Spirit* from stern to stem. Not the usual booted clomp of the men I know. The rhythm is lighter, less steady, as if the walker isn't sure where he wants to go.

It can't be a tourist coming to visit. Tourists never visit the island so early in the season when it's still so cold. And they don't come on foot. The harbor on the mainland is said to be far from any town, so people always arrive by car.

Superstition makes me crouch on the ladder connecting the lower pier to ground level. I sneak a peek over the edge, and a shaft of sunlight blinds me. It leaves the impression of a shadowed figure drifting off the boat and onto the road. A long coat skims its legs and flares in a gust of wind. The figure stops to cast a look about the whole of Keele's Landing.

It's a woman. By herself. A woman who doesn't know the island. Who might not know anyone here. Who seems to be looking for something.

5

It used to be that every time a woman came to the island by herself, Aidie would insist she was my mother. I tried to be skeptical when Aidie played her game, but if a woman arrived who had a certain look and was a certain age, the suggestion didn't seem impossible. Maybe my mother had gotten better. Doris talks about how her husband was an alcoholic but kicked the bottle right before he died. And Peg has mentioned how some of her island patients had to overcome "depression" or "hormonal imbalance."

Maybe my mother missed me. Maybe she'd searched the whole country, stopping at nothing, until she found me.

When I was eight, nine, ten, I secretly hoped that she'd show up one day. But there comes a time, as Peg says, when we must accept that the sea is the sea and always will be.

❧

The woman walks toward the FoodMart and slowly scans the surroundings. With the light silhouetting her, I can't see her face or true coloring. After a few minutes, she walks in the other direction, passing the ferry.

Hesperos closes and locks the ramp. He approaches the woman and asks her a question, which I can't hear. She shakes her head, and Hesp smiles and salutes her in a comic way, then ambles off to have lunch with the fishermen.

It's always been Hesp's job to deal with the passengers, and Jonah likes it that way, so there *is* a possibility — if Jonah was distracted or busy — that he never saw the woman boarding or disembarking. Jonah's van still sits by the pier, and I wonder what's delaying him.

The woman walks down the road that leads either to my house or to the rest of the island. I very quickly scramble down the short ladder and back along the lower pier to the escarpment below the FoodMart. When I turn to look again, the woman has arrived at the edge of town. She stops at the split in the road.

One road leads to the rest of the island. The other goes right to my house. She doesn't move for a long time, but stares into the distance.

Jonah always says that with experiments there are results you expect and results you don't expect. In order to eliminate the extraneous, you have to investigate all the data, even the most unlikely. You have to believe it's possible that the impossible has just happened.

~

As I watch her linger, an urge overwhelms me. I want to follow her. To run up and introduce myself. Something I never do. Not anymore. Not since I was ten. But then she turns and heads to Peg's. She opens the door and steps inside. I run as fast as I can toward the diner and have to stop myself from barreling through the door. I pause, take a breath, and walk through it like a regular, unremarkable person.

The woman stands in the middle of the diner while everyone smiles and waves at her. I can tell they're as taken aback as I am.

She's covered in fuzzy brown clothing: a soft brown scarf is wrapped around her neck, a half-tuque of the same material caps the top of her head, brown-red hair curls from underneath it and around her face, a tight long coat — soft and brown as well — swings down her body. She has a mouth that looks like it wants to be kissed and hazel eyes that owl around. Doris would say she looks "fancy," but I think she looks like a jackrabbit pretending the wolves can't see her.

Either way, she's the most beautiful woman I've ever seen.

Doris is the first to say something. Doris is always the first. She pats her bleached-yellow bun and pushes out her giant boobs. "Well, skinamarink, you're our first guest this year!" She calls out to the back, "Randy! Fire up the grill. Our first guest of the season is here!" Doris beams at the woman, her red lipstick already messing up her dentured teeth. "Welcome to the island, honey."

The tourist doesn't say anything, but looks as pale as a breaking wave.

"Well, don't just stand there, come on in!" Doris ushers the woman to the nearest table. Transfixed, the tourist lets herself be moved. "Ooh, aren't you chilled through? A nice hot cup of coffee will do just the trick." Doris knows tourists always prefer coffee. She introduces everyone while she grabs a menu and brings it to the woman. I slip into a back booth where I can watch her without being noticed.

"This here is Peg," Doris says, introducing the last adult. "She owns the diner, and also our only B&B, which is that pretty house over there and a place you're more than welcome to visit." Doris points out the window across the street. Peg's house is the biggest on the island, made of brick and not the usual painted shingles or siding. It has three stories and a front porch. "Peg is also our local nurse, saver of lives and curer of illness."

"That's a bit much, dear," Peg says. "But I'm certainly around for anyone who might get hurt or sick."

On the ground floor of Peg's house, there's an examination room where you might lie as a patient until Peg can decide if your injury or illness is serious enough for Dr. Thomas in Kingsmith.

The tourist's face drains paler. Peg must notice, because she says, "Would you like a visit, dear?"

The woman startles and shakes her head. She pulls off her hat. Static ruffles her brown curls into a matted halo.

"And what's your name, miss?" Doris asks with a raised eyebrow. When the woman doesn't speak, Doris says again louder, "Miss …?"

"Oh." The woman tilts her head. She says, "Luellen."

"Well, hello, Miss Luellen." Doris sets a cup of coffee in front of her — reward for a job well done. Then she points at me. "And I almost forgot to introduce our little doll." She smiles. "Miss Luellen, this is Gemma."

I can't help it; I hold my breath.

"Gemma is our angel," Doris says.

A blush eclipses me so fast I don't have time to look away.

"Your angel?" the woman asks. She looks at me and repeats my name: "Gemma."

Something happens between us. Our eyes connect, and her face softens and I feel myself smile. A true smile, not one conjured to be polite. She sees me. Will she say something that will change my life?

"And where are you from, Miss Luellen?"

Doris's voice breaks the connection between us. The woman looks down at her coat. She begins to unbutton it. "Toronto."

It's like I've run a great distance for no reason except to feel it in my legs. I'm not sure anymore what to do with myself.

"Oh my, Toronto." Doris hates Toronto. Thinks it's too snobbish. She says as if we hadn't heard, "Miss Luellen is from the big city."

"Please, call me Marlie." Marlie doesn't look at us as she fumbles in her bag. "Well, I guess I should …" She pulls out a computer. Many tourists bring computers with them. She sets it on the table in front of her and opens it.

Doris waggles the menu. "We have a lovely breakfast if you want."

"No, I …" Marlie says, blinking. "I should really do some work."

"Oh, so you're here to work?" Across from me, Peg brightens and sits up. "It's a lovely place for it. Very peaceful. Right, Gemma?" I nod, and Peg looks pleased. She leans across the aisle. "Are you a writer then, Marlie?"

Marlie taps at a computer key. "I don't … well, yes, I do use it to write and things like that, but not —"

Peg gives an excited wave. "A writer! How wonderful. What are you working on then?"

Doris nudges Marlie's arm. "Is it like Alistair MacLeod or Lucy Maud Montgomery? There're some wonderful Maritime stories."

Marlie taps a different set of keys. "Well, no, but —" She watches her screen.

"Oh my, this is really, really wonderful," Peg says, eyes shining. "We've had some visiting politicians, a few doctors, many, many teachers. There was a forensic scientist once. And several historians. We've had a few photographers, and a minister who was thinking of settling here back when there was still a church. Mind, we're look-ing over the whole of fifty years now. But never once did we have a writer." She takes a long, appreciative breath.

Doris leans in, also excited but not as much as Peg. "If you want to know anything about the island for your book, just ask me. I'm a, what do you call it, a *wellspring* of island trivia."

Marlie stabs another computer key then slumps back. "You don't have Internet here."

"I can tell you this," Doris says. "There are more widows and widowers on the island than you can shake a stick at. But no mischief, if you know what I mean. We're a loyal bunch." Sometimes Peg has to remind Doris that city folks don't want to hear all our business, but Doris never remembers that part.

"What about cell service?" Marlie says, pulling a phone from her purse. But Doris doesn't hear her, just keeps sharing island trivia. Marlie puts the phone to her ear. I notice tears start to puddle along her lower lids. "No service." She wipes her eyes and drops her phone back into her purse. "I'm sorry to bother you," she says, interrupting

Doris. "But I was looking for the famous lighthouse? It's up on some cliffs?" She casts her gaze from one adult to the other, not to me. "I had a link with the directions," she says. "But now it's lost in the, um, ether."

"Oh, well," Peg says, instantly excited, "as long as you're here to see the lighthouse, you should ask Jonah to give you a tour."

With a start I remember Jonah. I notice that his van is still parked on the road by the ferry.

"That's okay," Marlie says, shaking her head. "I don't need a tour." A small tremor vibrates over her hands, and she cups one over the other. "I just want to know where the lighthouse is."

"It has some very interesting history," Peg says. "You may well want to include a few lighthouse facts in that book of yours. And please don't worry — a tour is not a bother at all. In fact, Jonah is *supposed* to give tours."

"Jonah?" the woman repeats his name the way she repeated mine.

"Jonah Hubb — that's Gemma's father — he brought you over on the ferry. He and Gemma live up by the lighthouse." Marlie's eyes drift over to me again. As she looks at me, my breath flutters and doesn't work as it should.

I'm Jonah's daughter. Peg has revealed the truth.

"You live by the lighthouse?" Marlie asks me.

I can hardly speak. "I do."

Marlie's mouth rounds into a silent *O*, then she says, "That must be great."

"It is," I say.

"Jonah is a lovely man," Peg adds. "Especially when you consider all he's been through." She gets the far-off, pitying look she always gets when she remembers my history.

Doris says, "Jonah's not one to get caught up in all our island shenanigans. No, he keeps his head down, works hard, doesn't speak an unnecessary word, doesn't poke his nose in. If he gives you the gears, you can't take it hard. It's who he is."

"Although," Peg says, "he has quite a lot to say about animal behavior and such. What is it again? Oh yes — *ethology*."

"Yeah," Doris says, rolling her eyes. "Or all that stuff about genes and evolution. Don't get him started." She swats a hand through the air.

"When Jonah first came to the island way back," Peg explains to Marlie, "he was our lightkeeper. But then we lost Henry Jasper, captain of our little ferry, a few years later and Jonah took over. We're lucky to have him. He's something of a genius, I guess."

"And easy on the eyes to boot, eh?" Doris says, slapping the table in front of Marlie and adding a wink. "Now, doesn't an island tour sound like a wonderful plan?"

I picture myself showing Marlie around: *This is my house, this is the yard, this is the Rock Pit, this is the best place to look at the stars, this is the lighthouse, this was my favorite tree for climbing when I was a child.*

I check on her, but she only stares into her cup of coffee.

"You heading back on the afternoon ferry?" Doris asks her. "Last run leaves at two, for your information." She nudges Marlie's arm again. "But you know, you don't *have* to leave. In fact, we hope you'll consider staying on for a few days. There's a whole world of wonderful waiting for you here."

Peg's eyes mist up. "That's right. No one ever visits in the spring. It would be just lovely to have you stay for a bit."

Marlie looks up from her cup. Her eyes are clouded, her expression vague.

I surprise myself by saying loud enough for everyone to hear, "I'd be happy to show you the lighthouse. I know it really well."

Marlie composes a smile. "No, that's okay," she says.

I turn my face to the window. Is it possible to be hot and cold at the same time?

"You're very sweet to offer, though," she says. "Thank you."

A queasy feeling grinds up my stomach. It pleats upwards, through my chest and into my throat. It makes me lightheaded and dizzy. If I faint, Peg will make a fuss.

I push myself up from the table. I'm not the least bit certain I can stay upright. "Excuse me," I say. Without looking at anyone, I creep to the back of the diner and into the ladies' room.

≈

In the bathroom, I stare at my reflection and take deliberate breaths until the sound of my breathing is the only thing I hear.

I recognize the urge inside me that grasps for something I can't have. That invents a hope that will crush me when it doesn't happen. It's a terrible urge, and it makes me terribly angry at myself.

Wouldn't it be nice if mirrors were like the mirrors in stories? The ones that tell you what you want to hear no matter the consequences.

≈

When I go back into the diner, everyone is bustling about and chatting too quickly, and Doris is wiping a table. "She didn't even eat," Doris says, not to me but to everyone. "Typical. City girls never eat."

The booth where Marlie was sitting is empty.

I go up to Peg. "Where is she?"

Peg pats my cheek. "Oh, my darling dear, turns out our new friend wanted to take a tour of the island by herself."

"By herself?" I say, embarrassed, defeated.

"Yes," Peg says, smiling. "Isn't that lovely?"

"Mark my words," Doris says, putting on a fresh pot of coffee, "that was definitely the face of heartbreak."

I run without thinking to get my bike from where I left it, hobbled on the ground near the FoodMart. I wheel it down the road through Keele's Landing.

Like a dropped length of string, the road home weaves into the distance away from me. Through fields, into woods.

I don't see Marlie anywhere along it, but I'm certain she's heading toward the house. It was the lighthouse she asked about. *The famous lighthouse on some cliffs.*

I jump on my bike and push for momentum, but in my sloppy hurry, my pant leg gets caught in the chain. It tumbles me and the bike into a pile on the gravel.

I don't even stop to think about bruises or cuts, but gather myself as quickly as I can. Crouched over the tangle, I yank my pants out of the chain. Again, too messy, too fast, and the chain pops off the sprocket.

I rage with frustration. An easy fix, but a taker of time. I crouch to sort the mechanism, seething, swearing under my breath.

"Gemma." My name from a voice I don't recognize. "Are you all right?"

Before I can check who it is, I feel the pressure of a hand on my bent back. Someone I don't know touching me. I jerk my head up.

It's Mr. O'Reardon's son, Scotty. After five years away, he's come back to the island.

⤳

I was eleven the last time I saw Scotty. He seemed old to me then, a man just turned twenty, someone who could make everyone laugh, and mostly me. He was the last of the islanders' children, and so spent his school years on the mainland, living with an aunt. He came back when his mother got sick, and stayed a while after she died. When he was sixteen, he left school for work, but for the next four years he came back to the island every spring and stayed for a month to keep his father company and help with chores — the only grown child who returned on a regular basis. I rejoiced in his company. He had the energy and humor to play with me. Tag or hide-and-seek or running piggyback.

Scotty's mother had been sick for a long time before she died. When she left the island for the last time, I was five and didn't understand what was happening. I watched from the windows of Peg's Diner as Scotty cradled her arm and escorted her from their house to his father's pickup. She leaned against him. Fallen branches from a tree. I mostly remember Scotty's wincing face, tears not there but drawn in deep lines around his eyes and mouth. He seemed so grown-up, but now I understand he was just a boy. Soon after, Scotty and his father and a bunch of islanders went to her funeral in Fredericton. Because I'm not allowed to leave the island, Jonah and I didn't go.

Scotty and his father taught Jonah how to climb at the Rock Pit. As the lightkeeper, Jonah has to maintain the lighthouse, and that means once a year he has to rappel down its sides and repair any crumbling stone, then whitewash it to keep it pretty for tourists. When I was ten, Scotty taught me how to rock climb too, and it was amazing. We climbed the Rock Pit every day of his visit that summer, and then every day of his visit — his last visit — the summer after that. He taught me how to set the rope and lock off the gear, to rappel down, and to climb up by balancing on jutting ledges, reaching my fingers for holds that he called "crimps" and "jugs," "pockets" and "slopers." Even to fly up using mechanical ascenders, pulling myself up and up. I felt like a spider spinning its web. Like I could stick to the sky.

Scotty married a woman in Fredericton five years ago who never wanted to come to the island. Everyone whispered that twenty was too young for a boy to marry, and Doris still grumbles as she serves pie in the diner that you can't trust a woman who won't know her husband's home. That's how I forgot about Scotty: a strong, joking, helpful young man who'd gone his own way.

≫

Scotty has one hand on my back and stands so close to me that puffs of air from his mouth mix with my own. His red hair shines golden in the hazy light, his eyes are as blue as compressed ice, his chest and arms fill out his winter coat.

Breath clots in my throat. All the atoms in the universe seem to gather around us, as if the only reason the island was created was to hold Scotty on this day.

There's no imagined world more distracting than the one that has someone to love in it. Someone holding you and whispering your name.

"You need to sit down, kiddo?" he says. "Can I help you to Peg's?"

I shake my head. "No, I'm fine, thanks. Just winded is all." I sound like a child, like a baby, and feel terribly stupid.

To forget myself, I bend over my bike. Scotty scrambles to help me, but I don't let him. I release tension from the rear derailleur and pull the drooping chain back onto the teeth of the sprocket, then lift the back wheel off the ground and crank the pedal until the chain catches again.

"Hey," he says, "you got the hang of that pretty good."

Trying not to grin like a fool, I get up and lean my bike against my hip. I hide my greasy hands behind my back, secretly wiping them on my jeans. "It's good to see you, Scotty. It's been a long time."

He chews his lip and contemplates the ocean. "Yeah, too long."

"When did you get in?" I don't know how I could have missed his arrival, having sat in Peg's Diner every day this week.

"Yesterday. On the afternoon run."

Yesterday afternoon Phyllis Ketchum had asked me to help fill shelves at the FoodMart. Every spring I help her unpack, and even though it's always the same cans of tomatoes and stew and boxes of pop and chocolate, it's like those things from far-off places bring along some exotic information. My way of being a tourist.

"Right." I nod at him like everything makes sense now. "I was doing inventory."

"Right." He nods back at me. Then he does something that he used to do every time he saw me: he tousles my hair. Back then, it was another thing he did that made me laugh. Today it melts me so quickly, I actually sink a bit, and his fingers get tangled in the long strands. I have to pretend I'm ducking away from him. Have to pretend I don't like it.

"Sorry, Gemma. I guess you're not a kid anymore. How old are you now?"

"Sixteen. Well, sixteen next month." I try a smile. Sincere. Grown-up.

"Almost sixteen. Wow. Pretty soon you'll be older than me." He gives a kind of snorting laugh. The idea that we'll soon be adults together also fills me with unspent laughter.

I say, sincere, normal, "So, did you bring your wife home to meet us?"

Scotty contemplates the ocean again. After a swallow, he says, "We split up."

"Oh," I say. Barely a word, mostly a sound.

"It's all right. It wasn't working." He shrugs. "Can't say I didn't give it my all."

Then he smiles. Light from inside him shines on me like a light-house, and everything brooding in me floods out. My body, my head, everything illuminates.

I say, not smiling but feeling it swell, "I'm sorry, Scotty."

"It's all right, kiddo." He gives another laugh. "It's all good."

"Well, that's good." I give a laugh too, and it comes out like his. He checks the ground and bobs his head. Like him, I bob my head.

He aims his thumb behind him. "I gotta help Dad with the lobster traps." He bobs his head again, then says, "Hey, you wanna come? Yours are always the luckiest traps of the season." He says it with a wink, like we both know it's a worn-out line meant for a kid.

And I want to go with him. But there's a woman on her way to the lighthouse, and I still don't know who she is or what she wants. I say, "I have to go home for a bit. Rain check?"

He leans back on his heels and gives me his best smile, which is any of them. "For sure. Cool. See you later then."

"Cool. See you later," I say, my own smile heating me up. Scotty wheels around and walks down the road the other way, and I watch him, hoping he'll glance back one more time.

Jonah says in science a coincidence is called "a law of the universe." Without the coincidence of everything being in exactly the right place in the right way, the universe would be dead.

I pedal up the road as fast as I can. Even though I should still have the advantage, the woman is nowhere in sight.

A picture of a mother I imagined long ago comes to me unbidden. Her eyes lighting up when she sees me. Her pulling my head in to lean against her neck. A mother who is always there.

Marlie Luellen could be just another tourist. Someone who doesn't belong here. Someone irrelevant to me. Or she could be here for some terrible reason, some wretched purpose hidden under softness and jackrabbit eyes. Or it could be something else. Something she's uncertain about, something that scares her. She looked scared. And that's something I can understand.

I urge my bike on, not worried the way I should be, but hopeful the way I want to be. The hill pushes at my feet. The faster I try to go, the slower I move.

&

No one is at the house. Wind swishes through the dead grasses and scratches bare branches against the windows. I see it the way Marlie might see it: an old forgotten place, windows like black holes, peeling paint, no garden. Nowhere a person would want to live.

I drop my bike at the front stoop and notice my greasy hands and smeared jeans. I check with the house, weighing if I should use up more minutes to change and get clean.

A tapping sound comes from my bedroom window, and I look up. Aidie is tapping the glass, her finger like a bird or insect, fluttering to get out. Her face barely clears the ledge, but I can see she's tied up with excitement.

Already I feel better.

In the beginning when my reflection was the only child I knew, Aidie looked exactly like me. She dressed like me and grew like I did. When I realized she wasn't real and never would be, she didn't disappear, but only stopped growing with me. I expected that one day she wouldn't be there anymore when I looked for her, but that's not what happened. Instead she became more vivid: her hair grew darker and is sometimes braided, one tooth developed a tiny chip, and a dot of a mole showed up under her right eye.

I tried to forget her as I got older, but I never could. I tried to banish her, but she wouldn't go. No matter what I do or how I think, she never goes away. Sometimes I wonder if I'm as crazy as my mother.

I decide to make myself presentable and so I run inside. Upstairs in the bathroom, I wash my hands and face. Dirt trickles off me into the basin and slithers down the drain.

You have to find her. Aidie's voice echoes from my bedroom. *The tourist, I mean.*

"I know that's who you mean, Aidie." I scrub the wetness off with a towel and rearrange my scattered hair. "I'm going to look for her right now."

I run across the hall and into my room, pulling off my dirty clothes. Aidie sits cross-legged on her pillow in my closet, cuddling her little stuffed mouse. I reach over her to grab my favorite pink hooded sweatshirt and white jeans.

Hesperos does all my shopping for me on the mainland — Jonah gives him money, and Hesp goes to the mall in Moncton and stocks me up for the year. Doris says that because Hesp has so many girl-friends to help him, he has very good taste. She also says that he sure knows how to stretch a dollar. The white jeans are too precious to wear any old day, so I usually save them for special occasions like someone's birthday.

She came for you, Aidie says.

"Don't get ahead of yourself. It's never what we think."

She could be someone's mother.

"Her name is Marlie Luellen. And she has much darker hair than me, and darker eyes." I raise an eyebrow at Aidie. "So I think you're stretching it a bit."

Not everyone looks like their mothers.

I've flipped through photo albums in people's houses, I've seen their pictures, and Aidie is right — not every kid looks like their parents. It's just that I've pictured my mother for so long, her blue eyes and fine brown hair have become real to me. They can't just change on a whim.

Jonah once said she was very beautiful.

Jonah doesn't talk about my mother because the memories make him sick and angry. But there are some things he *must* tell, mostly because the islanders made him tell it. So my story about my mother is strung together with small, rare knots of facts and long garlands of fantasy.

The facts are these: when I was very young, just a few months old, my mother kicked Jonah out and told him to go away. Broken-hearted and thinking he had no choice, he left my mother and me behind. But he had it in his mind that if he found a wonderful, quiet place, he'd convince her to join him, and we'd begin a new life and she'd be happy again. He found the island and befriended the islanders and got the lightkeeper's job. Everyone said that because

Jonah kept so much to himself in those early days, only coming to Keele's Landing to stock up on provisions, they didn't know he'd left behind a troubled marriage. But eight months later, in late June after my first birthday, just when the weather was getting really warm, he became "despondent" is the word Peg uses. He came into town every day for a week, but he wouldn't talk to anyone. Then one day he took his van, drove onto the ferry that Henry Jasper was still captaining, and went across to the mainland. Didn't tell anyone where he was going or why.

A week later, he came back with me. Everyone was so smitten with me, so excited, they hardly got the details of what had happened. But Jonah told them bits and pieces. How when my mother had kicked him out the year before, he hadn't known how sick she was. That all through the winter, stuck on the island, he'd had a bad feeling. That it was killing him to know I was alone and vulnerable with her. That he'd made a terrible mistake and wasn't sure how to fix it. So in June he went back to convince my mother to come to the island, and she went into the most terrible rage he'd ever seen. She confessed to awful crimes, broke meaningful things, and scratched and clawed at him until he thought he was going to die. Peg said he was so shaken he wouldn't even let her dress his wounds. He said my mother had threatened to kill him, threatened to kill me, and then she ran away. Ran away before my father could get her "the help she needed." He was scared for our lives and left the town they'd lived in to bring me here. To safety. To quiet. To goodness.

She is beautiful and bright, Aidie sings. *She has terrible rages. She ran away. No one knows what she might do.*

The words always repeat in my mind, like a song no one wants to sing. *Beautiful, terrible, away, beautiful, terrible, away.*

I crouch in front of Aidie. "What if she wants to hurt me?"

What if she's better now and wants to protect you?

"By keeping away?"

Yes. Until she knows it's safe.

"You're a shameless dreamer."

What if she's ready to take you off the island and bring you to the world?

"No, it's impossible. Besides, her name is wrong."

Aidie takes my hands. *Maybe she lied about her name.*

"Why would she lie?"

To keep you safe until she knows what to do.

"No, Aidie. Remember what Jonah says."

That scientists have to watch they don't bend their data to fit their hypothesis.

"Exactly. We don't know anything about her."

Aidie smiles. *We will.* She closes her eyes and her cheeks bud pink. *She's so beautiful.*

"Okay, enough," I say, readying myself to go.

Aidie reaches up and smoothes the hair around my face. *I want you to look as beautiful as her.*

"We both know that's impossible."

I can try.

"Yes." The silky feel of her hands soothes me. I stand up and do a quick twirl. "How do I look?"

Like someone's daughter.

I giggle like a much younger person. Like having a mother should turn me into a child.

Aidie sticks out her hand. *I have something for her.* Inside the curl of her fingers is her stuffed mouse.

We promised to always tell the truth. "That's pretty ugly, Aidie."

Aidie pushes the mouse toward me. *It doesn't matter.*

I don't want to, but I take the mouse and stuff it in my pocket. "You're very sweet, Aidie."

Aidie lays her head on the pillow and smiles at me. Her smile gives me the courage to carry on.

8

*M*arlie Luellen's eyes are closed and she lies on the ground under the lighthouse at the very edge of the cliff. If she rolls over, she'll go right over the edge. The lighthouse looks like a sentry keeping guard, or a bystander waiting for the worst to happen.

I run to her and crouch on the ground and touch her cheek. Her face is so peaceful, her body so relaxed, she could be taking a nap. But she's out cold.

As carefully as I can, I wrestle my hands under her arms. She moans, and her head lolls. I tighten my grip and yank on her arms, but her body weighs more than I expect. The very real possibility of dropping her, her body plummeting to the sea and splintering on the jagged rocks, is too terrible to imagine and gives me strength I don't have.

I manage to drag her several feet away from the edge, from the lighthouse. Red dust eddies around us and makes me want to cough.

I settle her in a safe spot and cradle her head in my lap. The sun disappears behind some clouds, and I feel the cold for the first time. It's very quiet. The wind has died, the birds have stopped calling, and the waves at the bottom of the cliffs sound very distant.

Strands of hair stick to Marlie's eyelashes and inside her mouth. I stroke it off her face and into order. It's as thick and soft as a blanket.

What feels like hours later — because it's so quiet and cold — Marlie flutters her eyes open. They don't see me, but search the haze of clouds and stop on the smothered sun. After a few moments, her lips part and she sucks in some air.

Words are in her mouth: I can see her tongue curving to form them. "I wanted to see the light," she finally says. "Just once." Her voice is faint, and I nod to encourage her. "You never loved me."

"I do." It comes out before I can think.

"I didn't see it. I never see it." Water gathers on her bottom eyelids. "I'm so stupid."

"No, you're not."

"I wanted the baby."

The word shocks me. I say, as loudly as I dare, "The baby?"

Marlie's eyes shift over, and she seems to properly see me for the first time. Her pupils contract into tiny spots, each like a period at the end of a sentence. When she speaks again, her voice is changed. "Where am I?"

I smile at her like a mother. "With me. Gemma."

"Gemma?"

"I think you fainted."

"Fainted?" She closes her eyes, and a tear drops off her lashes. She says, "I guess I missed."

"Do you remember me?"

She nods. "From the diner."

"Yes, from the diner."

"Gemma." She looks directly at me and reaches her hand up. Very slowly, she strokes the whole length of my hair. Goosebumps pop up all over my skin. She says, "I'm sorry."

Everything inside me goes still. "It's okay."

Her eyebrows rut together and she closes her eyes.

I long to lay my head beside hers and also close my eyes. "We should go back to the house," I say, trying to remember what Peg would prescribe for a faint. "You should rest where it's warm."

Marlie's fear rises and wanes and rises again, and I can scent it like an animal. "No," she says. "I really need to go back."

"In case it makes a difference," I offer, "my father isn't home."

Marlie winces.

"You need to get warm," I say, desperate to keep her.

After a long moment, she says, "Okay."

&

I drop her purse on the living room couch — it's as heavy as a baby — and head straight for the kitchen. Marlie follows slowly behind me. My white jeans and pink sweatshirt are ruined — dusted with red from crouching on the ground by the lighthouse.

I run water from the tap into a glass. "Faints are usually from bad blood flow or dehydration," I say, imitating Peg. "You should drink some water." I hand her the glass.

"Thank you." She gulps the water down quickly. The soft glugging of her pharynx defeats me. It's such an intimate sound, like I'm seeing a very private side of her and I should feel humble and unworthy.

"You have a nice house," she says.

"Do I?" I wish I spent more time cleaning this morning.

"Yes. It's very cozy."

I repeat the word in my head: *cozy*. Almost another language. "Thank you."

She wipes her mouth. "Are you alone?"

I wonder if she thinks I'm too young to be alone. There's never been a stranger to the island who's guessed my real age, always putting me younger by enough years to make me and everyone laugh. If someone was looking for a girl almost sixteen, they might not see her.

"Jonah," I say, "my dad, he runs the ferry between the island and the mainland. When you were on it, you might have seen him?"

I wait for her reaction, but she doesn't have one.

She doesn't take her eyes off me. "And your mom?"

The question nooses my neck. If, like Aidie says, she's protecting me by pretending she doesn't know me, how long will it be before she reveals herself? And if she's here to do wrong, if everything she's doing now is a show, how long will it be before she attacks?

"I don't have a mom."

"I'm so sorry."

"She's not dead." The thought alarms me. The only possibility I never considered. "She ran off when I was a baby."

"Oh." She tries to hold my gaze, but I look away. I guess it's better to have a crazy mom than a dead one.

I check the time. The afternoon ferry would have left already. I say, "You missed the last ferry of the day."

She doesn't respond, but stares into the empty bottom of her glass. I take it from her and put it into the sink. I lean against the counter to steady myself. With my back to her, I say, "I don't know what you want to do, but visitors always stay at Peg's B&B."

"Oh," she says, and then she says it again, "Oh, oh," and her eyes roll back and her knees bend in. I run to catch her, and she leans on me as I lead her to the couch in the living room. Her body is cool and soft, but very heavy. "Sorry, Gemma," she says again. "I'm so sorry."

"You need to rest." I guide her down to the couch and pick up her feet one by one and pull off her soft suede boots and ease her legs onto the couch so she can lie down, then I cover her with the wool blanket.

She watches me closely and says, "Thank you." She shivers and burrows under the blanket. Her eyes blink closed.

"I'll make you some tea," I say, going back to the kitchen. "That'll warm you."

But when I come back with the tea, Marlie is asleep.

I remember Aidie's old mouse and pull it from my pocket. I lay it on the blanket close to Marlie's head where I can feel the warm certainty of her breath.

≫

I flick on the light in the back room. Stacks of cardboard boxes line the walls. I'm not supposed to look into the boxes, but over the years, I've opened each one. They're filled with ordinary things, items we've both grown out of, like textbooks Jonah never reads or toys and clothes I'm too old for.

Every now and then, I'll pull something out of a box and turn it over, hoping that maybe it holds some news of my mother. Nothing is quite as lonely as squeezing an old wooden spoon and expecting words to fly out that will answer your questions.

In the furthest corner is a box I find curious. *Experiment LLB* is written in black marker on one corner. The only thing in it is a baby blanket, bright green and printed with cartoon frogs, with a clear plastic soother clipped to one edge. I always wonder why the blanket isn't with all my other baby things but in this one box, on its own. I've never heard Jonah speak of Experiment LLB, and never seen it written on any of his many journals. Not that this means anything, but it's a question.

For the millionth time, I open the box and hold the green frog blanket to my chest. Even though I'm too old to take comfort, it feels lovely to rub the soft cotton on my chin.

After a long while, I repack it and put the box exactly where it's supposed to be. Next I do what I came here to do: check the old fold-out cot. Despite its faded mattress, it might be comfortable enough for Marlie.

I go to the laundry closet in the kitchen and get clean sheets, a blanket, and a pillow, and bring them all to the back room. I release the bars of the cot and open it, then dress it as nicely as I can.

Soon Jonah will come home. No matter how determined he is, Jonah won't be able to hide if he knows Marlie. He's been thinking about my mother for as long as I have.

When the cot is made as inviting as I can make it, I join Marlie in the living room. She's still asleep on the couch, so I sit in the chair opposite her. After a while, I drink her tea.

9

The sound of the front door jangling wakes me. When I open my eyes, Jonah is staring at us. Actually, he's staring at Marlie, who's still asleep. I jolt to immediate attention.

Jonah walks deeper into the room so he can stare more closely at her. "What's this?" he says, as much to himself as anyone.

Anxiety and eagerness muffle my voice. "She came on the morning ferry. You didn't see her?"

Jonah looks only at her. "The *Spirit* was acting up. I was busy."

I repeat what I'm supposed to know. "This is Marlie Luellen." But it's a test for Jonah. "She's a writer from Toronto." I watch carefully for his reactions — his cheek movements, his pupil dilations, his color.

Nothing changes.

"Oh," I say to no one. My breath unwinds like a dropped spool of thread.

Maybe I have to face the truth: that Marlie is just another tourist. A meaningless occurrence.

Jonah says, not looking at me, "A writer from Toronto? What kind of writer?"

"I don't know."

"A reporter?"

"No." Disappointment holds me under water and I don't have the power to fight it. "Invented stories. Like Lucy Maud Montgomery."

Jonah thinks for another minute then says, "And she's taking a nap?"

"She's sleeping off a faint."

"A faint?"

"I found her by the lighthouse. Out cold. I brought her here when she came to, and she fell asleep."

"I see." He looks at me for the first time. "Okay. Well, Peg should have her under observation —"

A high *ting* interrupts him.

Reflex makes Jonah jerk his head around and check the kitchen. I follow his gaze and see the red glow of the alert light blinking above the back door.

Before he started his vole experiment, Jonah insulated the back-yard lab and had it temperature controlled. He installed the alert system and set up timed feedings and reward devices and cameras that monitor the voles twenty-four hours a day. If anything goes wrong or changes, the alert lets him know. If it goes off when he's not home, it tings once a minute until he comes back. I'm not allowed to turn it off, but have to note the time it started and mark it down. I'm not allowed to go into the lab because "human contact must be kept to a minimum or the whole experiment is ruined."

Jonah checks through the window. "Storm's started."

And then I remember down at the lighthouse when I was holding Marlie: muddy clouds rolling in, a change in the wind, a sudden hush. Now I hear the tick-tick against the windowpane. "Ice storm?"

Jonah looks back at Marlie. "I don't have time for this." His eyes narrow, annoyed. "I have to check the lab."

"It's okay," I say. "I think she just needs to rest."

Jonah leans first on one leg then the other. "Ferry is likely stranded tomorrow."

"We have plenty of food and an extra room."

"Extra room? Where?"

I lead the way to the back room and flick on the overhead light.

With the cot all dressed up in clean sheets and a blanket, it looks comfortable. Pushed off his guard, Jonah crosses his arms. I cross mine too. "Marlie needs help," I say. "We have to help her."

"No," he says. "I don't think that's a good idea."

The alert gives another *ting*. Jonah glances at the blinking light. The voles are always more important.

I never tell Jonah what to do; life is easier when I go along with whatever he wants. But he will say himself that being curious about a thing — a cocoon, say — means you're there to see it split and offer its butterfly. I want to rip the cocoon open. The thought terrifies me.

"We need to help her," I say.

"I have to go," Jonah says.

The couch creaks, and we both turn to look. Deep in sleep, Marlie has rolled onto her side. She pulls the blanket under her chin and Aidie's stuffed mouse springs from the woolen folds onto the floor. I take a breath and don't look at it. But Jonah has seen it. He steps forward and picks it up. I want to lunge in and protect the mouse, but I fight to still my legs. If I touch it, it will only make things worse.

"We have no choice," I say, staring at Aidie's mouse hard enough to boil milk.

"No, Gemma," Jonah says, "we have a choice in everything we do."

Ting. The red light blinks.

"You don't think about both sides."

"What do you mean, both sides?"

"The two sides of a story. You don't think about the other side."

"There aren't two sides in this. There's only what's right."

"No," I say, biting down. "There's only what's right for *you*. You only ever think of *you*."

Jonah looks at me, shocked. "This isn't about *me*."

"Yes, it is. It's always about you."

Ting.

"Gemma, that's enough." The mouse twists between Jonah's hands, its plump body thinned to starving, its tail binding the blood in his finger.

"No, it *isn't* enough." I lower my voice. "You need to do the right thing. The thing that's *not* best for you. The thing that will help someone else. For once, that's what you need to do."

Outrage distorts Jonah's face and his hands strain apart. He starts to say something. "If you don't stop —" But the tail of Aidie's mouse rips off and droops in his hand. In his other hand, the body with its pointed ears and stitched whiskers is reduced to nothing.

In an instant, all fierceness inside me is gone.

Jonah looks at the broken mouse like it's garbage, then throws the pieces to the floor. His face smooths into a smile. "Gemma," he says with deliberate calm, "you've lived your whole life on the island. You've never been exposed to the negative aspects of the real world."

I can't look at him, but only stare at the dismembered parts of Aidie's mouse.

"And that's because I protect you," he says. "We live here because I do what's best for you."

I don't let any expression come over my face.

"Do you think," he says, "I would have lived *here*, like *this*, if I were choosing for myself?"

Ting.

"This is for *you*," he says. "Do you see that?" I stare at my feet. "*Do you?*"

Jonah lets the room go quiet while I consider my mistake. Tonic immobility. When an animal under threat pretends to be dead.

But I rouse myself. Just a little. "We can't just throw her into the storm. What if she gets hurt? Or dies? Everyone will blame us." I pause. "Everyone will blame *you*."

Jonah looks from me to Marlie. The muscles in his face twitch and contract.

Ting.

Ice rain beats at every window.

After a moment, Jonah approaches Marlie. I don't say another word but watch him carefully. He ignores me and bends over and lifts Marlie from the couch. She flops a bit in his arms, and he has to secure her against his chest. He carries her to the cot in the back room and, very carefully, lays her down. He arranges the sheet and blanket over her and tucks all her parts underneath. When he's sure she's fully asleep, he wheels around, heads into the kitchen, and goes through the back door to his lab.

Nothing — not rage, not the weather, not any person on earth — can stop Jonah from protecting his experiment. A moment later the alert light goes black and the *ting* stops.

I check on Marlie. Her sleeping face is so trusting. She's just an ordinary girl.

I shut the door, pick up Aidie's mouse, and go upstairs to my room.

10

It doesn't take me long to reattach the tail. I sew a hundred stitches so it will never come off again. I nuzzle its mousey nose and apologize for Jonah's behavior and my sharp needle. Its threaded eyes stare back at me, unblinking.

When I'm done, I return it — rattier than ever — to Aidie's pillow in the closet. Before Aidie can say anything, I turn away and fall into bed. Outside, the night goes dark and ice rain continues to tap hard against the house.

Aidie taps my shoulder. I ignore her.

Jonah is lonely.

"No, he isn't." Aidie knows as well as I do that Jonah has his voles.

That's why he's so angry. That's why he squeezed your wrist. You remind him that he can't love your mother.

"I'm tired, Aidie." I close my eyes. "Go to bed."

That's what keeps him here. Loneliness. He doesn't know anything else.

"That's ridiculous. You don't know what you're talking about."

You're lonely too. That's why you love Scotty. You want him to touch you.

"Stop!" There's real violence in my voice. I yank the blanket over my head to contain it. But, like lightning, Scotty appears. I see him and feel him as surely as I've ever known any person alive. He stares into my eyes with his blue-blue gaze. His hands reach for me and soothe my skin. The realness of it is tormenting. It makes me reach my body up against the sheets. Against my will.

I toss the blankets off. Aidie is still there, waiting.

Why is Marlie here? she says. *Who is she?*

"I don't know."

You have to find out.

"I don't care who she is. She's nobody."

Maybe she's running away from something.

Frustration clings to me. It fuels my anger. "Maybe she's here to ruin everything."

Don't say that, Gemma. She's just sad.

"How do you know? When you're sad you can't fall asleep, and she's out cold."

Maybe she's enchanted.

"By what?" I say, irritated. "Her sadness?"

Yes.

"I want to go to sleep now, Aidie. Please, just go to bed."

Marlie knows what it's like off the island. Better than anyone. She can help you.

I bolt up. "You don't think he'd let me leave if I could, Aidie? We don't stay here because Jonah is *lonely*. We stay because," and I separate my words as if she were slow, "I'm — not — safe — off — the — island." Aidie and I lock eyes. I say, "Do you think I want to be here forever? Talking to you about the same stupid, unreal things? You're the reason I'm crazy!"

The color drains from Aidie's face. She looks like an old black-and-white photo.

I roll away from her and make my back a solid wall. I can hear the feeble wheeze of her breath marking time. *In and out, in and out.*

It doesn't take long before I hear the hollow, creaking steps of her walking back to the closet and then the rustle of her crouching on the pillow and cuddling her mouse.

Before she closes the door between us, she says, *I'm sorry.*

Even though the door is closed I say, "I'm sorry too."

❧

In the morning, I can tell by the opaque glaze over my bedroom window that the house is frozen solid with us inside it. Everything will be iced over from the storm: the doors, the windows, the flues. If the rain has stopped — and the quietness makes me think it has — then we'll have to jimmy our way out.

I get dressed in warm working clothes and go downstairs to make breakfast. The door to the back room where Marlie is sleeping is still shut.

Jonah is in the kitchen on the phone. The long yellowed cord is a necklace from the phone down to the floor and back up to his ear. Before I come in, he says goodbye and hangs up.

"Is the ferry grounded then?" I say, squeezing past him to the fridge.

"It is," Jonah says. He picks up his cup of tea and looks out the back window, which is crystalled over with ice.

"How are the voles?"

"Fine." He stares through the crystals toward their home.

I pull out the cast iron pan, put it over the burner, and oil it. While the pan heats up, I put three slices of bread into the toaster and crack six eggs into a bowl. We usually just have toast or cereal for breakfast, but eggs will get us ready for a day of heavy work.

Jonah clears his throat. "Did she say why she came to the island?"

I look at him carefully. "No."

He puts a finger to the windowpane. "Her driver's license confirms her hometown." I glance back into the living room — Marlie's purse is still on the couch where I left it. I know it's not right for Jonah to be rifling through her things. "Turns out," he says, "she didn't give you her real name."

"Her real name?" I say.

"She gave you her first name, but her last name is Frasier, not Luellen."

As I fork the eggs into a froth, I remember Marlie lying by the lighthouse, a tear rolling from her eye, her words about someone who never loved her.

When they come here, tourists don't need to pretend they're someone else. They never bring sorrow with them. They're too busy taking pictures and being delighted with the scenery.

"Maybe," I say, testing Aidie's theory, "she's running away from something."

He taps at the ice-glazed window. "Like what, for example?"

"Like maybe she's running away from something sad," I say. Then I repeat Doris's word. "Heartbreak."

"*Heartbreak*?" Jonah says the word like he genuinely doesn't understand it. "Interesting." He stares at the whipped eggs in the bowl and says again, "Interesting."

The oil in the pan sizzles, and I splash the eggs in and scrape them into a scramble. Jonah stares at my work for long enough that the eggs set and the toast pops up. "All right, then," he finally says. He goes to the back room door and gives it a polite knock. "Good morning, Miss Luellen." I notice he uses her alias. "Breakfast is ready."

I divide the eggs and toast onto three plates. Jonah grabs a plate and leans against the counter to eat because there are only two chairs in the kitchen. Before long we hear movement from the back room, the creaking of the cot, footsteps shuffling along the floor. The door opens, but very slowly, as if she's afraid to come out. Marlie's hair, rumpled and fuzzy, is the first thing we see as her head ducks around the corner. Her eyes peer out, wide and sleepy all at once. She looks first at me and then at Jonah. Then she comes out from behind the door.

I prepare myself. Here they are: Jonah and Marlie, face to face. Aidie's words come back to me: *Jonah is lonely*. Is it possible?

Marlie blinks at him and says, "I'm so sorry."

"We're iced in at the moment," Jonah says. "After breakfast, Gemma and I have to work on getting us out and doing a storm cleanup. If the weather holds, we can have Peg take a look at you afterward. Otherwise, you're welcome to stay."

"I don't know what to say," Marlie says. She gives herself a cautious hug. "Thank you."

I put her plate down on the table and wait for her to sit. She comes slowly toward the kitchen chair. "Smells delicious."

To encourage her, I lift my fork to my mouth, as if I'm showing a small child how to eat.

"I'd be happy to help," Marlie says as she sits. Jonah and I look at her. "With the storm cleanup?"

"Of course, Miss Luellen. We'd appreciate it."

"Please," she says, lifting a forkful of eggs to her mouth, "call me Marlie."

11

Jonah has to jimmy open every door, and when we finally get outside it's obvious how much work there is to do to clean the grounds. Branches have fallen everywhere, broken from the weight of rain falling and freezing. Ice encases every surface and each branch like a clear chrysalis, the imprisoned things still visible and preserved inside. But already it's warmer, and soon the ice will melt.

I give Marlie an old parka of Jonah's and a pair of his galoshes so she doesn't ruin her city clothes — her flowing brown wool coat, her elegant, precise brown boots.

We get the wheelbarrow from the side of Jonah's lab and walk the perimeter of the yard, clearing branches and debris and piling them into the bucket to dump somewhere out of the way.

We free up the road to Keele's Landing until the road clears the woods, then we clean the path that leads to the Rock Pit.

The Rock Pit is a huge geographical basin with ancient red rocks bundled over the ground like bunches of grapes in a bowl. On the north side of the basin, the pit ends in a long wall of high, red-rocked cliffs. On top of the cliffs, a plateau of grassy dirt stretches into another thick wood.

The cliffs of the Rock Pit are where Mr. O'Reardon taught Jonah to rock climb and where Scotty taught me. As my eyes wander over the familiar rocks and cliffs, I remember Scotty helping me with my climbing gear, tousling my hair before slipping a helmet onto my head, securing a harness around my waist and making me giggle, clipping me to hooks, teaching me how to knot the rope that slides up and down the surface. Keeping me safe. Which was a nice feeling.

Marlie startles me by exclaiming that the Rock Pit is the most beautiful place she's ever seen. It calls to mind that the world is very massive, with so many places and parts that will forever be unknown to me. Only real because in theory I know they're there. If Marlie says the Rock Pit is the most beautiful, there is some consolation in that.

❧

By the time we've cleared the path to the lighthouse, warmer air has already started to melt the ice. Everything is streaming and wet, birthed anew.

We get to the clearing at the end of the path and Marlie stops and stares up the full length of the lighthouse, entranced by it.

The lighthouse is so tall that when I was young I used to think it was for getting in and out of the sky. I was sure that one day I'd be able to climb to the top of the tower and jump to the nearest cloud, then hop from cloud to cloud until I'd explored the entire planet. When I learned the lighthouse didn't touch the sky at all, it didn't feel like the truth.

In bed at night, its steady blinking reaches me through my bedroom window and I let myself get hypnotized by it. The rhythm is exactly the same as when you cry yourself to sleep: *waa, breath, waa, breath.*

"This is where I found you," I say to Marlie.

"Yes, I know." Her smile wavers. "Guess the view got the better of me," she says. Then she turns abruptly to Jonah. "I was told you give tours?"

Jonah starts. "Of the lighthouse?"

"They told me in town it's something you do. That I should take a tour."

"For your stories," Jonah says, observing her. "Yes, I heard you're a writer."

She doesn't look up but eyes a crumpled blade of grass on the ground. I remember the diner and her uncomfortable squirming when Peg called her a writer. There's also the proven fact that she invented a last name for us. *Who is she?* Aidie had asked. *And why is she here?*

Jonah sets the wheelbarrow down and pulls off his gloves. "I'd be happy to give you a tour."

"You don't have to," Marlie says, flustered. "I just heard it's something you do. It sounded interesting."

"You're right. It's very interesting." Jonah searches for the key on his fob. In front of the tourists, Jonah always makes a big show of "unlocking" the door to the lighthouse. The truth is, he always keeps it open, but because it's supposed to be locked, he pretends that it is. The only thing Jonah really cares about securing is his lab behind our house.

He pushes open the door and starts his lecture — how the British overpowered the Mi'kmaq and Acadians three hundred years ago and brought in militia and built the lighthouse. How they abandoned the area later and left behind settlers. How the lighthouse is controlled now by the Canadian Coast Guard from far away and has an uncertain future because of lack of funding.

Inside the lighthouse it's dark and close, like being caught in a pipe. Jonah flips a switch and fluorescents flicker along the walls. It's all very plain, walls painted white like the outside, rows of wooden ladders and platforms leading up to the top. On the ground floor, some shelves are loaded with flashlights, rain gear, old compasses, maps, and all the equipment for rock climbing: harnesses and ropes, rappel devices, quick draws, ascenders, and wonky hinged hooks called carabiners. Beside the shelves, there are a few framed copies of the original lighthouse designs. Marlie studies the drawings while Jonah lectures. Even though I know the drawings by heart, I study them too.

When Jonah finishes his rehearsed speech, he leans back to look up the ladders. "Why don't we go up?" he says.

Marlie hesitates. "It's so high."

"It's very safe," he says.

"All right," she says in a small voice. "Sure."

Jonah wipes his palms on his pants and leads us to the ladders. I invite Marlie to climb up between us. As we climb, my face is so close to her feet that I can watch the faded rubber of Jonah's old galoshes split in skinny lines. I want to move my hand from the wooden rails of the ladder and touch one of her legs. Maybe the back of her knee. But I don't.

We climb in silence. At the top, the ladder disappears through a small opening. When we climb through it and out onto the landing, Marlie looks around the Watch Room. It's surrounded on all sides by tall windows, and Jonah tells her that in the old days the Watch Room was for the keeper to check the condition of the seas or to watch for the approach of warships. Above the Watch Room, there's one more ladder that ends at a trap door that leads outside. The Gallery and Lantern Room make up the platform and housing for the giant beam of light.

At first when Jonah opens the door, the wind almost slaps it down on top of him. But he pushes his shoulder hard against it and forces it open. He climbs through to the top and secures the panel, then checks for ice. When he's certain the surface is clear, he holds down his hand for Marlie to take. After a second's hesitation, she does. I wonder what it feels like, their two hands touching.

When I climb through, the hot eye of the lighthouse glares at me, then blinks away. Like Marlie, I gasp as the wind hits me in the mouth. The sea rolls green in the gloom far below, as odd as a different planet, and hazed clouds press close enough to almost swaddle us. The wind shoves me against the rails, and it starts to feel good. Like I could die but won't.

Jonah surprises me by leaning toward Marlie and asking, "So, where did you come from?"

"Toronto," she says, her curls tumbling around her head.

"Yes," Jonah says. His hands grip the rail in front of him, and I wonder at the whiteness of his knuckles. I take a step back so I can observe them from a better angle. Jonah says, "You have family there?"

"Just my mother." Marlie grips the rail too. "But she's very sick," she says. "I had to put her in facilitated care."

"I'm sorry to hear that."

"MS," she says. "She's had it for years, but she keeps getting worse. I took care of her for a while, but it's too much for one person now."

"That's very hard." Jonah shakes his head. "You have no one to help you? No husband, no partner?"

"Not right now. Not anymore."

"I understand." Jonah moves the hand closest to Marlie from the rail into the air behind her back. He stares closely at her. "So, why are you here?"

Furtively, I lean in.

"For my writing?" Marlie says, uncertain, unclear.

The wind gusts in louder, and Jonah leans closer to Marlie. "But if the story is fiction, why the island?" His hand is hovering behind the small of her back, so close it almost touches her. "What's so important about the island?"

Marlie shivers. She searches for the starting point of the wind. "To be honest," she says, and I lean even closer, "I was interested in the cliffs."

"You were interested in the cliffs?" Jonah's hovering hand lands on her back. Something about it disturbs me. Jonah never touches people.

"I think we should go," I say.

But they don't hear me. Instead Jonah's hand flexes as a slight amount of pressure is applied to Marlie's back. "Why?"

Marlie presses against the rail. "They're so ..." She seems to allow his push. Seems to want it. "High."

"Yes. They're unusually high for this part of the country." Jonah holds Marlie against the rails and watches her for five seconds, ten. But she doesn't say another word, only grips the rails and trembles slightly.

Jonah's profile grabs my attention. It's set in its usual way: brow pinched with observation, broody eyes peering out, jaw gritted tight. But the thing that startles me is that it's such a *nice* face. Nicely shaped lips around even, white teeth, eyes that trick you into thinking they're every color, wavy, dark hair. And he has a strong body too, tall and lean.

He's like the Russian nesting dolls that Peg collects. A matryoshka. Different for whoever he's with and whatever is being discussed. And maybe that's why people don't understand him. But he's a handsome man. And maybe that's why people trust him.

After a few minutes of no one talking or looking at each other, Jonah's hand drops to his side and his face relaxes. "The Milky Way," he says in a gentle voice, "has over two hundred billion stars in it. Did you know that?"

Marlie seems surprised. "Sure, I guess."

"I'm being impertinent. Of course you do. But, in reality, we have no intuition for that kind of number. Evolution hasn't equipped us to understand it."

Marlie looks at him.

"If you take the finest pen," he says, "and make the tiniest mark on a piece of paper to indicate a star location, the next tiny pen mark would have to be sixty kilometers away. That's how far apart the stars are. And there are over two hundred *billion* of them."

I remind myself that Jonah doesn't take note of the constellations or know any of the stories behind them.

"The space, the numbers involved, people refuse to accept that we can't understand them. Because we feel very ..." The wind lashes his hair around his face, but he doesn't seem to notice. "We have tremendous egos with respect to one organ." He taps his temple. "The brain. And the only reason I understand it is because I build a crutch — a prosthetic, if you will — by creating this model to help illustrate what it means."

For the first time, he truly looks at Marlie, and she smiles as if she recognizes him from a long time ago.

"I'm sorry," he says. "We don't get a lot of visitors up here. Small talk isn't ... well ... it isn't really my ..."

"No," she says. "It's fascinating."

A secret gaze connects them. It thrills and confuses me. Jonah smiles back at her and his face transforms. They look beautiful together.

He says something else, but the wind roars up and drowns him out. Marlie mimes that she can't hear, so he leans in so close that the tip of his nose disappears inside her curls.

Jonah *is* lonely. He must be. I don't know how I never noticed it before.

When he pulls his face away from her ear, they both turn to leave. He must have decided that it's too dangerous for us to stay.

꙳

As soon as we get in the house, Jonah throws more logs onto the living room fire, rearranging and prodding them with the poker. Even though the house is colder than usual, it feels warm to come inside.

Marlie pulls off the old coat and galoshes of Jonah's and puts them where they belong. She helps me take off my coat and hangs it neatly on a hook.

"Would it be okay," she says cautiously, "if I took a bath?"

Jonah keeps his face turned toward the fire, but I can see his ears flush red.

Marlie steps toward him. "If I have to stay until morning, I should probably clean up." She laughs a little. "Is that okay?"

Jonah says to the fire as he stokes it, "Yes, of course."

"Great," she says.

Jonah closes the fireplace screen and turns to me, his color back to normal. "Gemma, go upstairs and run Miss Luellen a bath. And find some clean clothes for her to change into. Yours will be too small, so it'll have to be something of mine."

Marlie says, "Thank you so much."

I blush for some unknown reason and run upstairs without looking at either of them.

⤳

Marlie disappears inside the bathroom before the bathtub has even partly filled. I find Jonah in the kitchen setting the kettle on the stove and lighting the burner. He seems to be planning something — it's clear in the way he starts and stops moving.

I perch myself on the edge of a chair, hoping he'll forget I'm there and talk out loud to himself. Something he often does. It's one way I get to know what's deeply on his mind. But he surprises me by turning and looking directly at me.

"I think you should go to the FoodMart and get us something nice for dinner."

I reel at the unexpected proposal. "Like what?"

"I think I'll make a roast. With potatoes, yes. And boiled carrots."

The surprise of it is almost enough to make me sick. Jonah has never cooked a proper meal in my life. "Okay," I say, as if a menu is something we plan every day. I pull money from the grocery jar and get myself ready to go out again.

"And take your time coming home," he says as I head to the door. I look back at him. "Yes," he says, turning to grab the kettle that has just started to whistle. "I think Miss Luellen needs a proper rest."

12

*C*hoosing the potatoes and carrots at the FoodMart is easy. The roast is not so clear. It's the first time they've had fresh meat in stock since before the winter. Every piece looks bright and bloody. I've only ever known Randy at the diner to cook meat, and that's usually hamburgers charred black. Despite my worry, I pick a wrapped hunk and take everything up to the cash. I pretend to be too busy counting money to properly answer Phyllis Ketchum about how everyone is doing up at the house.

Outside, I gather my bike and ride it around the back of Peg's Diner so none of the other islanders can stop me and ask questions. Safely out of sight, I straddle to a stop. Jonah said I should take my time. Riding into town and buying groceries went faster than it ever has before. Time always plays tricks on you when you least want it to.

"Hey, kiddo," a playful voice calls out to me.

My head snaps in his direction like a bird heeding a call. Scotty O'Reardon is standing in his yard, Mr. O'Reardon's binocular case in one hand, the other hand flopped on the head of Mr. O'Reardon's dog, Biscuit. Scotty is even more dazzling than I remember, than I dreamed in my bed.

Biscuit bounds up to me, his tail wagging his entire body. I can't help smiling as he slobbers all over my hand and then rears back on his hind legs to slobber all over my face. I give him a hug and order him to settle down.

"What're you up to?" Scotty says, a heartbreakingly tilted grin on his face.

I push the bag of groceries deep into my bike basket. "Nothing."

"Well, Mitch Follows just called. Says one of the buoys from the south side of Crescent Bay isn't there anymore. I told my dad I'd check it out, set a new one. Want to come along?"

I glance toward the road leading back to my house. If I could choose any way to take my time getting home, I would choose Scotty.

"Yes," I say, "I want to come." I climb off my bike and push it along after him.

∻

Scotty reaches his hand out and helps me climb onto the boat. Something I've never needed before, but take anyway. It's such a handsome hand, not gnarled like the men on the island but strong and assured. Last night's dream comes back to haunt me, that very hand touching me, and I have to hide my face from him. My skin is so hot, I wonder if he can feel it.

After I stuff the grocery bag with the roast and vegetables into the hull, Scotty offers me a life jacket. I notice there's a tiny ball of white thread caught in the stubble on his chin, and I have an overpowering urge to reach up and brush it off. But I know I can't touch him. I busy myself putting on the life jacket instead.

My heart thunders wildly. *Boom-boom, boom-boom.* Like a kid jumping on a floor.

"You okay?" Scotty asks. He unmoors the boat and drops the rope at my feet.

I swallow and nod. "Yup. Perfectly perfect."

"Good to hear." And we float away from the dock.

I wish so much that I could be my older self. Wear her clothes and speak with her voice. I want my hands to have her sure fingers and maybe nails painted red. I wish I could wear jewelry, maybe like

Marlie, silver chains and transparent colored stones dangling into the dip between my collarbones. Could have hips that push back and forth when I walk. I'm still so miniature, baby nails at the ends of my fingers, ribs poking through my T-shirts. I want another me to be here in front of Scotty now. I want him to see her.

Scotty starts the motor. The engine is very loud and makes it almost impossible for us to talk. I sit on the bench and bundle up, putting my gloves back on and pulling the hood of my parka over my tuque. Today the water is very flat and the boat makes the only waves. Sparks of light flare off each crest.

Standing behind me like a protective wall, Scotty navigates the coast, avoiding the rocks on the shoal. Biscuit looks like he's going to barf. I pat his head and he gives me his drooly paw to hold and I stroke the thin tendons around his nails.

It doesn't take long for us to take the boat from Keele's Landing to Crescent Bay, maybe ten minutes. As we get closer, the lighthouse appears on the cliffs. It looks a bit like it's getting ready to jump but can't make up its mind.

Scotty steers around the shoal and, sure enough, one buoy is gone while the other bobs lazily on the other side of the cove. Scotty cuts the engine and drops anchor. He pulls the binoculars from his bag and spreads his feet for balance. We rock gently as he scans the horizon, turning in a circle to inspect the ocean in every direction. He says to himself, "Strange. That buoy just up and disappeared."

I say, "Can I look?"

"Sure thing. Let me know if you find anything." He passes me the binoculars and bends over to grab the buoy he brought along to replace the missing one. He tethers and weights it and secures the lines.

I aim the binoculars toward the shallows along the cliff under the lighthouse where most days the waves crash hard enough to break things, but today they lap and loll. If I find the missing buoy, it could be like a present from me to Scotty. I hear myself say, "Please please please," out loud, and it's so humiliating, I bite my tongue.

Just as I'm about to give up, something flashes in the middle of the cliff. I aim the binoculars toward it. It takes a while before I track it, but then I do: on the sheer side of the rock face, several feet below the lighthouse and above the sea, a human head is pushing its way out of the rock.

It's so impossible, I shake myself and refocus the binocular lens and aim it carefully at the cliffside below the lighthouse. And there it is again: a whole person climbing out of a crevice in the rock.

As I ease my breath so I can focus without trembling, it becomes clear — even though his features look as small as a doll's — that the person pulling out of the crevice is Jonah. And that the crevice isn't a natural phenomenon at all, but a perfectly square window. The kind of stone window you might see in a textbook about medieval castles.

Jonah continues to pull himself out then up the face of the cliff, and then I realize he's tethered in the climbing gear. When he passes higher, a large dead ball of weed flaps over the window and closes it off like a thick, wooly curtain.

He inches himself up the cliffside until he arrives at the top, where he pulls himself over to the foot of the lighthouse. He catches his breath, then collects the rope and bundles it around his arm. He brings all the gear to the lighthouse and goes inside, then comes back out a moment later empty-handed.

Before he turns to walk up the path to our house, he takes a moment to check the sea. I start back, wondering if he can see me. But his expression is as even as the tide.

After he's gone, I scan the cliffside. Everything is usual, like nothing at all has happened. My hands start to shake, and I drop the binoculars to my side.

"Okay, kiddo," Scotty says loudly behind me, making me jump. "All set over here."

I turn around and see the new buoy bobbing in the water like the old one.

Something like an egg is in my throat. If I swallow I will crack it.

"What's wrong, Gemma?"

Consequences flip though my mind — consequences to Jonah, to me. Jonah values his privacy. He demands it. He won't want me blurting out what he's clearly trying to hide.

Still I say — and my voice is so far away it might be another's — "Did you ever hear of any structures around the lighthouse?"

"Other than your own house, no."

"Or in the rock under it?"

"A structure under the lighthouse? In the rock? No, that's impossible." Scotty chuckles. "But *there's* a plan. Coolest man-cave ever. Escape everything that wants to bleed you dry, and only come out when you're ready to face the world." He gives another chuckle. "Why?"

My voice shakes as I speak. "Because I think I saw something."

"Yeah? Like what?"

"Like a window in the rock."

"No way, man. Your imagination is playing tricks. Living on the island your whole life'll do that to a person." He grins like it's a joke. When I don't respond, he extends his hand. "Let me look."

I pass him the binoculars, and he puts them to his eyes and scans the cliffs.

"Do you see the big clump of weed?" I say.

"Yeah, sure. About twenty feet down from the lighthouse."

"The hole is behind that."

Scotty keeps the binoculars steady on the same spot for a long time. "Sorry, kiddo," he says after a while. "Don't see it at all." He pulls the binoculars away and looks at me. "I've never heard anyone mention anything being in the rock. And our family's lived here a few hundred years. Are you sure?"

Because I can't stop shaking, I sit down on the center bench and hold my hands together. Biscuit puts his drooling face on my knees.

"I'm sure," I say. "Jonah was coming out of it."

A betrayal. My first.

"Like, coming out of a *hole* in the rock?" Scotty says.

"Using the climbing gear and coming out of a hole cut like a window."

Scotty stares at the area again, swaying slightly with the boat. "Huh," he says. "Maybe he found something."

"Yeah, maybe."

"You should ask him."

I blink against a refraction of light. I always wanted a real friend. Someone I could tell my version of events. The islanders so often talk over you in a rush not to forget what they're going to say. Or are too busy listening to the chatter in their own minds. But Scotty is different. Scotty has always been different.

"I don't think that'll work," I say. "I used to ask him all the time if we could find my mom."

"And what happened?"

"He didn't like it."

"Yeah ... I guess I kinda figured that." Scotty looks at me for almost as long as he searched the cliff for the window, then he looks away and says, "Remember when you were little and I'd come back to visit and we used to hang out at the Rock Pit?"

I'll never forget it. "Yeah."

"Well, I used to have this crazy idea and it wouldn't let go." He shakes his head as if the idea is still there, rattling around. "Those were the days when I was sure I could save the world. I just wanted to help you."

He wanted to help me. A terrifying amount of love swells my heart.

"I got this idea that we should know where your mom was. She was supposed to be dangerous, right? I just wanted to know for sure that she wasn't going to show up one day with, I don't know, a shotgun or something. Or, it coulda gone the other way too, right? A lot of time had passed. Maybe she …" He stops and grips his hands together.

"Maybe she got better?" I say. Scotty is the only one who thinks the way I do.

"Exactly."

He doesn't continue, but cracks his knuckles. I say, "Did you do something?"

"I needed more information," he says. "I asked around. You know, stuff like, 'Did Jonah ever mention anything else about his wife?'"

"And did he?"

"Took a while, but Peg remembered something. When Jonah first came here with you — you remember those stories, right? We used to talk about it sometimes? How your mother kicked him out and he came here, but he got stuck on the island because of the ferry not running in the winter? How he started freaking out about you being alone with her — I'm sorry, Gemma, is this too much?"

I shake my head, anxious to know how the story ends.

"And he went back to check on things, and she flipped out and ran away? And he brought you here?"

I nod.

"Okay, so anyway, when he came back with you and everyone was asking him what happened, well, Peg told me that he was super-agitated about the whole thing, and there was this one time —" He stops and checks with me. I give a breathless nod. "— one time where it spilled out. He said her name."

"Her name?"

"It slipped out, is the feeling Peg got. But he said it." He looks at me. "You wanna know? Because I can stop. This whole thing might be way outta line." He shrugs. "Or maybe, screw it, maybe you should know. Maybe it's about frickin' time."

"Yes, it's time."

"Shannon," he says. "Her name is Shannon."

The name draws a picture of a mother I used to imagine. The one whose arm I could lean against, whose hand would stroke my head, whose eyes would see me. "What happened then?"

"So," Scotty goes on, "now I had something to work with. I went to the mainland and searched online. Googled her, the whole bit. Shannon Hubb — it's not the most usual name. But I couldn't find her. There was nothing."

I look down. Scotty keeps going. "Then later — you know that national parks gig I got after I left the island?" I nod without looking at him. "Well, it takes our crew all over the Maritimes. Everywhere we went, I'd ask people if they knew Shannon Hubb. Those coastal towns are small, right? Not much bigger than here. But no one had ever heard of her. Not just that she had a family and had run off, but nothing about anyone named Hubb."

I want it to make sense, but it's so mixed up I can't understand it. Like seeing and not recognizing your own hand.

"Gemma," Scotty says carefully, "if she doesn't want to be found — or," he adds more carefully, "if no one wants you to find her — as harsh as this sounds — you might have to give her up."

I remember that Scotty also had to give up his mother.

He puts his hand on my shoulder. My heart beats inches away.

"I'm sorry, Gemma," he says. "You okay?" I nod. "Anyway, point is, if you wanna ask Jonah about a hole in the cliffs, I think you should ask him. And if you don't, I will."

He makes it sound easy. But already the idea of asking Jonah *anything* pulls me away from daydreams about my mother and into nauseating impossibility. Like Doris says, "Sometimes we don't want to know what we want to know."

I busy myself with the binoculars, grabbing them from the bench, pushing them into the case, putting the case in Scotty's pack. Scotty starts the motor, and I turn my back on him as he steers us out. Biscuit tries to give me his paw. When I don't take it, he lays it on my boot.

13

Jonah's roast turns out well. We eat in the living room around the coffee table because there isn't enough room for all three of us in the kitchen. With lit candles placed here and there and a fire blazing in the fireplace, the house almost looks romantic.

Once or twice, in a surge of nerve, I start to ask Jonah the question about the hole in the cliff, but the necessary words won't come out. More than that, I want to ask him about my mother, who is more real to me now that she has a name. *Shannon.* And that question doesn't come either.

Apprehension upends my stomach, and I can only pick at my food and pretend to enjoy it. Marlie, on the other hand, eats everything and gives profuse compliments and thanks. Jonah lights up whenever she speaks. He basks. "You're welcome," he says. "You're very welcome."

Marlie tells us a bit of what it's like to live in a city. Jonah asks her if she's ever troubled by the "disassociation of society." She says she's never thought about it, but that it's "ironic" he brought it up. When he asks why it's ironic, she gives the faintest shrug and lowers her lashes.

He tells her his ideas on Darwinism. "Darwin said — and I'm paraphrasing here — in the distant future, man will be a far more perfect creature than he is now." Marlie listens with interest. "But we have to do our part. Because we're at a dangerous precipice, you see. We don't rely on each other to survive anymore." He adds for emphasis, "The tribe is *dead*."

After dinner, Marlie pulls out her phone and takes pictures of us with it, then shows us the images on the screen. The oddness of how we look makes us laugh, even me, despite my uncertainties.

It used to be that Jonah didn't allow anyone to take pictures of me. Even so, Peg and Doris have a full album of them. The first photo is from not long after I arrived on the island, after Jonah went back to save me from my mother. I'm just over a year old with a chubby, smiling baby face, with red gums and tiny square teeth, with wisps of hair sticking up. Apparently Jonah fussed a lot about people taking photos, so everyone assured him they wouldn't do it anymore. Peg's photo taking became "our little secret."

There are pages and pages in the album of me growing up: Peg and Doris adoring me, sometimes Jake and Finey Roberts or Hesperos or Randy playing with me, sometimes even Scotty when he was home for a visit, and my birthday celebrations with the islanders surrounding me. The album stops when I'm five because Peg's camera — which was very big and strange looking — broke and she never got it fixed.

But today Jonah doesn't seem to mind that Marlie is taking photos. Maybe he's forgotten why it once seemed so important. When I examine the images in Marlie's phone, I notice I'm not a child stuck in the past anymore — and I'm also not the face I see in the mirror every day combing knots from my hair and brushing my teeth. I'm a funny thing with a skinny face and bluer eyes than I thought. It reminds me of the old snapshots of Peg or Doris from their "heyday," as they call it, and how they don't look anything like they do today, as if it's two different people.

I study the photos of Jonah and search for hints of myself — in his eyes, the color of his hair, the angles that draw his chin and cheeks — but I don't see any.

"Who do I look like?" I want to ask him. "You or Shannon?" I want to see his reaction when I say her name. But I don't have the nerve. Not yet.

※

We all go to bed early, and I leave my curtains open so I can watch the stars. Aidie climbs under the blankets with me and takes hold of my hand. I'm relieved and thankful to have her. I dabble my fingers over hers, which are so light I hardly feel them.

Shannon is a nice name.

I smile despite myself.

It sounds like a person who can get better.

"You can't tell that by a person's name, Aidie."

Marlie will be your friend and she'll help you leave the island so you can find her.

Aidie never worries about what other people want. She's like a fairy who turns everything she sees into candy, then keeps it all for herself.

"Maybe I don't want to leave."

That's because of Scotty.

"No." I flick her thigh. "Shut your mouth."

She giggles, and that makes me giggle too.

Marlie and Jonah will fall in love, and Jonah will feel safe, and we'll get off the island. We'll find your mother and she'll be happy and you'll have a normal life. Wouldn't that be wonderful?

"You're crazy," I say, teasing.

Why can't we hope for something nice?

"Oh, Aidie." I snuggle against her. "I wish I could dream like you."

You just have to imagine it, she says, nuzzling back.

I check through the window. The night sky is clear now. A long time ago, I used to wish upon stars. Then I found books on Jonah's shelves that described the planets and solar systems and how the constellations were named for gods and goddesses. It felt good to study. Something I could explain to Jonah if he cared to listen.

"Look over there," I say to Aidie. I draw my finger over the points of light. "Those stars make up Virgo. Virgo is hard to see without lines connecting the lights, but she has an arm up over there and a fat bum sticking out over there." Aidie claps her hand over her mouth and giggles again. "No, listen. Virgo is for women, the life-givers. But she's also Persephone. Persephone was stolen by Hades and was taken to live with him in the underworld. Persephone's mother never gave up looking for her. But when she finally found her daughter, she had to make a deal with Hades. That they would share her. So for half the year Persephone stays in the underworld, and in spring she comes back here. It sounds terrible, but it's supposed to be the seasons. Or the cycle of life."

So Persephone agrees to live with Hades?

"I guess so."

So she's always sad, either living with him or waiting to go back?

"I never thought about that. The books don't say." I put my cheek against hers. "Don't think about it if it makes you feel bad. Look," I point. "Virgo is watching over us right now. If you want, you can wish upon her star."

I will, Aidie says. And she closes her eyes and her lips move as she makes her wish.

14

The next morning, the weather is clear enough for the ferry to run. Jonah surprises me by suggesting Marlie stay on for a few more days so she can rest and recover, and Marlie surprises me by saying she'd love to. She says she'll use the extra time on the island to pay us back for our kindness.

Marlie says she wants to cook dinner for us and prepare some casseroles for the freezer, so Jonah offers to drive into town and back before the morning ferry run so he can stock us up from the FoodMart. He says he'll go alone so we're not "subjected to the prying curiosity of the islanders." I picture Peg and Doris with their hearts full of questions.

After Jonah comes back with the groceries and then leaves again for work, Marlie and I organize ingredients. Slowly, I begin to feel more comfortable around her, more myself. It's an odd feeling, and I try not to be too suspicious of it.

She shows me how to make casseroles with fresh vegetables and beans and herbs, with fresh chicken and beef, so Jonah and I can take them out of the freezer anytime we want. I taste the cooked dishes before we freeze them and tell her how delicious they are. We put one pan in the oven to eat when Jonah comes home for lunch.

When we finish cleaning up, Marlie looks around the kitchen. Her drifting gaze lands on me and I wait for her to speak, but she just lingers on me, on different parts of the kitchen, on our heating lunch. A tenderness comes into her eyes and her eyes begin to well. I want to say something of comfort, but I can't think of anything. She turns abruptly and excuses herself to go to the bathroom. Confused and curious, I follow upstairs and wait for her in my bedroom. Aidie only peeks out of the closet once, and that's to put her finger to her lips and encourage me to hush.

After a long while of quiet, Jonah comes home. He calls hello and no one answers. I wait for Marlie to respond or come out, but it's only quiet behind the bathroom door. Eventually, I go downstairs to see what Jonah has to say.

I find him standing at the counter, his back to me, working on something with intense concentration. Before I get all the way into the kitchen, something about his meticulous movements makes me stop and hide myself behind the wall.

Peering carefully around the corner, I watch Jonah push a little pill from a blister pack into a bowl and then grind the pill with a pestle. He seems to be conscious of going fast. Or of not being caught. He checks the fineness of the powder and then carefully tips it into a glass. Then he pours water over the powder and stirs it, checking the bottom for residue. When he's satisfied, he places the glass on the kitchen table.

I press myself against the wall and wait to see his next move, but he just cleans up his utensils, sits down at the kitchen table, and protects the glass between his hands. Because his back is to me, I creep partway up and then run back down the stairs, pretending I was upstairs all along. I pretend to be surprised to see him, but he doesn't acknowledge me. I sit at the kitchen table across from him and wait for him to drink the water, but he doesn't do that either. He just sits like a rock in the chair, staring at the glass.

When Marlie finally joins us, the hair around her face is damp as if she recently splashed water on it. She looks tired, and maybe a little as if she's been crying.

Jonah lights up when he sees her. He lifts the glass and passes it to her. "I thought you looked a little pale this morning," he says. "So I got this for you from the health food store in Kingsmith." Kingsmith is the closest town to the mainland ferry docks. But I never knew Jonah to be interested in health food stores. Or to notice people looking pale. He says to Marlie, "It's supposed to be very beneficial."

"That's so considerate," Marlie says, smiling. "Thank you." She tastes the water, and Jonah smiles as he watches her. She gulps some more and wipes her mouth. "Bitter."

"That's health food for you," he says.

She circles the glass. "The whole thing?"

"The whole thing." He smiles an odd and unnatural smile.

A bad feeling lights up in the pit of my stomach. I don't say a word as Marlie nods and drinks the rest.

❧

After Jonah leaves for the afternoon run Marlie asks me if we can explore outside. She says the day is so beautiful, it might be nice to take advantage. I agree, and we get dressed in our coats and boots.

Only now do I notice how really warm it is out. I usually love the smell of spring coming, mossy and fresh, making me want to inhale forever.

Marlie asks if she can use our wheelbarrow, and I take her to where it leans against Jonah's lab. I consider telling her about the voles in their enclosures living their ordered lives just on the other side of the walls, but then I wonder if Marlie would consider it cruel. For the first time, it occurs to me that maybe it is. So I say nothing and just follow as she takes hold of the wheelbarrow and pushes it down the path to the Rock Pit.

"What are we doing?" I ask.

"I have this random idea," she says, gaining confidence. "Is it bad if I move a few rocks from the Rock Pit to the lighthouse clearing?"

"I don't think so. I mean, I think it's okay."

She smiles again and pushes on. At the Pit, she begins to inspect rocks. She picks one, a round ball-ish rock, and rolls it to the edge of the path. She looks around again, finds another one, and rolls it into the path too. I ask if she wants help, and she says I should roll the rocks into the wheelbarrow, so I tip the wheelbarrow and push them in, one by one. They're heavy, but the round shape makes them easy to propel. Marlie arrives with another rock and then another, and I heave those into the wheelbarrow too. Breathing heavily but energized by the warm day, we push the wheelbarrow up the path toward the house and then down the path toward the lighthouse.

Near the lighthouse, Marlie stops and examines the clearing. She walks around, standing first here and then there, inspecting the ground and the views. I don't interrupt because I can see purpose in her movements. While she muses, I make my way to the cliff edge where Jonah climbed up yesterday.

Curiosity compels me to hold on to the lighthouse and lean over the edge. Right under the lip of the rock is an anchor Jonah must have set up for quick and easy descents: a short sling hooked off two bolts, with two carabiners knotted in the center. A thick electrical cable is clamped beside it, running from the lighthouse, then down to the large clump of weed and then through it. A few climbing bolts are lodged in the rock alongside the cable.

From this angle, I can't see the square opening that Jonah crawled from, but I know it's there. Far below the weed, waves crash up the base of the cliffs, and they are reminders of danger.

"Gemma, not so close to the edge!" Marlie's call startles me and pulls me back. "You scared me," she says, her hand clasping her stomach. She motions me over, and I push the wheelbarrow to her so we can tip it and roll the four rocks onto the grass. Working carefully, she rolls one to mark each compass point: south, west, north, east.

The window in the cliffside reminds me of an old mole hole I found a long time ago on the far side of the lighthouse and turned into a secret-keeper. I covered the hole with a square of moss and marked it with three speckled stones from Mrs. Dalhousie's garden. Hidden inside is a small metal jewelry box Mr. O'Reardon gave me when I was ten. It holds three childhood treasures: a silver bird earring I got from a tourist who I thought was my mother, a key I found in the grass by Jonah's lab, and a ring Doris gave me that came inside a clear plastic ball. All things that, at the time, I didn't want Jonah to see or was afraid he'd forbid me from keeping.

"There," Marlie says, wiping her hands. "A sitting circle."

"Just for sitting?" I say, already appreciating the logic of having a dry seat to admire the coastal view or enjoy the breeze or watch the comings and goings of the *Spirit* far away down the coast.

"I thought it might be nice to have a meditation circle here." Marlie laughs. "Something I could leave behind that would make you think of me when you see it."

I feel myself soften. "I won't forget you, Marlie."

"Ah," she says, teasing, "don't make promises you can't keep."

She indicates a rock, and we each sit on one. She pulls a strand of dead grass from the ground beside her and lets it flutter in the air.

I think of things to say. Like Jonah, I'm not at all familiar or comfortable with small talk. "When you were in the diner," I finally decide to ask, "everyone said you were a writer — are you?"

She takes a deep breath and exhales it, then she starts to laugh. "No," she says. She doesn't look at me but keeps laughing. "It felt good, though, I won't lie, when people didn't label me plain old Marlie, booze-slinger at Joe's Dive, loser with nothing going for her. But transformed me into —" and she raises a finger "— Marlie Luellen, writer, tragic waste of potential."

I laugh too, and we laugh a little until it peters out. I say, "I'm sorry about your mom being sick."

"Oh. Well." She sighs. "I pretend every day is just a normal day." She hesitates then shrugs. "Most days, that seems to work." She touches my arm for a brief second. "I'm sorry about your mom running away when you were a baby." I look down, and she says, "I never knew my dad, either."

"Really?"

She nods.

"Coincidence," I say.

"What?"

"That we both have parents we don't know."

"Oh, right. Yes."

"Jonah says coincidence keeps the universe alive."

"Does it?"

"Like the sun and moon, for instance. They're such different sizes, but they look about the same in our sky."

"I never thought about that before."

"That's coincidence. The sun is four hundred times the size of the moon, but the moon is four hundred times closer."

"Wow," she says. "You and your father know the most interesting things." She looks at me. "I guess you're pretty close."

I think about it, but don't have an answer.

"You're lucky," she says and smiles wistfully, maybe thinking of the father she never knew.

I say, "Who didn't love you?"

Marlie's smile slips away. "What?" A warm breeze gusts in and lifts threads of her hair like marionette strings.

"The person who didn't love you."

"Oh." Her smile is gone. "That was a mistake." She speaks so softly her words barely touch the air. "And I guess you only see your mistakes after you make them."

I almost hear Aidie's voice: *Marlie will be your friend and she will help you.*

In the distance, the *Spirit* gives off a white glimmer as it navigates the strait toward Keele's Landing. I note the arc of the sun and realize it's almost 4:00 p.m.

Before I can ask about the mistake, something slams into me with so much force it knocks me over. Marlie lets out a scream, but I'm already giggling because Biscuit is licking my ears. My laughter reassures Marlie and she smiles as Biscuit and I tackle each other. After a few minutes, Biscuit gives up and rolls over so that I can scratch his belly. I do, and his smell wafts into my nose. Someone whistles, but Biscuit ignores it, too enthralled by my scratching.

"Must be Mr. O'Reardon up for a visit," I say to Marlie. "Even though the islanders never come by."

"They don't?"

"They say it's too far."

"That's funny," she says.

I picture the rest of the country, the way it appears on maps, and remember how vast the distances are between other places.

Biscuit noses the ground not far from the sitting circle and starts to snuffle and scratch at a hollow. "Look at him go," Marlie says. "Must be something in there."

"Probably some old carcass." I go to him and pat his behind. "Let's go, boy." But Biscuit is intent on his digging. Huge gobs of red mud shoot out at us. "Stop it, Biscuit," I order. But Biscuit is stubborn: a dog with a bone. Marlie steps back, out of the way. "Biscuit, stop." He ignores me, and his digging becomes more insistent. The little well of dirt becomes a bowl. I scold him again, "Biscuit!"

Now Marlie tries to persuade him, "C'mon, boy!" She snaps her fingers at him. "C'mon, get away from there. C'mon, boy. Let's go." She bends over and starts to push at his flank. I shout at Biscuit again, but Marlie angles between us, pushing at him. Biscuit begins to growl — I can't tell if it's at her or from the stress. He doesn't look at her, but his lips curl back and the growl twitches through his body and shivers all the way up, right into Marlie's pushing hands. It isn't until I see his twitching muscles that I realize Marlie could be in real danger. Biscuit doesn't know her, he's a big animal with sharp teeth, and he's stubborn about something that's on *his* property — which is the whole of the wilderness. His claws dig deeper into the ground and still Marlie keeps shoving him. I watch them closely, shaken into silence.

Then, as if we've sent a distress signal to the whole of the island, another whistle, sharper this time, sounds through the woods. Mr. O'Reardon, calling from the house. This time Biscuit heeds it. He stops digging, his snout comes up out of the mud, and his whole body relaxes. Mr. O'Reardon whistles again, and now Biscuit charges toward it. Marlie and I brush dirt off our pants and, without looking at each other, head back up the path.

15

When we get to the top of the path, my heart stops. It isn't Mr. O'Reardon at all, but Scotty. He brightens when he sees us, and his face becomes a wash of gold. He doesn't wear a coat and his chest and arms are proud under his plaid shirt.

I can't speak, can't even smile. A bond was forged between us on the boat — Scotty caring enough to look out for me, me accepting his help. The most painful happiness I've ever known.

"Hello!" Scotty calls to us.

Marlie goes to shake his hand and introduce herself. The sight of their hands holding each other, even for a short moment, makes my heart falter.

"I'm glad to finally meet you," Scotty says. He smacks Biscuit on the side. "And I guess you've met this vile mutt already." His eyes don't leave Marlie's face, which I notice again is very beautiful. "So, Marlie — Peg and Doris tell me you've come to the island to write a book. We'll have to read it when you're done."

Marlie glances at me and lets out a laugh that I'm supposed to share.

"I hope I'm not intruding," Scotty says, lifting the vinyl cover on his truck bed and reaching for a crate, "but Doris made me bring up her signature dip and a few bottles of her homemade wine."

"Homemade wine," Marlie repeats. "Aren't you sweet."

"Sweet?" Scotty puts his hand to his chest. "Aw, man, jab to the heart." His face beams with a grin. Dimples appear on both cheeks.

"Well, I'm sure it won't compare to your city cocktails, but Doris means well. We can't be turning our noses up."

"I'm not turning my nose up." Marlie laughs. "I love homemade wine."

"Well, good." Scotty leads the way to the house. "Makes two of us."

Scotty sounds different when he talks to Marlie. And then I recognize it: even though he hides it well, he still speaks to me like I'm a child.

I'm overcome with a sudden urge to reach into the crate and smash Doris's homemade wine to the ground. Instead I run ahead of Scotty and open the door.

Still laughing, Marlie comes up from behind. She stands close enough to him that her coat brushes his arm.

I don't know why, but then I hate her.

❧

Scotty holds the crate steady as Marlie takes out a platter of dip and a box of crackers and the bottles of wine and sets everything on the kitchen table. Every time Marlie nears the crate and bends over it, the top of her head almost touches Scotty's. I hang back, unable to speak.

When the box is empty, Scotty puts it aside and starts to open drawers, pushing around utensils, looking for something.

"Gemma and I were going to make chicken for dinner," Marlie says, putting a cracker in Doris's dip. "You're welcome to stay, Scotty." She looks at me and says, "I mean, if you think it's okay, Gemma, and that Jonah won't mind?"

I nod and shrug and shake my head: *Scotty is welcome, it might be okay, Jonah will probably mind.*

Scotty gives up on our drawers and pulls a Swiss Army knife from his pocket. "Well, we'll see what Jonah says when he gets back." He finds an attachment and uses it to open one of the bottles of wine.

Marlie sticks the dipped cracker in her mouth. She closes her eyes while she tastes it. "Oh my God, this is really good."

"I know," Scotty says, also grabbing a cracker, dipping it, and sticking it in his mouth. Also chewing and smiling. Only staring at Marlie. "Told you."

The thing about Scotty is that he's comfortable with everyone.

He opens a cupboard and finds three glasses. He pours wine into two, then turns to find me in the doorway and waggles the third glass at me. "What do you want to drink, kiddo? Milk, juice, pop?" I open my mouth but nothing comes out. I shake my head. He passes a glass of wine to Marlie. Smiling, she takes it, but I notice that when she brings it to her lips, she hesitates. Another thought seems to come to her mind as she observes the swirling redness in the glass. "You reconsidering?" Scotty says, laughing. "Go on, it won't bite." And Marlie's face clears and she takes a long sip.

Scotty urging Marlie to drink reminds me of Jonah urging a glass of health food water on her. Everyone trying to feed her like she's some chick dropped from its nest.

"Not bad," she says, swallowing. "Not bad."

Scotty pumps his arm in mock victory. "That's two for the home team."

"Oh, the home team has way more than two points." Laughing, Marlie turns to the fridge. "Come on, Gemma, let's get dinner started."

I push myself away from the sureness of the doorway. Marlie takes chicken pieces from the fridge. She finds the box of flaked cereal she asked Jonah to buy, and I get a bowl from the cupboard. Scotty sits at the kitchen table with his glass of wine. "I hope this doesn't embarrass our Gems here, but I hope you know how important she is to us."

I keep my face turned to the counter, trying to concentrate on following Marlie's recipe by crumbling cereal for the chicken.

"Of course I do," Marlie says, slicing the meat into long strips. She gives my arm a jokey nudge. "It's very apparent."

"The islanders don't want their girl to be blinded by city lights. Lured away. You know?"

That much is clear to me: the islanders don't want to lose their only child. Everything in my life has been colored by that wish.

"You gotta take good care of her."

"Of course."

They both look at me at once. Before I can say a word, Jonah arrives home.

⌇

Again, we eat gathered around the living room table. Biscuit falls into a deep sleep in front of the fire. Scotty is comfortable and funny and tells us stories about touring the Maritimes with the Parks crew. I notice he doesn't mention his wife, and no one asks him about her either.

Jonah doesn't act like himself, pretending instead to be a man who enjoys people gathered in his house, a good-natured man who always drinks glasses of wine and makes small talk. He sits close to Marlie, like he wants to be near her. He pays attention to everything she does and has a response for everything she says.

The feeling that something is wrong touches down on me again. Like a cyclone dropping, warm air meeting cold, whirling and twisting, it ripples and fans through me.

We eat chicken and peas and carrots and a salad, the adults opening more bottles of wine and pouring it into their glasses and soon laughing at things that aren't funny. I notice that Marlie pays equal attention to both men, and they respond to her attention like they're competing for it. A game — or trick — I'll never be able to learn.

I bring my empty plate to the kitchen. An open bottle of wine sits on the table. I check to make sure everyone is preoccupied in the living room, then take a mug from the cupboard and dribble some wine into it. I put the mug to my lips and a tiny bit splashes up.

Sometimes, outside Peg's diner, people drink beer. Once I snuck a taste of that too, but this is different. I like the beer better, the coldness of it. I drink a bit more of the wine. It's very warm and sour.

Feeling bolder already, I pour more into the mug and take it with me into the living room and drink from it. Right in front of all of them.

Marlie jumps to her feet and says very loudly, "Hey, music! Can we maybe use your shortwave radio, Jonah?" She stumbles a bit, but rights herself.

Jonah opens his hands in a friendly way and I go to the kitchen to get the radio, bringing it to the coffee table and turning it on. It's set to the weather report because Jonah checks the sea and weather every morning.

Marlie kneels in front of the radio and winds the knob in circles. Bits of sound, music and voices, jabber here and gone and swoop around the room like agitated birds. Biscuit starts up, sure he's meant to protect us, but then flops down again, too lazy to care.

Marlie stops at a station with very aggressive music. "Oh my God, I love this song!" She turns the sound louder and starts to jump around like a kid, punching her arms and pumping her head and pretending to kiss the air. Scotty and Jonah watch her and also pump their heads.

I drink more wine from the mug, a few sips at a time. More and then more, getting warm and warmer.

The music makes my body hum and hurt at the same time. It spurs my body to wriggle and move about. I start to dance too, but not the way I learned from the islanders with hand clapping and foot stomping. Like Marlie, pumping and wiggling and twisting. Maybe Scotty is looking me up and down. Maybe I'm the only woman in the room. The best woman.

My whole body feels warm. Like sap burbling up from a tree and sliding down itself.

Scotty gets up and collects the dirty dishes and tries to move around us. When he passes me, I dance for him. I want desperately to grab hold of him and wrap myself in his arms. It takes enormous effort to stop myself, effort that feeds my feverish dancing.

He doesn't look at me, but continues on to the kitchen. Soon I hear water running into the sink and smell dish soap bubbling. I drink more wine and imagine the hot water bubbling over me.

Marlie grabs my hands — my hands that are spread in the air waiting for someone to take them. Like I hoped Scotty would, she pulls me close and swings me around, turning me in the loops of an old-fashioned waltz. The smell of her hair and the feel of her hands and the warmth of her body make me ache and ache for Scotty. Like the music, Marlie twirls me in circles, around and around, barely missing tables and chairs and Biscuit's sprawled body and Jonah's tapping foot.

She's like the witches in fairy tales, enchanting and enticing us to our deaths.

"Well," Scotty says from the kitchen doorway, everything behind him clean, "I should be heading home now."

"No!" I say, unwrapping myself from Marlie's arms so I can face him.

"Sorry, kiddo. Lots to do tomorrow with the old man."

Marlie keeps dancing but flutters one hand at him. "Hey, Scotty, thank Doris for the wine for me. Tell her I really needed that. It really hit — the — spot." She mimes hitting spots.

Scotty chuckles. "Will do, Marlie. And thanks for dinner. It was delicious." Scotty heads to the front door. "Good night, Jonah. It was a blast. Night, Gems. See you around." Biscuit jumps up and follows him out.

Panicked, I try to think of ways to stop Scotty, but my head is so fuzzed and warm that no thoughts come. I follow him to the door and watch him walk out to the drive.

"Stop," I remember I could say to him, "you didn't ask Jonah about the hole in the cliff!" But Scotty doesn't hear my imaginary pleas; he ushers Biscuit into the truck and climbs in after. He turns one last time and his expression is gentle and kind. He raises his hand to me, then slams the truck door and drives away.

16

Instead of going to the living room right away, an unreasonable urge leads me to the back room. I throw on the light. Her things are everywhere: the bed I made for her when I invited her to stay, Jonah's old clothes that she borrowed, her purse and its contents scattered on the floor, her computer and phone plugged into an outlet.

My heart is racing and I heave and pant. Momentum left over from the dancing, from losing Scotty.

Rage builds inside me. Mysterious rage, because I'm not angry at anything that I can name. I yearn to pick up her things and smash them against the walls.

In a blur of not thinking, I push through the room, scooping away imaginary waves of air, and make my way to the box in the corner. *Experiment LLB.* I open it and pull out the green frog blanket and dump my face into its reassuring softness.

My shoulders buckle as I sob. But it's not real sobbing. Another part of me is laughing. And so I sob and laugh and bury my face in the blanket.

It's all so strange. So ridiculous.

Then another unreasonable urge takes over. I don't care anymore.

❧

The living room flickers with firelight. Jonah and Marlie sit together on the couch drinking wine. Jonah listens to Marlie and nods as if hers is the most important talk he's ever heard. Like she's offering original ideas on Darwin or something. When he speaks, his words come out, like Marlie's, mushed and unclear.

I say, my voice also unrecognizable, "What's Experiment LLB?" Jonah hardly seems to hear me, but raises his eyebrows at Marlie as if he's waiting for her to answer.

Marlie says, "It's so cool you do experiments." Jonah gives a tight and unfocused smile — the kind people give when they're not really listening. "I love that," Marlie says.

"No." I wave the green frog blanket at him. "The box with the green *baby* blanket in it." The wine spins me around. "What is *that* experiment?" I throw the blanket at him, but it just plops to the ground. I want to laugh hysterically.

Marlie looks at me, then at the blanket. She wears a sloppy grin on her face, and I can see she also wants to laugh but is stopping herself.

"What's in the hole?" I say to Jonah. His attention fixes on Marlie's knee, the one closest to him. I say, "What is it? The hole?" Like them, my words come out like mush. "Is it a secret?"

"Yeah, what was that?" Marlie says, rolling her eyes. "He kept *digging* and *digging* at that hole."

"No," I say. "The hole in the *rock*. In the *cliff*."

Marlie says, "It really freaked us out."

Jonah, his eyes unfocused and wandering, tips his glass of wine at Marlie.

It's like I'm in another world, trying to speak through the atmosphere. I turn my back on them, sick and exhausted all at once.

≈

The coldness of the bathroom floor startles me awake. I stare at the intricate design of black and white mosaic tiles. I don't remember how I got here. The tiles dig into my face and, when I get up and look into the mirror, I see their imprint on my cheek.

My mouth is dry but my head has stopped spinning. I wonder how late it is.

I creak open the bathroom door, afraid to alert Jonah, or anyone. I want desperately to get back into my bed and burrow into its warmth. In the hall, I notice that Jonah's bedroom door is still open. The muffled sound of a woman crying surprises me.

The sound draws me to the top of the stairs and then down enough of them to peer into the living room. The reflection of the ebbing fire flickers orange on the walls. Shadows repeat the shapes of the chair and couch and double up the picture frames. The living room — in color and in dark.

The muffled crying gets clearer as I creep closer, and the stairway becomes a tall, skinny peephole. Through it I see:

Marlie, tears streaking her face like cracks in a bowl, bends over Jonah. She pulls at his clothes and kisses his mouth, and Jonah leans away, his hands in the air, not sure what to do. Then he kisses her too and now he touches her body. Cautious, unsure. Not a scientist anymore. Firelight shines on them. It scratches over their clothing and then over their naked skin.

17

I push myself into my closet and curl into a ball on the pillow beside Aidie.

Aidie has her mouth open in a scream. She screams so loudly no one can hear it.

I try to make sense of what I saw. Not what Jonah and Marlie were doing, but what it means to them. What it means to my future.

Aidie balls her fists and pounds them into her belly. She pounds them against the wall.

"Stop it, Aidie." I try to pull her hands to stillness, but she fights me. *What's happening, what's happening.* Her eyes are crazy.

"Don't worry," I say to calm her. "We'll figure it out."

Aidie's face strains with red and the veins around her eyes worm up. She screams again, and the sound drives into my mind. I'm about to clamp her mouth shut, but Aidie takes a gulp of air — and then she bites down. Just as abruptly, as if she's bitten fishing line to release the catch, the struggle against me is over. Relieved by the quiet, I relax my grip on her.

Aidie turns to face me and her eyes light into mine. She says in a low, clear voice, *Jonah did it.*

"What?"

You saw him. The way he looked at her. He was planning it.

"No, Aidie. He wouldn't know how to plan that."

He pays too much attention to her. Makes special drinks. Makes small talk. He doesn't work in his lab so much.

"It's because he's lonely. Like you said."

He's planning something. He's going to hurt her.

My body braces. "What are you talking about? This is what you wished for, Aidie. He and Marlie are falling in love. It's going to be wonderful, remember?"

Aidie looks at me with sorry eyes. *You don't know what being in love means.*

Anger floods me. "No, *you* don't know what love means, Aidie." I lurch to my feet and tower over her. "You live in a closet."

He said he left you with her when you were a baby.

I lower my hand. "What?"

He was on the island for seven months by himself before he brought you here. He told everyone he left you with your mother so he could find a safe place to live. You were alone with her the whole time he was gone. Nothing happened to you.

"Because she got worse when he went back to get me."

Scotty said there were no Hubbs anywhere. No Shannon Hubb —

I clap my hands over my ears.

And no Jonah either. The islanders always say, "It's a good thing Jonah had his papers so he could take over the ferry when Henry Jasper passed." Where did he get his papers if Scotty couldn't find any sign of him anywhere?

"Scotty didn't look everywhere. He missed a place." It feels treacherous to doubt Scotty. "Or," a new thought occurs, "maybe Jonah made up all the names. To protect us."

Jonah is making everything up.

"You're just saying that because you're angry."

You have to get out of here, Gemma. Like that girl said last year — you have no future here. You're just one of Jonah's voles.

"Why are you doing this to me?"

Because now I remember.

"Remember what?"

That he hurts people. He hurt you.

"He didn't hurt me, Aidie!" Without meaning to, I glance at my wrist. There's only the faintest ring of brown.

I reached across him when he was reading a case study. *Stop*, he said, his eyes no longer running over lines of text but stuck on one word. Only two long bones — my ulna, my radius — held the pressure of his squeezing fingers.

And he hurt me too.

"No, he didn't!" I push the closet door closed, but Aidie pushes against me. "You're crazy, Aidie!" I spit her name into the dark. "Nothing you say makes sense. Just like Jonah."

Aidie pushes harder on the door. *I'm not like Jonah.*

"Go away." I push back, but Aidie is almost as strong as me. I can hear her grunting and mewling. "I want you to go away," I growl at her.

Aidie cries through the door, *I'm not like Jonah!*

How do you stop what you can't stop?

"I'm sick of you always being here," I roar at her. "I hate you!"

And just like that, the door closes and everything goes quiet.

Out of breath, I slump against the wood. Tears I didn't expect sting my eyes and I stumble, blinded, through the dark and into bed.

18

An hour later, I hear the sound of the bathroom door squealing open and knees thunking to the tiles. Then retching.

Waking out of a fitful sleep, I have to work to remember where I am. I sit up, my eyes adjusting to the dark. Across from me, the closet is closed.

I push myself to my feet.

The closet door is like the doors in dreams: a moonlight shadow in a wall of black. Somehow, I arrive in front of it. My hand is on the knob. The first time I've ever been scared of opening this door.

Only one vision would be more terrifying than finding a monster. And that is to find what I see now: nothing.

Nothing on the pillow. Nothing beside or behind the hamper. Nothing around my hanging clothes.

Aidie is gone.

The sound of retching rouses me and pulls me away.

❧

I step into the hall. Jonah's bedroom door is still open and dark. Empty. The bathroom door is partway open, and I can see Marlie bent over the toilet puking.

I let myself in behind her. She's like a wounded rabbit in an open field. Any anger I held against her is gone. Any anger I ever felt is gone. I smooth Marlie's hair from her face and hold the strands away.

When I was little and got sick, Jonah would bring me down to Peg's and I would stay with her nursing me until I got better. Peg is an excellent nurse: she puts a cool folded cloth on your head and lets you rest for days and days, feeding you herbal tea with honey and a bay leaf and two peppercorns floating in the bottom, and when you're a bit better, toast with butter, and later mashed bananas. By the time Peg is done with you, you hardly remember you were ever sick.

Marlie stops puking and sits back. She gets up very shakily and bends over the sink to rinse her mouth. She tries to smile at me through the mirror, but puking-tears are running down her face. They make her look terribly sad.

When she vomits again, we start over: her thunking to her knees in front of the toilet, bending over and retching, me holding her hair back and out of the way. We work like that for ages, up and down, puking and waiting and puking and waiting, until finally her stomach is empty.

Shivering, she brushes her teeth and says she needs to lie down. Because it's closer and easier than climbing down to the back room, I escort her to my bedroom and help her into my bed. Like an unseeing invalid, she doesn't protest, just lets me pull the sheet and blanket over her body and smooth it down.

I go downstairs to grab a bucket from under the kitchen sink and get a clean washcloth from the laundry closet. On my way back upstairs, Jonah's sleeping body catches my attention. He lies across the couch with the wool blanket draped across him. The dying embers of the fire light his face and his expression is slack and innocent. A face I've never seen on him before. A boy's face. Or the boy inside the man. For a moment I stop and admire it. If Jonah has never had happiness before, I want that for him now.

I leave him to his dreaming sleep and go upstairs to Marlie. I carefully dab her face with the washcloth, then push the bucket against the bed beside her. I'm about to leave and put myself in the back room to sleep when Marlie takes my hand and pulls me to a stop.

"You want me to stay?" I ask. She nods.

Even though I'm not sure I should, I climb into the bed beside her. I don't know how to lie beside a real person, so I stretch out on my back and stare up at the ceiling.

≈

I wake out of my next sleep and find the silhouette of a person at my window. The sky beyond the silhouette is gray and still — so early, the sun is only starting to rise.

I wish it were Aidie. Aidie, who knows everything about me, who loves me even when I'm dismal and sad. My only friend.

But I know, even as I wish it, that Aidie won't come back. Maybe, probably, forever.

Loneliness gushes through me, rushing over everything and unearthing more loneliness. So much buried inside me, getting dredged up.

I climb out of the bed and step toward the silhouette. It looks unfamiliar as it stands against the bluing sky. As I move nearer, I pretend this is Aidie grown up. A future Aidie who's returned to tell me that all the worries I feel right now are nothing and will soon fade away. *You'll get over it*, she might say. *So many beautiful things will happen to you.* And the loneliness inside me would dissolve and relief and joy would grow in its place. If I knew it would all be okay one day, I could stand anything now.

Only when I'm close enough to touch her do I begin to see the strands of her hair and the color of her skin and I allow myself to accept that this is Marlie. A real person with no insight into the future.

She stares into the yard, her face pale and her eyes glassy. I begin to realize she's still asleep, like when I found her by the lighthouse and she spoke to me without knowing. I think of Peg's stories about sleepwalkers, people who can get up and bustle about without any idea of what they're doing or where they are, with no memory of it after they wake.

I put a hand on her shoulder and say, low and careful, "Marlie? Wake up."

But she doesn't recognize that I'm there. I follow her gaze into the yard.

Jonah is at the open door to his lab dressed in his climbing clothes. While he often gets up early, it's usually not as early as a springtime sun. He pulls an empty cardboard box off the grass and collapses it into a flat square and stuffs it into the garbage bin outside the lab door. Before the box disappears into the bin, I notice black marker scribbled on one corner. I don't have to look too closely to see that the writing says *Experiment LLB*.

On Jonah's back is a stuffed knapsack. Sticking out of the open top are rolls of cardboard sheets. He often special-orders large rectangles of white cardboard from a supply shop in Moncton. He uses them to track his experiments. When I was younger and they arrived in the mail and lay in bright blank piles on the table, I longed to paint them over.

Now Jonah reaches through the lab door and pulls out a large shovel and pitchfork, then he closes the door and locks it. He walks away with the tools, his stuffed knapsack bobbing on his back, and makes his way down the path toward the Rock Pit.

Curiosity and dread land on a scale inside me — first one side heavier, then the other.

Marlie turns from the window, still without looking at me, and glides like an omen toward my bed and slips into it. She rolls away from me, away from the light rising through the window, and pulls the blanket under her chin.

I follow quickly to the other side of the bed so I can check on her. She's fast asleep now, as if nothing had happened. The rhythm of her breath is regular and even. Good breathing, Peg would say. I touch her cheek and the temperature feels right. I stroke my hand down her hair. So soft, touching it brings comfort.

I go to my closet and find some clothes. Aidie's pillow is still empty.

I try not to think about her as I pull on my pants and a sweater, but words she would say come anyway: *Sometimes getting mad breaks things that ought to be broken.*

But Aidie isn't here talking to me.

19

I run downstairs and quickly pull on my coat and boots. Outside,
I race down the path to the Rock Pit until I find Jonah on it, walking
with purpose, using the pitchfork and shovel as walking sticks. He
doesn't look left or right or back. Dew-frost splinters under my feet, and
I follow like a deer in tracks, far from him so he won't hear it breaking.

When Jonah gets to the Rock Pit, I crouch down into a bush, ducking my head so the thorns don't cut me. He wedges the shovel and
pitchfork under a rock several feet from the path, levering it up and
out of the way. When the rock is flipped on one end, I notice it's a very
particular one, identifiable by a pattern of crystal on its surface that
looks exactly like a smiling face. Squinty, laughing eyes; round nose;
divots and flecks arranged into a friendly mouth. The upended rock
teeters and wobbles for a few seconds, as if it's trying to balance on its
head, then slowly keels over. Jonah crouches and digs into the hollow
and pulls up five or six smaller rocks. Then he reaches very deep into
the excavated hole. With both his hands he pulls out a chest about the
size of a tackle box.

I'm too far away to tell what the chest is made of or what it looks
like in detail, but it's precious enough to Jonah that when he brushes
the red sandstone dust from the top, his hands twitch. He seems to
take a breath or two during which he stretches and clenches his hands
a few times. Then he unlatches the lid. I wonder if it's a Mi'kmaq or
Acadian antiquity he's looted for himself.

His hands keep twitching as he turns to his knapsack and opens it. He digs past the rolled cardboard sheets and pulls something else out. Because of the bright green color, I know right away that he's brought along the baby blanket — the green frog blanket I've smoothed against my cheek a hundred times, that has a soother attached to it, that was hidden inside the box marked Experiment LLB.

Jonah spreads the blanket on his lap. Then he turns to the chest and pulls something out of it. A wrapped bundle that seems very light. He lays the bundle gently on top of the green frog blanket. He removes string from it that has rotted to bits and peels open the cloth. The cloth is so dirty and old it flays like stiff cardboard flaps, but something about it looks familiar in a way I can't quite understand. Jonah stares inside the folds of cloth for a long, long time. He even raises his thumb to one eye and then the other and rubs at his lashes. It occurs to me that he might be crying.

After a while, he closes the cloth flaps of the bundle, places the bundle inside the green frog blanket, and sets the blanket and bundle together back inside the chest. Very carefully, he closes the lid. He gets up and rearranges all the small rocks back inside the hole and then covers it with the larger one. He grabs the shovel and pitchfork and, cradling the chest, jumps from rock to rock until he gets back to the path. I push myself deeper into the bushes and freeze, and he walks right past me like I'm not there at all.

When he's far enough away, I pull myself out of the bush and go back up the path toward the house. I catch him as he's coming out of his lab again and locking the door behind him. Again, I duck out of sight. The tools aren't in his hands anymore, but the knapsack with the cardboard rolls is still strapped to his back and the chest he pulled from the rocks is still under one arm. Jonah doesn't go into the house like I expect him to, but walks down the path to the lighthouse. Again, I follow far behind and as quiet as a shell.

He continues toward the lighthouse, skirting the hole that Biscuit started digging yesterday, but which seems a lot bigger today. Jonah eyes the hole, but moves on. The white tower is waiting for him, quiet and watchful.

I hide myself behind a tree as Jonah goes through the lighthouse door. He comes out a moment later holding the climbing gear. He puts on the harness and then bends down and finds the anchor and sling that he attached to the edge of the rock face. He connects his safety line and then the rope to the sling. Then he picks up the coil of rope and throws it down the cliff. When the rope is settled, he takes a length of it and feeds it through the rappel device. Then he snaps the rappel into his harness and tests that all the holds are secure.

I study every move he makes, determined to memorize it. He takes out some netting and wraps it around the chest and straps it to his back, making room for the knapsack with its rolls of cardboard. Jonah looks very strange now, like the hunchback of Notre Dame or something. Like a monster and not a man.

He moves very slowly as he takes his contorted body over the side of the cliff and follows the rope. I can hear the labored huff and puff of his breath. For the first time, I get scared. I realize the rope could snap or he could lose his balance and fall to the ocean. I know if that happens, he will die. It's the hardest thing for me not to scream at him to stop.

The wind is strong when he climbs over the cliff. When the wind is high around the lighthouse it sounds like voices howling in pain, many many voices. More than you can count.

Jonah's body and then his head disappear over the ledge. When I can't see him anymore, I run to the edge of the cliff. I grip the wall of the lighthouse and, holding tight and bracing my feet, I stretch my neck out and look far over the edge so I can see where he's going. I'm just in time to see Jonah's feet push through the big clump of weeds wedged into the cliff and then into the cave underneath it. His body wriggles in next.

The high wind on the cliff chokes me. The cliff falls so violently below me, I think it might reach up and grab me for balance. At the bottom the waves crash then stretch far up, taunting me like devil's fingernails.

My heart stops racing when I understand that Jonah is safe. But I also know I can't keep gawping down the cliff anymore — Jonah has only one route out of the cave, and that's up toward me.

I rear back out of his sight and collect my thoughts. My attention shifts to the secret mole hole on the far side of the lighthouse that hides my old jewelry box. My memory spins around the childhood treasures inside it and the fact that one of them might be of significant value.

Spurred by a certainty, by the sense that I'm doing something inevitable, I run to the hole. It's been ages since I've looked at my jewelry box, but I still remember all the things inside it: a silver bird earring from a tourist I thought could be my mom, a ring Doris gave me inside a plastic ball, and a key I found four years ago wedged in the soil by Jonah's lab.

I move aside the three speckled stones and crumble the dried seam of dirt that covers the secret hole, then reach down into the darkness, deep to my elbow. I almost don't recognize it when I pull it up. All the paint has scratched off the metal, and it's covered in rust. I can hear the key clank around inside.

I open the box and reach past the plastic ball, but something catches my skin and makes me stop. It's the earring — a beautiful little silver bird with wings spread like it's ready to fly.

She was very pretty, that tourist, almost as pretty as Marlie. What made me pay attention to her was the color of her eyes, which were almost like mine. She'd come to the island by herself, and I was in Peg's Diner doing my lessons when she arrived. Immediately I felt a magnetic pull, so I got up and followed her around the diner, watching as she ordered a cheeseburger and fries, noticing that she had a strange accent. When she sat down to eat, I stood by her booth looking at her for a very long time before she noticed me and smiled. After looking at each other for a few minutes, she opened her hand to me. Lying on the center of her palm was the tiniest, most perfect silver bird. She asked if it was my earring, and I told the truth even though I didn't want to. She could see that I admired it and said that since she'd found it in the grass by the keeper's house, I should have it. I was so happy then, so certain.

The key is the last item in the treasure box. I slip it into my pocket and go back to the house, on the lookout for anything suspicious.

Outside the lab door, I hesitate — I'm anxious to see if the key fits the lock, but I don't want Jonah to catch me. There's no point searching his lab unless he's guaranteed to be gone for a long time — like on the morning ferry run. I decide to hide in the back room until he leaves for the day.

Just as I'm about to go into the house, there's a rustle and blur of movement through the woods by the drive. I freeze and stare into the caged branches. I half-expect Jonah to come charging out, somehow returning more quickly than possible because he's read my mind. But the dark, lunging shape is only Biscuit loping toward me. His fur is matted and dirty, his eyes shining and eager. He comes up to me and nuzzles my hand.

"Go on, boy," I say to him. "Get back home now." Somehow he understands that this time I'm serious and he lopes away. As I let myself into the house, I see him head down the path to the lighthouse and imagine him intent on getting back to his newfound hole. I wish him well and shut the door.

I hide myself in the back room and hold the door closed with my body. The Experiment LLB box and its soft green blanket are missing. But something new has been added.

A small folded piece of paper balances on Marlie's purse. I know I should leave it, but I'm drawn to it. I approach, hoping I'll only have to observe it from a distance to know what it means. But the paper is in my hand and unfolded before I realize it.

Dear Marlie, it says in Jonah's most careful handwriting.

I look forward to seeing you when I get back from this morning's run. Always, Jonah

Words so slight, I wonder if Marlie will even know how meaningful they are. I remember his innocent boy's face when he was asleep on the couch. His sweet face.

I reorder the note and place it back on her purse.

Not much later, Jonah returns from the cliffs. Pressed against the door, I listen as he makes himself breakfast, as he hums tunelessly — an unfamiliar sound — and as he washes up and runs upstairs. I can tell by the clomp of his boots that he's in my room, probably checking on Marlie. Maybe kissing her on the cheek. Then there's the thump of him running back downstairs again and leaving out the front door. The van starts up and rumbles down the drive and into town.

20

The key from my treasure box fits into the knob of Jonah's lab door like a bulb in a socket. Turning it isn't so easy. It sticks and jams. But I keep trying. And pretty soon, it jigs right around and I hear the lock click open.

I push the door, step inside the shed, close the door behind me, and turn on the light.

※

The first things I see are the hooks securing the garden tools: the shovel, the spade, the pitchfork. Beside those is a single stack of shelves running the height of the wall, each filled with some kind of equipment: traps for capturing voles, buckets and sponges and gloves, cameras and monitors and flashlights, everything jumbled together. Beside that, there's a stack of divided shelves, each edge labeled and each cubicle filled with Jonah's research papers — studies upon studies that he found on computers on the mainland and printed out: *Reciprocal Altruism*, *Pair Bonding*, *Human Attachment*. I recognize the pencil marks and underlined text, having lost him to this work every night of my life.

At the turn in the wall, a single shelf is set up as a workstation with a stool tucked underneath and writing material on top: pencils sharpened and collected in jars, rulers and stacks of loose-leaf paper and blank journals, a stapler, a hole punch, some metal clips.

A small white box that looks like prescription medicine sits among them. *Clomiphene*, the writing says. It doesn't say what clomiphene is, so I look inside and recognize the blister pack and pills that Jonah crushed into Marlie's water.

On the third wall, I find the voles.

The whole wall is lined with enclosures from floor to ceiling, and each enclosure has some quantity of voles inside. Mothers with babies, or whole families, or voles by themselves. But most of the cages have two together. Each one labeled.

Generation 54, Generation 55, Generation 56.

"Critical attachment theory," I say out loud as if to explain it to myself.

For the first time I hear the sound: tiny, screeching, urgent pleas.

I peer closer, and bead-like eyes find me. Ears and front paws prick up. Little whiskered snouts twitch and worry.

Human contact must be kept to a minimum, I hear Jonah warning.

"Shush," I say to them as gently as I can. "Don't worry. I would never hurt you."

As if they understand and believe me, most of the voles go back to their regular existence. In one cage, two voles — a bonded pair — run to opposite sides and into small identical pens. When they stop moving, a hatch is triggered in the center of the main enclosure and a small cricket is released from underneath. The voles run back and grab the cricket together, then eat it so quickly I'm hardly sure I saw it. In another cage, two voles move to a water dropper. I notice the dropper is too high for them to reach with their mouths, but one vole stands up on its hind legs and pulls the dropper down with two paws so the other vole can drink. After the vole drinks, it reaches up and pulls the dropper with two paws so the first one can drink.

As I watch them, a burrowing love for the voles fills me. Love for their cleverness, their trust, their innocent beauty. But I can't decide if I'm happy they're safe and clean and well cared for — like Biscuit or any of the dozens of farm animals and pets kept all over the island — or if I'm sickened by the strangeness of their behavior and the smallness of their lives.

I turn to the fourth wall, the one behind the door. This wall is also stacked with shelves, but each shelf is lined with journals — all the journals that I've watched Jonah fill over the years. Like the other cubicles, each shelf-edge is labeled. *Darwin Methodology, Neo-Lamarckism, Neo-Darwinism, The Southern Red-backed Vole, Island History, Acadian History, Mi'kmaq History.* All subjects I know Jonah has researched. Still, I pull out journals and flip through them.

The last entry in the Mi'kmaq journal has an interesting story dated two years ago, and I read it.

To investigate the possibility of a Mi'kmaq cull by the British military some 200 years ago, I decided to explore the waters closest to the lighthouse. The coastline here is extremely shallow and pitted with rock deposits, making boat access impossible. The likelihood of an accidental burial ground never before discovered is high. There may not be any organic matter left, but there might be evidence of historical importance.

Striking a course 180° straight down from the lighthouse, my descent was slow. I took my time, carefully setting the bolts and anchor for the climbing rope. About midway down the sheer rock face of the cliffs, I found myself navigating a large clump of yarrow that grows from a fissure. As I rappelled past the mass of blooms, I lost my footing and found myself bouncing into the plant instead of around it. Trying to regain my balance, I angled my foot downward. It didn't land against a solid brace of rock, as I expected, but slipped past the foliage and through a hole. I released more rope, allowing myself to drop further, and found myself going through a small opening.

At first I was certain I'd stumbled into a natural formation. It was only when I unhooked the rope and stood to my full height that I noticed the opening is completely square. There are vestiges of rust on the top and bottom, a sure sign that at one point metal — probably iron — bars secured it. The window to a jail, no doubt, or a keep. As my eyes adjusted to the minimal light, I could see there was a floor of sorts beneath my feet; it is as level and smooth as any manmade floor. The natural wall of the cliff face behind me — the wall with the porthole — is abutted on both sides with walls made from stacked, handmade clay bricks. It was then that I began to understand this was no natural formation, but a carefully engineered chamber.

There had never been any talk on the island of a porthole in the rock or of a cavern behind it. In the architectural drawings that decorate the lighthouse, there is no hint of an underground chamber. Later, on inspecting from the water, I saw that through a combination of the fissure in the cliff and the overgrown yarrow — both natural accidents — the porthole is impossible to see, even through high-powered binoculars.

I shone a lantern around the chamber. Damp and mildewed, the outside wall leached moisture into the air and sticky streams of lime marked the brick walls. The floor is hard-packed dirt with virtually no decomposition in the centuries since it was laid. The chamber is about 10 feet by 12 feet and about 7 feet high and has only the one porthole to the outside — the one through which I'd come — for air and light. As I ventured deeper inside, I discovered a tunnel off the back wall a few feet wide and several feet long, which ends with a flight of stone stairs that leads to a trap door.

Never having noticed any sign of a trap door in the ground at lighthouse level, I calculated its approximate position relative to the lighthouse and I note here that above ground there is only dirt and vegetation where the entrance would be. I assume the lack of air and light has petrified the trap door's slatted wood and kept it in place, buried for two centuries. When the Brits decamped to more effective military strongholds, the place must have been locked away and forgotten like any other useless secret.

The good luck of finding such an unknown and secure room is not lost on me. If the lab behind the house is a sanctuary for the voles, here is a sanctuary for an open exhibit of the studies I would never risk exposing at the house. Even behind a locked door.

The cavern walls, while mildewed and damp, will provide an excellent backdrop on which to hang waterproof tarps, to which my large study-charts can be attached and displayed. Here, with past experiments ordered around me, I can examine the linear evolution of my work: how this experiment led to that discovery, how that discovery led to this experiment, and so on. As a result, the space will be a safe retrospective of sorts. A reliquary of my science. A gallery to showcase exactly what for me is the essential truth of life.

So, the hole under the lighthouse is Jonah's "reliquary of science." I can't imagine, with all the information stored and catalogued in the lab, what else Jonah is researching — and hiding — down there.

When I put the Mi'kmaq journal back on the shelf, I notice the section next to it is marked *Critical Attachment*. The first journal is titled: *Critical Attachment Theory: Developed from Abstract for Experiment LLB*.

"Experiment LLB," I repeat out loud. Black marker on a cardboard box: banished. Green frog blanket: banished.

The mother-child bond, the first page reads, is the most obvious example of human attachment. It guarantees that offspring survive and ensures the future of the human gene. But our tribes have also played an imperative role in safeguarding human survival.

In the old tribal model, access to robust reproductive pools was constant. Therefore, reproduction was cheap. But access to food was not guaranteed. Therefore, food was valuable. Now our food/reproduction value has inverted. Access to food is more reliable and access to reproductive partners — as every fertile man and woman retreats behind technology — is becoming more and more unstable. Now relationships are "too complicated." It's all pornography and vibrators.

The tribe is dead.

In our modern developed society, technology dominates every human interaction. And, as surely as any creature, technology needs to survive. So it too must evolve.

As our genes adapt to this "new normal," and as gene pools respond to natural selection, social detachment risks becoming the mutation that works. This mutation will become the "unit of selection" and it will certainly affect the progress of human evolution.

The "critical attachment" experiment using southern red-backed voles will serve as a model in the push to reshape (or salvage) genetic evolution. The red-backed vole is related to the prairie vole — a monogamous rodent that shows a high level of affiliative behavior — but the red-backed vole is a solitary creature.

If the results are as predicted, this new theory will save human evolution.

A slow shudder picks up inside me. Something uncomfortable and aching. I stick the journal back on the shelf, careful to arrange it in its proper place.

Uncertain now of what I'd hoped to find or what I'd hoped to feel when I found it, my eyes wander the hundreds of journals lined up in front of me. Like with everything Jonah, it's too confusing, too strange. Holding import that's just outside my grasp.

Sort of like a cavern — a *reliquary* — under a lighthouse.

My eyes land on another labeled shelf: *Experiment M. Luellen.* Instantly, I am stilled.

There's only one journal in the cubicle, and I pick it up. Inside, scrawled notes scratch over the page. Answers to questions I never heard him ask.

— 30 years old
— real name: Marlie Frasier
— from Toronto
— childhood in Chatham, Ontario
— mother sick with Primary Progressive MS, residing at Summer-field Extended Care facility
— father is "out of the picture"
— works as a barmaid, Joe's Local Pub, southwest Toronto
— has the "usual" amount of friends, "the kind you can go out for drinks with on a Friday night"
— no romantic attachments
— once enrolled at York University, Toronto, for BA degree, major in Sociology, never graduated
— claims to be a fiction writer, but no published work under either name

And then his summary:

Herein lies ample proof of Emotional Detachment Disorder. Loneliness and frustration have driven her here, providing a sound baseline for the experiment. She will be both willing to participate and easy to imprint.

Ice crawls up my spine, searching for a way in.

Page upon page of Jonah's observations come next. Everything he said to Marlie, exactly how he said it, followed by calculations of how he thought his words affected her. There are charts recording the amount of time they spent together — the exact hours, minutes, and seconds — and how, from Jonah's assessments, he thought those minutes made her feel. There are pages and pages of scribbled and edited versions of the letter he left for Marlie in the back room — most are profuse or exaggerated or sound like a person who speaks little English. And then there's one, identical, which he must have copied to leave her.

Then I find: *Experiment M. Luellen: How to Trigger Critical Attachment. Experiment successor to Experiment LLB.*

Generation I:

— Unlike Experiment LLB, gene history is not ideal. The action-reward system will be designed to override this fundamental deficiency. However, the living environment remains ideal.
— Controlled variables: social interaction, basic sustenance, cohabitation.
— Primary behaviors of interest: reciprocal altruism, contact leading to "love."
— Experimenter will be one-half of bonded pair.
— Experimenter must always maintain emotional detachment.

Generation 2:

— Incision in prophylactic begins the process.
— Clomiphene dissolved in water stimulates and boosts egg production.
— Administer the anti-estrogen for five days at the appropriate time in cycle.
— Inseminate around estimated time of ovulation.
— At human subject's fertile age, likelihood of conception: high. Of producing twins: high.

Clomiphene in water. Incision in a prophylactic. My breath turns to ash in my mouth.

— Two children. Pair bonded.
— When old enough, children will feed each other. Comfort each other. Speak for each other.
— Intellectual, physical, and psychological needs will be supported. Two minds will be available to solve every problem. Two bodies will meet every physical challenge. Each will have someone to "love," and each will have someone who "loves" them.

I slam the journal shut and stick it back on the shelf exactly how I found it.

Marlie is just *Experiment M. Luellen*. A baby — *two* babies — future experiments. Only studies that will keep Jonah busy. And only until they don't behave as they should.

I leave the lab as quickly and quietly as I came and lock the door behind me.

21

A fierce anger grows inside me; it's stronger than fear, changing the way my muscles move and the way blood siphons through my body.

I make my way down to the lighthouse without thinking about what I'm going to do next, but feeling the pulse of it. Along the path, Biscuit's hole almost trips me up, and I notice it's even wider than before. I glance about, carelessly wondering if Biscuit is still here.

Inside the lighthouse, I gather the climbing gear and the camping lantern. Outside, I put on the harness and clip the lantern to a hook on the back of it. Old memories ripple through my mind: Scotty tousling my hair before he put on my helmet, the feel of the rigid Rock Pit cliffs under my groping fingers, a summer sun warming my head, Scotty yelling out encouraging words: "To the left and up!", "Take it slow!", "You got it, Gemma! Way to go!"

Like I saw Jonah do, I crouch at the edge of the cliff and gather the sling that's anchored to the rock. With shaking fingers and questionable strength, I attach the center of the rope and my safety line to the double carabiners, then I brace myself and throw the rope down the cliff. The doubled-up cord unfurls and plummets past Jonah's secret hole, almost all the way to the water.

The sun has risen quite far by now and shines down the cliff like a flashlight. The sky is clear, and the wind has subsided.

I grab the rappel device and loop the rope into it, then make sure every carabiner is secure. The memory of how to do it comes back through the pressure of the equipment against my fingers. I turn myself around and let myself down. I feel the harness take my weight as I suspend my body over the cliff and into thin air and brace my feet against the rock. I test the rope again, then unclip the safety line and let it drop to my side.

Fear hits me now and bleaches out every other feeling. I go very slowly, extending my hands so I can feed the rope carefully through the rappel device.

Instead of dropping down, I walk the rock step by step. I let the rappel hold me, feeding the rope through it by fractions of inches. Already my hands are so cold and stiff, the rope feels rougher against them than I remember. Jonah's hole isn't far, but I know it's death if I make a mistake.

Then I see the mistake I've already made. I freeze, squatting against the rock, to assess the situation. When I looped the rope through the rappel device, I put it on backwards, threading the rope through the smooth side instead of the side with teeth. Now, if I lose my hold, nothing will stop me from freefalling.

Adrenalin courses through me. And then comes panic. Both together poison my concentration.

Instead of angling the rope to the side to control my descent, I straighten it. And, just as I feared, I begin to fall.

I fall fast. So fast, the rushing wind in my ears is thunder. So fast, I should be crashing onto the rocks. Waves should be splashing over me and dragging me out to sea.

Me dying and no one knowing.

My body jerks and flails about. My feet thrash for outcroppings to stop me, my hands desperately grab at the rope. One second passes, then two, but such slow seconds, it's like time is caught in amber. Something I can clutch and gape at.

And then — unbelievably, miraculously — I jerk to a stop. I skid forward, and my head bangs hard on the rock.

A terrible pain radiates from my right hand and down my arm. I dare myself to look at it, terrified I'll find half my body gone.

But my hand is still there, curled into a tight fist that's coiled with rope. Somehow my body took over and wound the rope around my hand. Somehow my wrapped fist jammed into the rappel device.

I very carefully tiptoe my feet against the cliff to brace myself against an outcrop. The pain in my hand makes me want to scream. I get heavier and heavier as my feet try to find a grip. A hundred pounds, two hundred, a thousand.

My left foot finally finds a toehold. And then my right. I let my feet take my weight as I huddle against the rock, breathing, making sure I still can. *In and out, in and out, like a metronome.* A mineral smell fills my nose. The most vital smell in the world.

When I've caught my breath, I check my right hand. Rope burn. Blood oozes out of a row of cuts. It hurts so badly I want to scream. But I hold myself statue-still against the cliff while the scratch burns then heartbeats inside my skin. I put my palm to my mouth and suck it clean.

When my hand stops throbbing, I secure the rappel, tighten the rope, and peer between my toes to see how far I still have to go. Only a few more feet and I'll arrive at the bush that grows over the window that leads into the cave.

❧

Because my body is so exhausted, I don't feel any relief when I slip through the window and fall into black. I don't want to get up and walk into the dark. I just want to wake up from a nightmare.

My hands shake while I unclip the rappel device from the harness, then the lantern, which I turn on. Its light envelops me in a green halo. Nothing is visible beyond the halo but deeper blackness. Captured within the beam is the furthest wall, and beyond that the opening to the tunnel that Jonah mentioned in his journal. Stairs climb upwards to a trap door that must lead to the fields above and the exact spot where Biscuit was digging. If Biscuit were to keep digging, if we were to let him, there's no doubt in my mind he'd eventually unearth the door.

There's a small electrical panel on the wall beside me, and it occurs to me that Jonah has wired the room. Which explains the cable running from the lighthouse, down the cliff, and in through the window. Details I was hardly able to take in until now. I shine the lantern over the panel and, sure enough, there's a switch beside it and an outlet below.

When I flip the switch, a plain bulb flickers on from a socket on the wall near the window. It bathes the room in light that looks almost pink because of the red rock. Since I don't need it anymore, I turn off the lantern and crouch to put it on the ground. Near my feet, I notice a long row of glass jars. Inside each jar is something Jonah once showed me in a textbook — a preserved creature. Like a plastic figurine floating in gold water — never breathing, never real — its mouth and eyes gape and its suspended paws grasp imaginary air.

Earlier generations of Jonah's voles.

Gone, then saved.

The observer effect: when you change results with the act of looking. Jonah thinks he withstands it, but every single thing he's touched has been altered.

I turn around to check the rest of the room. Cardboard sheets like the ones I saw rolled into Jonah's knapsack hang from the other walls. The sheet closest to me is edged and boxed with thick black marker. In the top corner is written: *Experiment Marlie Luellen*. Nothing is written in the space beneath.

The sheets next to it are covered with Jonah's journal pages. Graphs and studies covering every inch of cardboard. At the top of each sheet is written in black marker: *Experiment LLB*. The name startles me like a shriek in the woods. Is the answer to the question here?

As I step closer to get a better look, my foot catches on something. On the ground is the most beautiful chest I've ever seen. Wood overlaid with decorative copper plating. Delicate patterns of interlaced diamonds and whorls. The chest Jonah pulled from the rocks in the Rock Pit. Underneath, cradling it, is the green frog blanket from the box in the back room.

I crouch down and carefully lift the lid. Inside is the wrapped bundle that made Jonah cry. I see now what made it so familiar when I first saw him handling it: the bundling cloth is soiled and stiff from being in the ground, but underneath the decay, it's identical to the other green frog blanket. To my green blanket.

When I pick it up, the bundle buckles and jangles like a bag of gold. Even as I imagine the possible richness of a treasure, my heart starts to pound. My body begs me to stop, urges me to get away before it's too late. Aidie's voice, the memory of it, echoes in my mind: *You have to get out of here, Gemma.*

But my hands keep unwrapping.

Inside the cloth, bones clatter to disorder. Bones like the ones Jonah sometimes showed me after foraging in the woods, or in his textbooks as fine-ink drawings of skeleton parts. The difference is, these bones are miniature.

Too-small ribs and femurs and metatarsals and more and more slight bones laid out in a pile. And, last of all, the bones Jonah never showed me: a tiny human skull.

From the bottom of the cloth, a compressed star shines at me. My fingers reach between the bones to pick it up. It's an earring: a perfect silver bird with its wings flying open.

22

My eyes burn from staring at such exquisite things.

I don't need to find my old jewelry box to know this earring is the same as the one a tourist found in our grass years ago and gave to me, and I push it into my pants pocket for safekeeping. I wrap the bones up again, careful not to let the skull roll away, and bundle the frog blanket around it like mothers bundle babies, with its face free to the world. The skull's mouth is shaped into a smile, and the smile makes me forget I should be scared.

The bundle feels lighter than I ever dreamed bones would feel. I gently shush and rock the bundle around the room, not sure what else to do. Something about comforting the bones comforts me.

But Jonah's other hanging sheets call my attention. So many charts scribbled over with notes, so many notes marked with precise hours and minutes. I lay the baby bones back inside the chest and draw closer until the words take shape.

They are the plainest, simplest of words: *eating, sleeping, crying, 2:11 a.m., 8:04 a.m., 9:49 a.m.* Each moment reveals the next ordinary word: *burping, crying, diaper changing, formula.*

Babies. Two. Identified by two letters: G. and A.

Colic, nap times, rolling over, sitting, crawling, crying.

A terrible buzzing starts in my head.

G. and *A.* , over and over, everywhere.

My heart jerks and its beat stumbles into my mouth.

On the last sheet, the letters assemble into two full names: *Gemma* and *Adria*.

I feel myself rock back and forth. My brain spins circles inside my head. It reels me like a top. *Who's Adria? Who's Adria?* My brain screams the question so loudly I can't breathe.

The last journal pages pinned to the cardboard sheets describe the experiment. Pages and pages explain something that happened to people I don't know. Things Jonah did. My eyes blur the words, but still the meaning comes through.

> Twin babies. Weaned from mother. Gemma *and* Adria.
> Pair bonded. Four months old, five months, six months.
> Sleep together. Feed each other. Comfort each other.
> Limited human contact.

More and more notes with times and dates and babies' ages. *Ten months, eleven months, one year.*
Then:

> A. not eating. Crying. More crying. G. not able to feed her. G. eating well. A. still not eating. Experimenter intercepts. But A. only wants G. And G. not able to feed her. A. losing weight. Nothing working. G. unable — or unwilling — to help.

My hands reach up and tear the pages off the wall. Flesh tearing off bone and dropped to the floor. As if what happened can be undone without drawing blood.

As I rip and pull, another name hooks me: *Shannon*. Written in red along the thick spine of a video. Underneath is a date, also in red. October. Almost sixteen years ago.

The tape sticks out of an old VCR that sits on top of an old TV that used to occupy a shelf in our living room, but is now wedged into a corner of the cavern.

When I was very young, Jonah used to let me watch recorded tapes of children's cartoons. It was a way to keep me distracted while he worked. But when he asked Peg to take over my education, the TV was banished like everything else Jonah thought would spoil the integrity of my thinking.

Those painted, excitable children had been so real to me, and for days after they left I mourned. Cried by myself because Jonah didn't want to hear me. And that's when Aidie stepped through the closet and into my room. She was reaching out her hand and laughing — *Come on, let me show you something*. And I laughed too and took her hand.

It surprises me how natural it is to push the tape into its slot in the VCR and use the remote to turn everything on. A forgotten habit remembered.

A gasp of light illuminates the screen, and I start the video. It's a face, very close, the movements somehow slowed down. Eyelids very slowly blink, tears very slowly roll down cheeks. Her hand comes up and with aching slowness wipes a tear away, then moves, slowly, slowly, to cover her mouth.

It goes on and on. Just her face, tearful, listening, her fingers dabbing her eyes and mouth, running across her smooth skin, her eyes blinking, looking aside, looking down.

This is Shannon. I could watch it forever.

The video squeals and lurches and returns to normal speed. The picture opens up, as if I'd been hugging her and have stepped back for a better view. There's a man beside her, standing so close that their shoulders press one against the other. The picture expands. Shannon and the man are holding hands. Gripping each other's hands.

I'm aware of the sound of a man speaking in the background. Not the man pictured in the video because he's not talking, only gripping Shannon's hand and staring into space. It's a flat voice with a broad American accent describing events that have nothing to do with Shannon. "… an emotional plea from the parents."

The picture switches to the façade of a house. A large elegant place with an abundant garden. The picture widens and rolls to show that the house sits behind a high black gate, beside other similar properties and across the street from much smaller houses, more like the kind you'd find on the island, with broken porches and weedy lawns.

The flat voice continues to speak. "The small, close-knit community of Beachport is on high alert." The video shows a road sign — *Beachport, Maine, Where the sea takes your breath away* — then a large, bustling harbor set against a coastline, then people standing in a pretty town handing out or taping up signs. A photo is copied on the pages, but the video image is too far to make out what it is.

I wait, anxious, for the story to go back to Shannon, and it does. There's her face again, casting about, searching for some kind of answer, as the man beside her starts to speak. For some reason, I want to hate him — maybe for owning Shannon with his shoulder and his gripping hand — but his face draws me in. A true expression in his eyes, muscles slack with true emotion, voice speaking truly.

"We just want our babies back. Please, wherever you are, please bring them back to us."

My hand reaches out to the screen. But before I can touch him, the picture switches to another man. Formal in a suit, he sits in front of a blue screen, looking straight ahead, speaking to the camera. It's like he's talking directly and only to me: "That was Dr. Kevin Birkshire and his wife, Shannon. Understandably distraught after their twin baby girls, four months old, were stolen from their home. They are pleading for their safe return."

A photo comes onto the screen beside his face. His voice echoes in my head: *Twin baby girls, four months old, stolen from their home.*

"Anyone with information is asked to please come forward."

Two names appear underneath the photo: *Lindsay and Leah Birkshire.*

The photo gets larger and larger until it fills the screen. Two baby girls together: two little faces, two matching green frog blankets bundled around them, pink bows tied to scraps of hair, shining earrings dotting their ears. Shining silver birds flying off their tiny ears.

23

My body catapults and slams into the wall. Some part of me hits the bulb and smashes the glass. The room goes dark as I drop to the ground and curl into a ball.

My heart slaps so hard, it stings every inch of me and shakes me like a thousand hands. I can't feel or move. There is no sense in my head or sounds in my mouth.

Sweat covers me and turns me into a slug. Shivering and shaking, slippery, I cower on the floor.

Each second is a slide under a microscope: the clay wall, the clay wall, the clay floor.

Sunbeams through the window sting my eyes,

   pick their way down my body to my feet,

     move off somewhere else,

       leave me in shadow.

I am safe here. If I don't move, everything will be the way it used to be.

       ❧

I don't know how many hours later, the climbing rope brushes my face. My eyes shift from the floor until I see the rope dangle in through the opening. Something — maybe the wind outside — makes it move about. With no thoughts telling me to do it, my hand grabs hold.

All I see is my hand on the rope and then my other hand on the rope and then myself getting pulled off the ground. Somehow, I get all the way up and stand on my feet.

Somehow, I make it to the window and my hands find the ascender devices clipped to the back of the harness. I lock both ascenders to the rope like Scotty taught me — right one first, left one underneath — then attach them by their slings to my harness. My body pulls itself upwards until I'm standing on the sill. I turn around, ready to go up. The cliff is in front of me, the sea is at my back, wind swirls around me, maybe rain is coming, maybe heavy rain tonight.

My left foot finds the foot strap, my right hand lifts the clamp. I keep my weight hanging off the right sling and let my left leg do all the work. Up and up I go. No thoughts inside my head at all.

Wind races up the cliffs, and wind roars inside me. It makes me shiver so much I can hardly keep the equipment between my hands. It dries the tears and snot that bubble out, and I have to wipe the crust from my face so I can see, so I can breathe. The cliff rock blows cool, sharp air against my cheek. I don't know how I manage to climb, but somehow everything moves without my knowing.

The sun slips over the sky. Dusk is on me. On the island, time is a loop of sun always changing the light.

At the top by the lighthouse, I rip off the rope and harness and bend over, panting over my knees. I am a boat rocking.

I throw up. Everything comes out from deep inside me. It wrenches out of me, on and on, until I am empty. I spit into the grass.

There is still no ferry in the harbor.

⤳

The keeper's house is gray and old and looks like somebody left it out in the rain.

Jonah's van isn't in the driveway.

When I walk through the back door, the alert for the voles is blinking red and the alarm *tings*. Me trespassing into the lab must have triggered the system. Marlie isn't anywhere on the ground floor, but I hear her moving around in the bathroom upstairs.

The phone starts to ring. I walk into the kitchen and pick up the receiver. "Hello?"

"Gemma."

His voice — the fact of him — makes me recoil.

"I've been phoning and phoning." I don't say a word, and after a pause, Jonah says, "Bad news." He waits, then says, "Yes, I'm afraid … I'm very, very sorry to say that the ferry has run into some problems and it looks like, unfortunately, I'll be stranded on the mainland for the night." Nothing fills the space between us, and so he says, "I feel just awful about this whole … disaster." Jonah has never felt awful about being stranded on the other side. "Just terrible."

The vole alert *tings* again, and Jonah says, "What's that?" I open a drawer and take out the scissors. "Gemma?" With the phone still to my ear, I pull a kitchen chair to the back door, climb it, and cut the wires to the alert. "Gemma? What's going on?" The red flashing bulb goes dead. "Is Marlie there? Put her on the phone, Gemma. It's urgent I —"

The blades cut through the telephone cord, and two broken wires spill out like veins. The silence is cold relief. I stab the scissors into my pocket and reach for the grocery jar and empty it of all the money — small bills and coins — and leave the kitchen. I climb the stairs to my bedroom. The air smells sickening, like dust and mold.

I go to the closet and pull out my old schoolbag and pack it with the money and some clothes — I add my favorite pink sweatshirt and jeans, now soiled with red dirt. Aidie's stuffed mouse sits on her pillow. I stroke its downy head then put it in the knapsack.

Piled on the chair beside my bed are the notepads I used for my lessons with Peg. The top pad is the one I use now to while away the time. Random words and nonsense sketches. So much time filled up and wasted away.

I pick it up and an old book of maps tumbles down. For so many years, I'd pored over those maps, memorizing the cities and towns and routes to and from other places. Always dreaming about where my crazy mother might have gone. I add the book of maps to the knapsack.

I stand in front of the dresser and look at the person in the mirror, then pull the scissors from my pocket and snap the blades a few times. The silver metal shines and cuts the air.

An unthinking motor, I grab a hunk of hair. The scissors chop it off. I grab another hunk and another. The scissors cut and cut. Hair falls or floats to the floor. Soon the face underneath is free and the reflection looks back. Ragged head, dead eyes.

I touch an ear. A tiny scar in the lobe. I see it in the reflection. It was never in the reflection before. I touch the other lobe. A scar there too.

I reach inside the pocket where I hid the tiny flying bird and pull it out. I pull the lock off the back and stab the sharp end through the closed-up hole in my left ear. There is no pain when it goes in, but I do feel warm blood spurt over my fingers. The reflection in the mirror must feel something because its muscles wince and its skin drains to green while blood drips down its cheek and neck. I push the earring all the way through and lock it into place.

"Hey, honey."

I turn around. Marlie stands in the doorway, her hands crossed over her stomach, her eyes red and tired.

"I knocked," she says, indicating my door. "When you didn't answer I got worried. You've been gone all day. I looked everywhere for you." She drops her hands and steps closer. "Your hair."

My head is only ragged edges. It looks ugly and mean. I avert my eyes and stare out the window. The sun is setting.

Marlie takes another step. "Are you okay, Gemma?"

Stars already pin the deep blue sky. Jupiter picks its spot.

"I'm sorry about what happened last night. About the drinking."

Turbulence from the earth's atmosphere refracts their ancient light and makes the stars glitter.

"You have every right to be mad. It was wrong. And I'm sorry."

When I don't answer, she walks away. The sound of her feet creaking over the old floorboards signals her movement. To the bathroom, stopping, coming back again.

She re-enters my room with a dampened washcloth, a towel, a comb, then goes to the chair beside my bed and stacks the pile of notepads on the floor. She brings the chair to me and sets it down. She pats it: an invitation to sit. When I don't react, she very gently guides me into it, then capes the towel around me.

First she dabs the washcloth along the blood on my ear and neck. She murmurs quietly about how it must hurt. She tells me it'll be okay, I'm going to be okay. When the blood is cleaned away, she bends over and wraps her arms around me. She holds me for a long time, but I barely feel her warmth. She kisses the earlobe with the tiny bird earring. I barely feel her lips.

She picks up the scissors from the dresser where I set them. She runs her fingers over my ragged head, carefully lifting the chopped ends up, massaging it this way and that. "You have nice hair," she says and draws the comb through a small section. "I cut my mom's hair all the time, so you don't have to worry." The scissors start to snip. Thorny points drop to the towel and floor. Like the leftover bits from a paper snowflake. Marlie massages and cuts all over. In the reflection, the head between her hands is a moon in orbit.

Dreamy thoughts whirl inside, puddling over the darkness. *You don't have to do anything. Just like we hoped, a woman came to the island to find us. And we knew she'd take care of us with homemade casseroles and photos in cameras and cleaning blood off wounds and leaving kisses on ears. Everything can be the way it's always been, but better. No one knows except you.*

"I remember when I was six or seven," Marlie's voice breaks over my thoughts, "I decided to have this tea party. My mother wasn't big on celebrations because we didn't have a lot of money and she didn't believe in waste — this was before she got sick — but there was definitely something we were celebrating. It might've been my birthday, I can't remember. And I really wanted to set the table nicely. I found the pretty plates and teacups my grandmother who I never met had given us a long time before. I set every piece in its exact place."

She pauses to stroke my hair, then continues. "My mother didn't say anything when I put out an extra place — three plates, forks, spoons, saucers, and teacups — instead of two, or when I decorated the table with a bunch of junk we had lying around — plastic red and white rosebuds, sparkles from my craft kit, a string of purple beads I'd found in the street. But then she left the house, and when she came back she had this box of Tim Hortons donuts with her. That was a treat for us back then. I remember she made Red Rose tea, and we didn't say anything to each other while we waited for the water to boil. I couldn't talk — because, oh my God, this was going to be the most important day of my life." I let the innocent cadence of her voice lull me.

"Mom had half a donut in her mouth already," Marlie keeps going. "I hadn't touched mine yet because I was waiting. But then she asked, 'Who's the extra plate for?' I said, 'The plate is for Dad. Because it's —' I can't remember what it was. My birthday? Easter? '— and,' I said, 'Dad is going to visit today.' My mom stopped chewing and said, 'Has your father ever made an appearance here? Ever?' I said no. She said, 'So why would he come today?' 'Because,' I said, 'it's my —' whatever it was. And Mom said, 'He's never coming so just forget about it.' I got so mad. I was furious. I mean, what was the point of celebrating my birthday if we weren't all together? But I couldn't say that to her, right? And I couldn't eat any of those donuts, so I pushed away my plate and she finished the box."

Marlie puts the scissors down. They're littered with sharp bits of my hair. I reach over to pick them off, but instead the blades scrape off flakes of blood that have dried all over my thumb and fingertips.

"When I was sixteen," she says while she strokes my head, arranging angles of hair toward my cheeks, my ears, my eyes, "I found this photo. It was just after Mom was diagnosed with MS and I'd been doing this deep clean of our house. I think to make up for the fact that, from then on, her life would never be the same. And there was this box under her bed filled with photos of both of them together. They looked so young, so cool. Mom was completely different, about fifty pounds lighter with no clue she was going to get sick one day. My dad looked gorgeous, even though he was already an addict by then. I don't know how much you know about drugs and all that, but addiction is a terrible thing, Gemma. Anyway, in those photos, they looked like they would never go through a crappy day in their lives." She sighs.

"One of the photos was especially nice, so I took it," she continues. "Not that long ago, I met him and I tried to match that gorgeous photo to this old, sad man who showed up at my mom's hospital room. I walked in and there he was, stooped-over and skinny. He looked sicker than her. His face was, like, *decayed*.

"Mom introduced us by first names. 'Marlie, meet Finn. Finn, Marlie.' That's when I recognized him as my father whose photo I carried everywhere. I was kind of freaked out because he didn't kiss me or hug me or anything. And my mom was so tough. 'He's asking for money, Marlie. Don't give him any.'" Marlie imitates her mother's voice. "'He's a user and if you give him money he will die.' It terrified me — I'd never seen my mother like that. And I had to watch this shrunken old man shuffle away. Even as a grown woman, I was too scared to run after him."

Marlie pauses. I'm still petting the blades of the scissors. Splinters of hair flick off and flick back on again. A magnetic attraction.

"After he left," Marlie continues, "my mom told me the truth. That

Finn wasn't even my dad. She'd had this one-night stand and gotten pregnant. She didn't know who my father was, but she decided to keep me — I guess I should be grateful. When I was born, she didn't want 'unknown' on my birth certificate, so she asked Finn to sign as my father. Finn was her best friend back then, a boy in love with boys. An addict who wanted to help her. Signing my birth certificate was the one thing he could do." Marlie takes a sip of air. "I asked her why she kept telling me that Finn was my dad. She said she did it so I would never think she didn't want me. And I said, 'So instead I thought he never did.'"

She lays her hand over my hand that holds the scissors. "I still have his picture in my wallet." She pulls the scissors away from me, sliding them along the dresser and picking them up. "I don't keep it so I can cry over it. I keep it because I liked having a father. Even one who's not there."

You don't have to do anything.

"Gemma — are you okay?"

No one needs to know except you.

"What's going on?" she says. The scissors dangle casually from her fingers. In her world, everything *is* okay.

"I know why you came here," I say. It's all so clear now. Her nerves, her shipwrecked body on the cliffs. It was always clear. "You were going to jump."

She gives a reflexive gasp. A small, almost noiseless noise. "No," she says. But her face is pale and her eyes are rooted to the ground.

"You were going to end it." It sounds rougher than I intended.

Marlie blinks her eyes but says nothing.

There are hushed island stories of the ones who couldn't go on. Stories I'm not supposed to know. "Love," I say. "That's what you want."

"No," she says. Her breath catches in her throat. "Love is something I make up to feel better."

"Jonah doesn't love you either." Is it as cruel as it sounds? I don't know anymore. "Get out of here," I say. "You have to go."

The scissors fall to the floor — the crashing sound is so loud — and spin in circles at our feet. Marlie's face is snow melting. She says in a low voice, "Okay, Gemma. I get it." A sad laugh seeps out of her before she walks out of the room and down the stairs.

I didn't want to change into this person. I tried to stop it.

After a long, expectant pause, I push the towel off my shoulders and brush the last bits of hair from my clothes. I get my knapsack and strap it over my shoulders.

Downstairs, I find Marlie in the back room slumped on the cot. When she sees me, she holds a hand toward the door. "Would you mind?" she says. "I just need a minute."

"That's okay," I say. I make up a lie so she won't worry — those are the easiest lies because people also want to hear them. "Scotty is coming to get me and I'm going to stay with him." But I have to warn her too. "Go to Peg's until you can cross back to the mainland. Get out of here. Don't let him stop you."

"Okay. Thanks, Gemma." She keeps melting into something smaller.

I close the door between us, and it goes quiet on her side. Before I know it, I'm leaving the house and walking away down the road.

24

Only the crunch of stones in my ears. My feet and legs are wheels turning and I can't feel them. Hot wind pushes into my mouth and chokes me. Stars cluster above me. Bootes, Virgo, Corvus. The herdsman, the goddess of fertility, the spy. Lower down, the sparkling lights of Corona Borealis, Ariadne's crown. A princess caught in a love triangle: her and Theseus, the man she loved who might or might not have loved her back, and Dionysius, the god who married her with or without her permission.

The road feels miles longer than ever, probably because I don't know where I'm going. I'm not going to Peg. Not going to Doris. Don't want to tell anyone. Don't want to turn this into a story.

Fog rolls up the hill from Keele's Landing. Soon it will swallow me into itself and try to lose me. Even so, I keep walking toward it, the fog bundling and rolling over the whole of West Island and on its way to smother the East.

I close my eyes while I walk and picture the wind swooping in and raising the bottom of the mist, like dainty hands pulling up the hem of a flowing dress. I walk under it, certain and trusting that the weather knows where to take me. Hidden in its folds, I follow exactly where it wants me to go.

At the end, there's a dark tunnel, and I stop and crawl inside it and lie down, curling myself into a ball. It isn't a blanket, the fog, it doesn't keep me warm at all. But I coil myself inside it and lie as still and silent as a stone. Even when the rain spears the tunnel. Even when the drumming is so loud it trumps my heart. Even when I shiver with such conviction it's like someone is drowning me.

After a very long while, I fall asleep.

≫

Someone is shaking me, but not hard. "Gemma … Gemma." That name sounds so special in his voice. "Gemma … Gemma." I wake up and peer through crusted eyes.

Scotty is crouching beside me. He has his hand on my shoulder. "Gemma? You all right?"

I rub my eyes clean. Behind Scotty, I notice the rain has stopped and has left an incandescent cloud of fog. Raindrops literally stopped in motion, in time, hanging, waiting, and blooming with sunlight.

I uncurl myself and try to stretch, but it's too cramped in the tunnel. My eyes are so tired, they can hardly open. Scotty coaxes and leads me out. Only with his help can I stand up.

But it's not a tunnel at all that I found during the night: it's Biscuit's doghouse. I've never been inside his house before, probably because Biscuit never has. But it's a good place. Solid and straight. Mr. O'Reardon made it when Biscuit was a puppy, building it with plywood walls and real shingles on the roof and even a carpet on the floor. But Biscuit never wanted a place of his own.

"You all right, Gems?" Scotty is still holding my hand. I don't want to let it go.

"I'm okay, Scotty."

"Biscuit in there with you?"

Coldness makes me shiver. "No."

"Wonder where the bugger is." Scotty huffs his breath and pulls gently on my hand. "Let's get you inside and warm."

Before I realize what I'm doing, I throw myself at him. I hug him so hard his ribs press into mine. I imagine our ribs lacing together like pleading fingers. Scotty pats my back, and I put my mouth to his ear and breathe into it. I want my breath to go inside him. I want it to swirl around inside him until it turns into a ghost that stays with him always.

Scotty leads me by the hand back to the house and brings me to the living room couch. He puts five blankets around me, even one around my head. I never take my eyes off him.

He says, "If it makes you feel any better, you look cute as a button with your new haircut. A real young woman." He smiles at me encouragingly. "Getting all fancy on us are you, now you have a big-city lady around?"

Even though my heart is burning, I feel myself shiver under the blankets.

Scotty goes to the kitchen and pours a cup of milk into a pot and puts the pot on the stove. He stirs the milk and says, "You going to talk about what happened, Gems?"

I don't say anything.

"My dad is out looking for — Anyway, it's just the two of us here right now if you want to talk."

I shake my head.

Scotty puts down the spoon, "Okay, then." He won't force me. He whistles between his teeth and checks the temperature. Scotty is the only one who understands. Because he is my one true love.

When it's ready, he brings me a cup of warm milk and sits on the couch beside me. He puts his hand on the blanket over my foot. "It's going to be all right, Gems. Take it from me. Today's heartbreak is tomorrow's foothold."

When I don't say anything, he gets up and goes to the hall closet and opens its door. He pulls out a flat pile of folded clothes.

I love him so much. Maybe he's the only one in the world who can make me happy.

He hands me the flat pile of clothes. "These are Mom's. Hope that's not too weird for you, but you've got to get out of those wet things if you're ever going to warm up. Mom was tiny too. Not like you, mind, but she was a wee thing. Those should fit you until you get home and can change into your own."

When I take the flat little squares from him, my hand touches his. I pull off all the blankets very slowly and stare at Scotty. He steps back and opens his hand to the bathroom. I walk to it very slowly, tears crystallizing over my eyes. Scotty has given me Mrs. O'Reardon's clothes, the clothes his own mother wore when he lived with her.

His hand reaches behind me and pulls the bathroom door closed. I can hear him walk into his bedroom. He calls through the walls. "You want to wait here till your dad gets back? Or do you want to hang around with the ladies at the diner today?" I hear the loud clomp of him changing his sandals for boots.

I put Mrs. O'Reardon's old clothes on the edge of the bathtub. Then I take off all my own clothes. They peel away in wet, snaky strips. My bare skin is slippery all over. My body is rounder and softer than I remember. I touch my breasts. They are as soft and budding as foam on a wake. Already I feel warmer.

Scotty calls through the wall, "I have to go out today, check for some poachers that Dad got wind of. I can take you wherever you want, though." Being with Scotty would make everything all right. It would make everything better.

I feel warmer and warmer. I touch my bare stomach and feel the slippery wetness. Scotty calls through the wall, "Your dad should have the ferry fixed later today, and you can wait in town and go home with him. What do you say?"

The flat pile of Mrs. O'Reardon's clothes waits for me to take it up. I wonder how Scotty took the clothes off his wife. How he kissed her. How it felt when he lay on top of her, skin to skin. I could be a Mrs. O'Reardon. If I have to pick a name, that's the one I want.

My bareness is warmer than any clothes. I put my hand on the doorknob.

"Now that I think of it, Gems," Scotty calls, "I think we should run you to Peg for a quick once-over. Just to make sure you're healthy and fit."

In his bedroom, Scotty sits on his bed, back to me, pulling a fresh shirt on. His head tilts down so he can watch himself doing up the buttons. The hairs on the back of his neck are red and black mixed together, like the skin on stones. He says, calling, looking at his buttons, "You could also stay at Peg's house, have yourself a proper sleep. Don't want you getting sick."

I open my arms and, with all my love pouring out of me, I climb over the quilted mattress, the softness that will entangle us, and wrap my warm bare body around Scotty.

When he turns to me, he's smiling so very sweetly and he starts to open his arms to me. But when he sees my body, his face opens up. His mouth opens, his eyes widen, his eyebrows lift. A gargling sound comes from the back of his throat. If it's a scream he's holding back, I must be what I know I am: a monster.

Scotty jerks away from my body, pulling himself up and far away from me to the very back corner of the room. Turning away, he puts his hands on his face. Through them he says, "Get some clothes on, child. Quick, go get dressed."

"But, Scotty —"

"Now. Get some clothes on now."

His words hammer me into the ground, crumbling my insides. More scared than I've ever been, I run back to the bathroom and slam the door shut. I fumble to put on Mrs. O'Reardon's dry clothes. They hang off me like empty bags.

When I'm dressed, I come out of the bathroom. Scotty isn't in his room. I find him in the kitchen, a knife in his hand, cutting thick slices of cheese onto bread.

I don't know what to say.

"It's okay, it's okay," Scotty says, not looking at me. His back is to me, muscles knotting and working as he cuts the cheese and heats up a frying pan.

"I love you, Scotty."

He puts the cheese toast into the frying pan. Without looking at me, he says, "It's okay, Gemma." The toast sizzles and smokes.

"I love you more than anything."

Scotty looks at me then. His face is back to normal. "I love you too, Gemma. You know that, right?"

I choke on my tears.

"But you're young and I'm old. Too old for you. We love each other like friends. Or like a brother and sister love each other."

You don't belong to anyone.

Scotty picks up a spatula and turns his back to me. "I would never do anything to hurt you, Gemma. Ever." He presses the spatula onto the cheese sandwich. A burnt smell rises with the smoke. He says, "And that's not always how it works with grown-up love."

25

I used to think the inside of Peg's house was from a fairy tale. It has butter-yellow walls and lace-covered everything and china figurines and matryoshkas and stuffed pillows and silver teapots. We used to have tea parties in her parlor when I was little. Peg always poured the tea. We would eat shortbread that Randy made us special and we would talk in British accents. Peg's British accent was hilarious.

In my head I say goodbye to all of it.

Peg walks me through the yellow, lacey parlor and into the exam room. The exam room is the opposite. It has white white walls, silver trays on wheels, shining tools, and three cots laid out with clean sheets. Scotty follows us, quietly catching Peg up on what he thinks has happened.

I don't pay attention. The only thing that matters now is how I'm going to get off the island.

Peg sits me on a cot, sticks a thermometer in my mouth, and shines a light into one eye. The brightness doesn't hurt at all. She shines it into the other eye. "Everything looks lovely, dear," she says, cooing.

I will sneak on the ferry when it comes back, when no one is looking.

Peg wraps a blood pressure cuff around my upper arm. She sticks the stethoscope under the cuff, then pumps the monitor tight. It squeezes me good and hard. It wants to tell me something.

I will cross to the other side. I will go away.

We're all quiet as Peg releases the pressure and blood pumps down my veins again. She counts the heartbeats.

On the mainland, because no one will know me, I can be anyone I choose.

Peg rips the cuff off my arm and wraps the stethoscope around the cuff. Then she pulls the thermometer out of my mouth and checks it. "Well, everything seems perfectly fine," she says, smiling, relieved. Then she looks me in the eye, "But is it, my darling?"

On the mainland, I won't belong to anyone. Nobody's child.

"Gemma. Is everything all right?" Peg's voice shakes me out of my dream. "Did something happen between you and Marlie up at the house?"

I pretend to think very seriously, then shake my head slowly, as if I don't want to hurry the answer, "Nooo, everything is perfectly fine."

"So why were you wandering around in the middle of the night, and sleeping in Mr. O'Reardon's doghouse?"

I pretend to think. "Well, no reason, really. I thought it might be fun to explore." I wait for another thought. "But don't expect Marlie to stick around too much longer."

Peg and Scotty exchange a look. Peg says carefully, "Did you two have a fight?"

"Oh no," I say, already sounding like a different person, "Marlie and I are awesome. It's Marlie and Jonah who might have a problem."

"I see," Peg says to Scotty.

"If you haven't seen her yet," I say, "expect her soon. Make sure she gets on the ferry."

Peg gives a sorry nod. "All right, my darling. We will."

"So," I say, "I should probably get back to the house to say goodbye. Don't want to miss her."

Scotty pipes up. "I could drive up there and bring Marlie down."

"Actually," I say, almost ashamed at how I'm using her — *but*

I have to get away and nothing must stop me — "I think it's best if Marlie and I have a good heart-to-heart before she leaves us. In private. Up at the house." I look through Scotty, but I give him my nicest smile. "So I think I'll head back now."

"Let me take you up, Gemma," Scotty says, trying not to sound worried. "Don't want you to get sick, after all this."

And I will walk myself back to town, under cover. It's the ferry I need.

Peg nods, "I think that's best, Gemma. If we can't convince you to stay here, then I'd rather Scotty ran you up."

On the island, there is no such thing as a waste of time.

"Okay, thank you," I say.

Peg seems reassured. "Well, good." She touches the back of her hand to my forehead, then strokes my face. "But you call us the moment you need anything. All right, my darling girl?"

"All right, Peg." Before I follow Scotty, I take her hand — without squeezing it because I don't want to hurt her — and say, "I love you, Peg."

Peg's eyes tear up. "I love you too, dear. More than anything."

❧

While Scotty drives me up the road to the house, I look straight ahead, not saying anything. When we get to the last bend in the road, Scotty says, "When you feel better, Gemma, call me and I'll come get you and we can go rock climbing like in the old days, how 'bout? Get the cobwebs out. Sound good?"

Looking out through the truck window, I say, "That sounds great."

He stops on the driveway by the front door. "Do you want me to come in? Talk to Marlie?"

I shake my head.

Scotty pats my knee then pulls his hand back quickly. "Okay, then. Don't you worry yourself. It's not good for you to worry. Everything will be fine."

I grab my knapsack and get out of the truck, closing the door behind me. Scotty maneuvers the truck around the drive.

For the first time, I notice the seat beside Scotty is empty. No Biscuit slobbering on the window, staring at me through it, no barking down at the house, no trying to jump on me, no begging for hugs. "Where's Biscuit?" I say as Scotty drives the truck away. I call louder, "Where's Biscuit?" But it's too late, he's gone.

⌇

I don't go into the keeper's house, but only wait long enough to make sure Marlie hasn't noticed my arrival. There's no movement through any of the windows.

The house reminds me of Jonah. A nightmare picture of his face charges into my mind — distorted, a menace. And questions call: *What is he? How could he do it? What did I see and ignore for so many years?*

Memories flood in instead of answers. Or maybe they are answers.

Once I found him crouched in the woods, his arm flinging up and coming down, smashing something in the space between his bent knees. Because it was dinnertime, I was out looking for him. It was pouring, but summer rain, hot enough that the rain was welcome. The sight of his arm coming up and smashing down, veins bulging under his skin like knotted kelp, stopped me from calling out to him. Blood started to ooze out of his hand and arm and wash with the rain down his skin like an overflowing brook.

A twig snapped under my foot and he heard it. He froze, his bloody fist hanging in the air. On the ground between his feet, something was too broken to recognize. Very slowly he turned his head around. His eyes locked onto mine, and I couldn't see into them. It was like there was a black screen across his pupils.

I wanted to run away. I knew — *I think I knew* — that whatever he was smashing could also be me. But I was too shocked to move.

That's how I saw the blackness in his eyes roll up like blinds being pulled, and his skin cooling to its natural color. Himself again, the *he* that I recognized.

Completely calm now, he lowered his hand and stared at his smashed knuckles. After a moment, he wiped his fist along his shirt, leaving rusty streaks on the cloth. "The surveillance camera broke," he said. "I'm going to have to order another one." He didn't say anything else, and I just watched as the rain joined us together, silver links of chain from him to me.

Fear crashes over me and washes everything else away. It destroys confusion and fatigue. It kills outrage and sorrow.

If I leave, Jonah will be angry. He will forget himself, and he will fight for his survival.

I have to get away from him. I have to hold him off.

I begin to fumble with my things, opening my knapsack, searching for an answer. My fingers brush my sketchpad, and an idea comes to me. If I leave him a letter, if I appease him, he'll be relieved. All his troubles will be over and he will let me go.

I tear out a blank page and write.

Dear Jonah,
I know about my real family.
Don't worry, I won't tell anyone what happened.
Thank you for taking care of me.
Give my love to Scotty, Peg, Doris, and all the others.
Gemma

It's a terrible letter. Foolish and simple. But fear only allows so much.

I fold the paper in thirds the way official letters are folded, then I write his name on the top flap. So it won't fly off, I shove it in a crack in the concrete of the front stoop.

No one calls to me as I walk away.

26

A long the road, I compose a plan. How I'm going to get onto the ferry by running out of sight behind the cabs of people's trucks, then sneak into the engine room and weave myself behind the pipes. Sooner or later, the ferry will have to cross to the mainland. The fact that Jonah will be the one in control is an irrelevant detail. It has to be.

When I get to the bend that clears the woods, it's clear there's no ferry in the harbor or coming across the bay. If the boat isn't fixed yet, it could be a long wait to get off the island.

As I get closer to Keele's Landing, I move off the road and into the Roberts' field that flanks the south side. The hay grass is high and shelters me on all sides and I'm able to get almost all the way to the docks through it. From the edge of the field, I have a good vantage point for what's happening in town.

Jake and Finey Roberts are taking one of their habitual walks up and down the pier. John Woolit leaves the FoodMart with a newspaper tucked under his arm and crosses to Peg's Diner. Scotty's house is quiet and dark, even though his truck has arrived back. No Biscuit barking or running around the yard.

Through the window of Peg's Diner, I see Doris wiping tables and a few islanders eating lunch or chatting. I can even make out the dark shape of Randy working at the grill in the back and a bit of smoke rising from it and getting sucked up by the fan.

What would happen if I told them what I know? Told them everything, exactly as I found it?

Peg is at the window now, staring out over the water. Peg doesn't often stare out windows. She's always busy working or chatting with people. Inside the wide pane, her face looks very small and white. Almost like an ornament that decorates people's houses for Christmas. Now the diner is a giant snow globe with everyone sealed inside it. A lovely souvenir advertising the island. It just needs sparkling bits to rain down over everything. I imagine leaving with a snow globe hidden in my pocket, my friends caught and coming along.

But the vision shatters. Peg is falling. Her arms fly up and her head arches back.

I hear myself scream. I feel my feet run toward the diner. But everyone else is also running to catch her. Arms seem to come out of nowhere to grab and protect her. I stop short and crouch behind a pier marker to watch. Peg disappears from view, slumping out of sight below the diner's window ledge. Everyone crouches to save her, also bending out of sight. There's a loud *clop-clop* along the wooden planks of the dock as Jake and Finey Roberts also run to help.

I struggle with panic. It's possible that it was me who caused Peg's fall. Maybe my visit to the examination room was too much for her. Maybe she built up worries too heavy to bear.

As I try to decide between going and giving up my plan to help Peg, the white nose of the ferry across the water comes into view. On one side of me are the diner and Peg and everyone I love and care about, and on the other side is a chance for me to escape without anyone knowing.

Everyone in the diner sees the ferry too because the bunch of them get up and press their faces to the glass. Doris has Peg in her arms and gently cradles her toward a booth. Peg's head wobbles a bit to one side, but her eyes flutter open.

She's alive.

Inside the diner, the islanders talk urgently together. Randy is on the phone. For someone who doesn't get excited, he looks like he's getting ready for a fight, shouting orders, running his hand through his hair. I can't help picturing the islanders as a mob of angry towns-folk like the ones I learned about during history lessons. Scythes and pitchforks and torches gripped in their hands. Angry enough to burn down the castle and kill the king. A horde. A crusade. A revolution.

Then Scotty's truck races around the corner and Scotty jumps out. As brave and noble as ever. A man to love forever, even if he doesn't love you back.

When Scotty gets inside the diner everyone seems to relax, as if they know, like I know, that Scotty will save everything. Through the window, the townsfolk go back to being as old and frail as ever. Not a crusade at all. A pasture.

Scotty takes Peg from Doris, bending over her and coming up with Peg in his arms, carrying her as if she doesn't weigh more than a snowflake. Which she probably doesn't.

He carries Peg to his truck while the others follow, worried and pale. Doris runs ahead and opens the passenger door so Scotty can put Peg down on the seat. They gather around the door, talking and gesturing excitedly toward the incoming ferry. They're going to make Jonah take her back to the mainland so they can get her to the hospital in Moncton. Of course they have to. She's too sick to nurse herself. That means the ferry will have to turn around as soon as it docks. My chance to get away.

While Jonah guides the ferry into the hold and while Scotty and Peg and all the rest wait anxiously on the loading dock, I sneak along the lower pier below the docking bay to the small ladder at the end. The ferry slowly motors closer in front of me. Close enough that I can almost touch it. The sounds of the engine are so loud I can't hear anything else, not even the waves or wind. I can't hear any of the islanders around Scotty's truck. The smell of diesel fills my nose — crisp-fried eggs.

I wait as the ferry maneuvers in and stops and the engine idles and quiets. Now I can hear voices calling to each other. Jonah's voice too. He sounds agitated as he explains the last two days. "Fuel pump died en route to the mainland the other day. Took Namath Motors till today to get the right fuel lines. Took us till now to get the lines in."

I hear Hesperos's deep voice. "But everything is running smooth now."

Doris calls out, louder than everyone, "Well, you have to turn right around, boys. Peg just had a spell. We have to get her to hospital."

"I think we need to settle down first." Jonah is firm in his refusal. "Take a breath. I'm sure she's fine —"

Doris screams like I've never heard her scream before. "Now!!"

Hesperos answers quickly. "Naturally, we're going, Doris. Don't you worry." He works on getting the ramp down as the engines of the cars and trucks coming in from the mainland start up. They rattle off the ferry and drive down the road, mostly to the FoodMart. The only vehicle that will cross back to the mainland right away is Scotty's. So I have to figure out a way to hide on it.

I hear the clang and rattle of Scotty's truck driving into the hold and people's voices shouting one on top of the other, debating what should be done next. Who should go, who should stay, and why. That's when I climb up the ladder and hop across to the dock, crouching down so no one can see. I check the diner, which has the only view toward the boat, toward me. But no one is in the diner anymore — everyone is crowded on the *Spirit*, arguing together about the best options for Peg.

I sidle over to the open ramp and angle my head in to see. Everyone has gathered at the far end and are bundled around Scotty and Peg, trying to pretend they aren't as worried as they are. Jonah is off to one side. I can see he's anxious. I can see him glancing up toward the lighthouse, toward the woods that hide the keeper's house.

I dart out. I don't take even a second to imagine myself getting caught or having to explain to anyone what I'm doing and why. I run and pray that no one sees me.

And no one does. I get to the back of Scotty's truck, jam my foot on the bumper, pop up the bed cover, angle one leg then the other underneath it, and slide myself into darkness.

Even though the blood is pounding in my ears, even though the strangeness of the thing I'm doing is pulling my body in unknown directions, I can still hear the voices of the islanders on deck, discussing and worrying. An agreement is somehow made and their voices shush. Then everyone's feet move across the metal floor of the boat and I know they've decided who is going to which place.

I lift the bed cover high enough to see their backs walking away: Doris, Randy, John Woolit, Jake and Finey Roberts, five or six others. Hesperos lifts the ramp closed behind them and pulls in all the ropes and ties. I know that now Hesp will follow Jonah up to the bridge so they can ready the engine, and pretty soon I hear the grunt and groan of it gearing up again. The boat lurches as it takes us into open water.

My heart beats as hard as the waves that push at us. My first time on the ferry as it crosses the bay. After imagining it for so many years.

I check once more from under the cover. On the island, everyone is walking back to the diner, their heads weighed down with worry. The ferry chugs along, still slow and steady. The coast moves into the distance, pulled away from me like it's on a string and someone is dragging it just out of my reach.

High on the road from East Island, I notice Marlie walking, then running toward town, faster and faster, like maybe she can stop what is already spinning away.

Only now do I remember that we left her. That I left her alone.

27

*A*ll the way across the water, I think about them, hoping and wishing that everyone will be okay.

I remind myself that Peg's eyes fluttered, and that she held on to Scotty. She didn't seem frail the way Mrs. O'Reardon once had.

And surely Marlie understands that she needs to get away from the island. Last night she said that love was something she invented. She went to the back room to cry. She must realize she has to go home now.

A shape in the water pins my attention: just before the shore that edges the strait, a bright pond of algae quivers around a buoy. I recognize the markings: it's the same buoy that went missing from Crescent Bay.

I'm weighed down with disappointment, only now realizing that I hoped something remarkable had happened to it. That it might have travelled all the way down the Atlantic and into the Amazon. That it might have bobbed past a capuchin monkey. A three-toed sloth. A black caiman. But instead it's just another captive that didn't get away.

My stomach convulses, and I let out a sob. By instinct I cover my mouth and my hand fills with tears.

❧

We get to the other side, and I can feel the boat docking and Scotty's truck gearing up to drive off the ferry. From my hiding spot in the truck bed, I watch Jonah and Hesperos on the deck waving Scotty and Peg off, then getting right to the work of turning around and heading back to the island.

Jonah: the man who kept me from my real life. The only parent I've ever known.

I want to hate him. I can feel the *feel* of that hate.

Boxed inside me, it only needs to be smashed open to spill over everything.

≫

After dreaming about it for as long as I can remember, after studying pictures of it and picturing myself within the lines, after wishing for the feel of it on my skin, I'm on the mainland. This isn't the way I imagined experiencing it, but now I'm going to see the world.

The truck moves fast. Faster than I'm used to. Because I don't want to pull the bed cover all the way down and miss anything, the wind whips through the opening and lashes me with cold, sharp edges. Long bands of road roll past, flanked on either side by flat patches of tree-dotted meadow. Sometimes a small gas station or diner. Telephone poles counting off the miles.

I long to be able to touch the new ground, to be able to examine it and see what the grass really looks like, what creatures hide in these woods, what insects in the leaves. I want to meet the people and watch them in their lives. I want to fill up on all the things that I've missed.

But the steady road and speed lull me, and my eyes get heavier and heavier, and soon I let myself fall into the breathless nothing.

≫

When I open my eyes, we're driving down a street crowded with cars and trucks. They're swarming all around us, behind Scotty's truck, beside it. Cables hang from the sky over the road. Lights blink from them, red or green. Sidewalks are crowded with stores and businesses. A few people walk in and out of shops or along the sidewalk past them. The people look much like the islanders, also like many of the tourists I've seen.

But everything is so vast, so fast, so loud. A thin web of panic binds my heart, and I grab the wall of the truck. How stupid of me to think it would be easy to adjust to the outside world.

Scotty steers the truck into a driveway that leads right to a wide set of doors. I look up. The hospital is gigantic. Also red brick like so much else here, but a giant box of it. I've never seen such a large building, although I've tried to imagine them.

Through the truck wall, there's talking in hushed voices — mostly Scotty's — but I think I hear the faint whisper of Peg's responses. I hope I do. Truck doors open and slam shut and Scotty's voice gets fainter, and I assume he's carrying Peg into the hospital.

I check around the driveway and make sure there's no one to see me, then I lift the bed cover and jump out. Touching down on new land feels strangely victorious, maybe like John Cabot first arriving on Maritime soil after an arduous journey.

I inch toward the shadows of the hospital, trying to check inside, hoping to catch sight of Peg. If the outside of the hospital looked like a giant brick box, the inside looks more like a maze. Hallways and columns and doors upon doors leading to unknown places. Rooms inside rooms, like the rings of felled trees.

I edge closer and finally see Scotty bending over a desk, talking to a friendly-looking woman. Behind him, another woman already has Peg on a stretcher and is pushing it through a door into one of the mysterious rooms. The profile of Peg's face is very still: a tiny cheek rounding up, a sharp triangle of nose, thin lips stretched into a kind of smile. I think I see her fingers tighten around the bars of the stretcher — a sign that she might be awake, but no sign of how bad she is or might get.

I wait, ducked around the corner, until Scotty finishes talking with the woman. He finds a chair and sits down. Suddenly he looks old, like his face has lost its shape.

I want to run to him and hug him. To be hugged by him. But it's time to go. I know I could, if given the chance, stare at Scotty for hours, for days, for all of my life.

28

The air around the hospital is warm. It feels like spring has come early to the city of Moncton. Grass is already starting to green up, and the buds on the trees are already pushing through. I check the sky — clouds are a gray blanket pulled over the blue, but I can still calculate that it's around four.

I don't know where to go, so I make my way down the sidewalk. I have to fight the urge to run blindly. Or to succumb to the dizziness that wants to ride my vision and breath. I know where I am and still a voice inside me cries: *Where am I? Where am I?*

Two or three people pass me, and I cringe away, hoping — like a baby — that if I don't look at them they won't see me. Nothing is chasing me here, and yet it feels like everything is.

The sidewalk leads me to a wide excavated field surrounded by chain-link fencing. Two sides of the field are flanked by houses with small fenced-in yards. Giant yellow trucks stand at attention on the construction dirt, but no one is around to operate them.

I push myself under the fence and walk a ways into the broken-up field, then huddle against one shadowed edge, making myself small. Here I am, at the first stop of my escape, with no better plan than to hide in the shadows. Sleep presses at my mind, willing me to close my eyes and curl up. I've never felt so tired in my life. My only relief is that the unbidden panic has begun to ease off. Slowly, I feel like myself again, even if I don't know at all what that means.

I remember I haven't eaten in over a day, and my mouth is starting to get dry. I know already there's nothing to eat or drink in my bag, but that doesn't stop me from checking, fumbling my hands over the bunched clothes, my sketchpad, the stuffed mouse. At least I have a little money.

I can't risk running into Scotty, who would just take me back to where I can never go again. I decide to wait until it gets dark and then look around for a store or diner. I think I have enough money with me to buy a drink and a sandwich. But it'll be hours still before the sun sets. During a maritime May, the days are so long, each one feels almost like two.

I wait one hour, maybe more, trying not to think too much, watching out for people who might be watching out for me, stubbing my boot into the yielding dirt, designing houses and cities that are more beautiful, safer, than the ones I've seen. Another hour goes by and the clouds thicken and throw out some drops of rain. The rain marks my clothes, perfect round spots that dishevel the cloth.

I think about how far from the ocean I've traveled. Never thought you could leave such a huge thing behind. On the island, you're always aware of water, even when you don't realize it. It laps at the edges of everything. It soaks the air, sprinkling your skin and mouth. During storms, the wind drives it willy-nilly — sometimes the rain doesn't fall but skips sideways across the sky. As certain as dawn, water will get inside every house at some point, peeling open the plaster of ceilings and walls no matter how much people do to hold it off. Now that I'm conscious of having left the ocean behind, I feel dried out. I close my eyes and lift my cheeks and hope the piddling drops soak me through.

In the darkness behind my closed eyes, I remember walking through the Roberts' field on a dry summer day, my fingertips brushing along the tops of feathered grasses, my skin nipping like when someone breathes down your neck by mistake. Marsh-pink, musk mallow, wild geraniums whispered from behind the grass shoots, promising me with their glances that soon I would know. The light of the sun sparked over everything and wings fluttered through the sparking light, but in a way I could only just see out of the corners of my eyes. Brown and yellow butterflies, gray moths, maroon thrushes, white terns. In the distance the ocean blanketed the island as if a starry night had dropped from the sky. The air smelled warm and sweet at the same time. The sound around me was a shushing like a lullaby — not separate sounds but the music of everything together: wind and crickets and chickadees, mingling branches, seagulls beckoning now and again. Somehow goodness shone into every part of me. It lit me up and made me want to laugh. And I won't ever see that day again.

⤴

The rain has stopped. The sky above me clears and the raindrop stains on my clothes begin to fade. Clouds still muddy the horizon and the sun sets behind them. I feel my mouth dry out more and more, the emptiness in my stomach growing bigger than my stomach. I don't know how I'll ever move myself away from here to eat or sleep. My body only wants to huddle in the gloomy field. But something strange and beautiful happens: just before the light disappears behind the horizon line, there's a rip in the clouds and the sun peers through one last time. Its rays cascade red and purple across the clouds, and in the opening the sun is a hot bloodshot eye.

I'm mesmerized by the effect, hypnotized by its sinking, until a piercing shriek jolts me. Up the field, a group of five people bunched close to each other are squeezing under the fence. There's some pushing and shoving among them, a few more quick and sharp shrieks that assure me they're not scared or hurt or angry. They don't see me but move unintentionally closer, circling and pulling on each other: two girls and three boys, too old to be children, too giddy to be adults. Two of the boys have coats tied around their hips. The T-shirts they wear don't hide the tattoos painted all over their arms and up their necks. Drawings like in a kid's book: dragons and hearts and wild teeth and snakes and crosses and women's red lips. Stories painted all over their bodies, maybe more amazing than any stories I've ever read or made up. The pictures are easier to see on the skin of the white boy, but have more color and fantasy on the skin of the black boy. The other three are more covered with clothes and I can't see if they have similar stories on their bodies. One of the girls has blue hair and earrings looped all over her ears that jangle a bit when she whirls around the others. The second girl has hair almost as yellow as Doris's, streaked with black. Earrings are looped through her lips and nose and over her eyebrows and there's a diamond pinned to her right cheek under her eye. The third boy looks more like a prince than any boy I've ever seen. A boy so handsome, it makes me want to look away. I remember Scotty and his iceberg eyes and feel guilty. Just yesterday, I loved him more than I could bear.

The white painted boy stops moving to stretch his back, and all the others stop moving and wait for him. He takes a thin stick from his pants pocket and puts it in his mouth. A cigarette. He lights it and inhales deeply, then passes it to the blue girl. She inhales too and passes it to the diamond girl. The cigarette goes around the circle and everything they do slows down, as if they're blowing out agitation with the smoke.

Then diamond girl sees me.

Before I can move or run or even stand up, she heads toward me. She smiles so grandly, I think it's a mistake. "Hello, gorgeous," she says as she wanders forward. "Aren't you a kitten." The others trail behind her, also smiling, like they've been waiting for me all along and I'm just a bit late.

I don't move or say anything and they amble closer and closer, smiling so that all their teeth show. When they're close enough for me to touch, they crouch around me in a half-circle like a gateway of suspicious but hospitable elves.

Diamond girl touches my elbow. "Are you lost, kitten?"

I shake my head.

They all look so fancy in their colors and skin drawings and tight-fitting clothes. Beside them, I'm awkward and messy, still wearing Mrs. O'Reardon's baggy leftovers, her old beige button-front shirt and her gray pants strapped to my waist with a stringy belt. I wish I'd changed into my nicer clothes. Or even better, I wish I could color myself over with designs and costumes and sparkles in my face.

Diamond girl takes the cigarette from one of the painted boys and holds it out to me. "Wanna toke?"

But blue girl snatches the cigarette from her before I can take it. "Are you fucked, Mo? She's a baby." She looks at me and gentles her voice. "How old are you, kitten? Twelve?"

It occurs to me that the younger they think I am, the nicer they might be to me. I shrug.

Diamond girl punches blue girl's thigh. "I was getting high at twelve, Cal."

Blue girl rolls her eyes. "And is it something you'd recommend, Mo?"

Mo looks away, mad. But suddenly she shrieks with laughter. She leans toward me until her screeching face is inches away. "No, Twelve," she says, "it's *not* something I'd recommend." Now, more than anything, I want to try her cigarette.

Blue girl interrupts us with a satisfied grunt. "That's better," she says, looking at me with curious eyes. "What's going on, Twelve? You cool? Or you need a little TLC?"

Their bodies huddle closer around me. I want to move back, but the fence behind me blocks me in. I say, "TLC?" Without meaning to, I do sound like a baby.

"Tender loving care. We might look like gutter-punks, but we're cool." She takes my hand very carefully in hers. "I promise you can trust us." She inches her head closer to mine. "Okay?" I nod. "Cool. So let me introduce ourselves. This," she points to Mo, "is Monique. And these freaks are Tank, Justin, and Chisel." Justin is the prince, Tank is the white painted boy, and Chisel the black one — both of them as bony as chickens. "And me, I'm Calcutta, but you can call me Cal. Got that?" I nod again. "So what's your deal, Twelve?"

I don't know why I tell them. Maybe because their huddled circle feels almost magical, as if we're conjuring spells together. "I ran away."

They all nod like they understand. "Let me guess," Mo says. "Dumb-ass mom? Lame-ass school? Dad who thinks evil is for your own good?"

It shocks me that it's so easy for her to say. Maybe in all of us there's the sadness you hide from other people and the sadness you hide from yourself that other people see.

"The last one."

They all nod again. Calcutta squeezes my arm. "You wanna live with us? We can get you food and shelter better than being alone in this crappy mud hole."

"Except I have to get somewhere," I say quickly, by accident.

"Yeah?" Calcutta asks. "Where're you headed?"

"Beachport, Maine." I didn't know it until I said it.

"Beachport." Tank seems to recognize it. "What's in Beachport, Twelve?"

I don't need to run away with no direction. There is a place I can go. "My mother."

Justin tilts his head. He is as beautiful as a cloud. "How're you getting to Beachport, Twelve?"

From examining maps for so many years, I know the points by heart. "I need to get to the U.S. border at St. Stephen. Then cross it somehow. Then head down along the coast."

"Wow." Chisel whistles. "Ambitious."

Calcutta shakes her head. "Might be a bit too ambitious, Twelve. Not trying to discourage you. But that trip's got a lotta loopholes in it."

"I got here by hiding in the back of a truck." I don't tell them it was the back of a truck I know very well. "Figured I could get down all the way like that."

Calcutta looks at Mo. "She's too young to hitch."

"Sure as fuck right," Mo says. "She'll get busted or she'll get raped." She shrugs her arms at me. "Sorry. But that's the truth and you should know it."

I nod even though the true implications are vague, almost meaningless.

"You can't just hide in any truck." Chisel says. "You don't know where they're going. You gotta know their destination."

I hadn't thought of that.

Tank stands up. "She could catch out. Ride the rails to Island Yard in Saint John. The trains don't go on to the border from there, but she'd never pass the customs inspectors anyway. From Saint John, she could try and hide in a truck that's crossing the border. At least there she's sort of close to the States and she can wait for an American traveling home."

Riding the rails. It would be like a dream.

"Can't promise anything once you're stateside," Tank adds, "but chances of getting to Beachport are a lot better from the other side."

"406 at Gordon Yard would get her to Saint John in just over two hours," Chisel calculates.

"The 406, yeah." Tank says. "One gets ordered up every day. Leaves the yard in the morning, midday latest." He bobs his head. "Yeah, solid plan, man."

"If you ignore the danger of train hopping," Mo stands up, "the slim chances she'll find the right truck to highjack, the border crossing where they'll likely bust her ass and haul her back to Satan's spawn — because the system is *fucked* — and the ever-possible possibility that any asshole can just come along and *rape* her, yeah, I think you cooked up a super-solid plan there, guys." She sticks her thumb in her mouth and chews at the skin. "Fucking hobos." She kneels back down in front of me. "Please, Twelve. I beg you. Stay here with us and let Cal and me be your moms."

Calcutta rubs Mo's back. "Mo is right, Twelve. You'd be safer with us."

They all wait for me to say something. Even though I haven't known them for more than fifteen minutes, I do consider staying.

But then I remember a screen in the dark and its slow-motion characters: a mother, her mournful, pleading face, her fevered, searching eyes; a father, his hand gripping hers.

Hope ignites into yearning. I have to take a chance.

Cal grabs my hand and pulls me up. "Okay, then. Let's at least get you some food and a good night's sleep.

≯

The dusk gets gloomier as we walk and walk. It takes about as long as the trip between the keeper's house and Keele's Landing. But this route is down ordered streets, with houses and stores all along the way. The only trees are shrubs growing out of sidewalks or planted in people's yards.

I try to move my body like Cal or Mo. An arm pumping back and forth with every step, lips smooshed together, one foot turned slightly inward. I want to try on each piece of them. To feel more real than a person who's lost all description.

Cal stops us outside a small store on one of the corners. It looks something like the FoodMart, but smaller and with only a few aisles. There are rows of magazines and chocolate bars and canned food and cereal. It's more disorganized than the FoodMart and, like during our winters, there's nothing fresh like apples or lettuce on the shelves.

Cal scratches at her arm. "Dean owes me ten bucks. Think I should try and collect?"

"If we go in there," Tank says, shaking his head, "he'll just call the cops. He thinks we stole that loaf of bread."

"We *did* steal that loaf of bread," Mo hisses.

"We were hungry."

Cal paces back and forth. "If he'da given me what he owes me, we wouldn't have been hungry and we wouldn't have needed to steal that bread."

Justin shakes his head. "Sorry, Cal, but Dean told me he never borrowed ten bucks from you."

"He fucking did, Justin. He wanted to borrow my bike, and when I said he couldn't because I needed it, he said, 'I'll give you ten bucks,' and so I said okay. So he borrowed my bike. Now he owes me ten bucks."

"Dean's a denier," Mo says. "Also short-term memory issues."

"Is your bike even worth ten bucks, Cal?" Justin isn't making fun of her; he sounds reasonable.

Cal kicks her foot into the air. "Whatever. I'm hungry and he said he'd give me ten bucks."

"Twelve, cutie?" Mo elbows me. "You go in there and steal some ramen, would ya? Be a doll."

Cal pushes Mo. "Fucking, no! She's not stealing anything for us. Jesus H., I hope you never have a kid."

I check the store. It's so much like the FoodMart. I check back with the kids. They do look very hungry. So am I. I have some money, but not much and still a long way to travel. I step closer to the window. So many packages of food inside.

Mo angles past Cal. "The ramen, Twelve. It's on the bottom shelf in the second aisle."

"Shut the fuck up, Mo." Cal wrestles her back.

Mo challenges her. "It costs nothing, Cal. It's almost not even food."

"Don't do it, Twelve."

"The markup on that shit is criminal."

"I'm sure we have something at home."

"Yeah. Cockroaches and dead mice."

Before I know it, I'm in the store.

The light is dazzling. Even the dust on the cans seems to gleam. Canned pineapple, canned peaches, canned carrots, canned beans. My mouth waters.

The bottom shelf. Second aisle.

I pick up six packages of ramen. I know this food. I made it often for Jonah.

The plastic crackles under my fingers. I could shove the packages into my bag. Or down my pants.

I look around. There's a young man behind the counter who must be Dean. Like Phyllis Ketchum at the FoodMart, he also watches a small TV behind the counter. He's chewing on a stick of beef jerky.

It's like I don't exist.

I could shove the ramen under my coat. I'm a fast runner.

I look back at the kids outside. They all watch me through the glass. Me inside a snow globe now. Sparkling bits raining down on me.

I squeeze the six packages in my hands. I carry them to the counter and put them down. Dean startles, then scans the packs, ringing them through the cash. "6.71."

"Except you owe Calcutta ten bucks."

Dean looks at me for the first time. "Did Cal send you here to do her dirty work? What a joke. Send a kid to collect." He snorts. "What? You gonna break my legs if I don't pay up?"

"I'm just saying you owe her money and you should pay it back."

"How many times do I have to tell her: I. Do. Not. Owe. Her. Money. She musta been high when she got that idea in her head."

"Did you borrow her bike?"

He blinks down at me. "What's that got to do with anything?"

"She needed her bike for herself. You said you'd pay her ten bucks, so she let you borrow it."

Dean picks jerky out of his teeth. "Damn, you're cute."

He packs the ramen into a shopping bag and I grab it.

"You still owe her 3.29."

I turn and race out of the store and down the street. Maybe I stole the ramen, maybe Dean gave it to me. For the first time, the pounding in my chest feels good. Like dancing for your one true love. The others chase after me, shrieking with laughter.

≈

The first time I get scared is when we arrive at their house. It's like the other houses up and down the street: rundown, pieces of siding falling off, broken steps, crazy nonsense lines painted over the walls, closed curtains behind the windows or plywood nailed across them.

It doesn't scare me because it's so rundown and dark, it scares me because it has the same feel as the house I've known all my life. A keeper's house, full of secrets.

We don't walk through the front door, which doesn't look too inviting, but creep around to the back and sneak in one at a time through a basement window. Inside it's dark as night.

Tank leads us up some wobbly stairs to the main floor. Cal and Mo start lighting candles and the wicks flicker from the bottoms of Mason jars.

The place is a wreck, with painted doodles on every wall and garbage lying around, and mattresses or cushions here and there over the floor. It's warm, though, and the flickering light makes the walls and garbage look alive, like nature.

"You hungry?" Calcutta asks, pushing Tank toward the kitchen.

"Thirsty," I say, because that's the most pressing. Cal smacks her head like she's stupid for not thinking of that, and she reaches for a plastic cup from a cupboard with no door and pulls a jug from the counter. She fills the cup with water from the jug, and I gulp it down in five seconds.

"You look like — " Mo says, shrieking, "— c'mon, you guys, say it with me — " She coaxes everyone with a buffeting hand. They all say it together: "Like a rose in a shit hole!"

"That's it!" Mo jumps up and down, laughing her head off. "That's it! A rose in a shit hole." Everyone laughs with her. I think of Marlie and how she looked when she first came to the island. Like a jack-rabbit pretending the wolves couldn't see her. Like a warning of what was to come.

Calcutta pours me more water. Tank has put a fuel stove on the kitchen floor and he's setting a pot of water on the blue and yellow flame. Cal looks at me. "You like ramen?" I nod, now able to think of my hunger. "Good, because you earned it."

Calcutta arranges some pillows on a mattress in what I guess to be the living room and makes me sit on them. Mo joins us and we stretch out while Tank cooks us dinner. Cal says, "Tell me about your mom, Twelve."

A picture of a mother's face on a TV screen comes to my mind. Completely different from how I'd imagined her. "I don't know anything about her," I say with bated breath.

Mo slaps a pillow. Dust floats up. "You don't *know* your mom? Then why are you going to her? Moms can be as shitty as dads. Shittier."

Calcutta pats Mo's arm. "Let her speak, Mo." She turns back to me. "Go on, Twelve."

"She didn't have a choice that I left her." I brush some dust from my arm. "That's why we never knew each other. Maybe she's bad, I don't know. But I don't think so." I stare at a big cracked square on the wall that's painted over with swirling letters — *Free* and *Love* — and let myself picture the mother I used to picture when I was younger. Before I ever saw any videos or read any experiment journals. The brown hair and warm eyes, the too-high voice when she sings, the feel of her arms around me, the smell of lilacs on her neck.

"My mom kept dating assholes," Mo says, disgusted, "and kept losing us kids to Child Services. The last time I was allowed to go back to her, she'd set herself up with this guy who had custody of three of his own kids. They were these adorable little babies and Mom was crazy for them. And I was the ugly, awkward bitch that no one gave a shit about. When people move on, they move on, man."

"That sucks, Mo, and I'm not saying it doesn't." Cal turns and focuses intently on me. "But sometimes the real thing turns out better than we expect. Sometimes it's way better."

"Usually, though," Mo says, sitting up, "it's way worse."

Tank stops Cal from slapping Mo by calling out that dinner is ready.

≫

We sit cross-legged on the mattress and eat ramen from plastic bowls.

Chisel smacks his lips. "I could use a shot of Johnny right about now." He gets up and rifles through some plastic bags and pulls out a bottle full of brown liquid. He unscrews the top and takes a long gulp. I'm closest to him, and he hands me the bottle next. I remember the night with Scotty and Marlie and the wine. Nausea upends my stomach. But is it more dangerous to say no?

I take the bottle and drink a bit and pass it on. It takes a long time to swallow, threads of liquid burning my tongue and throat.

After dinner, we clean up "hobo-style," which means seeing who can throw their empty bowl the furthest. The *thwamp thwamp* of the bowls hitting the walls or cupboards or other pieces of garbage makes us laugh until our stomachs hurt.

Tank gets up and grabs a guitar from one of the dark corners. Pretty soon, everyone has some kind of instrument. Chisel has a bow that he twangs across a rusty saw. Justin arranges plastic tubs and beats on them with sticks. Cal beats on the ground with her hands.

And Mo sings in the loveliest voice I've ever heard. They give me a jar of seeds and show me how to shake it to the beat.

It's only when the loneliness ebbs away that I realize how vast a space it has occupied.

When I no longer have the energy to shake the seeds, I lie back on the mattress and slowly, very slowly, let their music set me adrift.

Once I open my eyes and see Justin and Calcutta kissing in the dark. Candlelight flickers over their mouths, glints and glances, then licks my mouth. As if their coiling breath is on my lips.

Once I open my eyes and see Tank trying to memorize or perform some words: "*There was never any more inception than there is now … Nor any more youth or age than there is now … And will never be any more perfection than there is now … Nor any more heaven or hell than there is now …*"

Once I open my eyes and see Tank and Mo and Chisel squatting around the fuel stove in the kitchen. Rubber bands are tied around their arms, needles stick into their skin. Tank pulls the needle away and arches back. He crawls along the floor, arching and rolling, getting closer and closer to me. I keep watch through slitted eyes. Soon his body is against mine and my nerves light up with a million tiny flames. "*More perfection, heaven or hell.*" I pretend to roll away in my sleep, but Tank's body presses in. His fingers are on my thigh. Antennae feeling their way. I don't move — I can't — but let his hand touch me. I close my eyes and will myself to go under again. Nothing I can do but stay a worm on a hook.

Once I open my eyes and Calcutta is beside me. Until morning, she lies close, her arm thrown over and protecting me.

29

It's Chisel who wakes us. "We gotta get to Gordon Yard. Rise and shine, lazy asses. The train's a-callin'."

Everyone is groggy as we get up. Tank is already warming up cubed pieces of old French fries and bread over the fuel stove. He cracks an egg over the whole thing and scrambles it.

I find the bathroom. It's a dirty, smelly place where you have to flush the toilet by spilling rainwater from a jug down the hole. The spilled water doesn't clean the bowl at all. There's no mirror to look into, but I wash my face and teeth and run my wet fingers through my hair. The shortness of it surprises me and almost plunges me back into shock. I clutch the edge of the sink and concentrate on the trip ahead. A train, a border, a coastline. Nothing but those.

I change out of Mrs. O'Reardon's clothes, fold them neatly, and leave them in a corner for another runaway to wear. I rummage in my knapsack for my own clothes, and carefully choose only mud-colored pieces so I won't attract attention.

Nobody speaks as we eat the fried scramble. The kids drink coffee, and I try some too. It's bitter and sandy, but it wakes me up fast.

Justin waves his phone at us. "I called Alana. She's bringing her truck around. She doesn't mind driving us to the yards and back."

No one says much as we collect our stuff and head out.

Outside, I notice it's about 10:00 a.m. Clouds still blanket the sky but don't look to be filled with rain.

We don't wait long before a shiny red pickup arrives. Justin steps to the curb and waves his hand. Cal nudges him and says, "Thank God she's hot for you, J, or we'd never get anywhere." Justin ignores her and waves at the truck again. The truck stops, and a very pretty girl smiles at us. The window rolls down by itself. "Hey, Justin." The girl looks at him meaningfully, then turns to the rest of us. "You guys train hopping again?"

"Nah," says Cal, opening the cab door and climbing in. "Only Twelve here." I smile at her. "The rest of us need to make some dough first." Mo and Cal climb onto the truck bench beside the girl, and I can tell she's disappointed that Justin isn't sitting beside her.

Justin, Tank, and Chisel escort me to the bed of the truck and we climb in. Chisel shivers and bundles himself against Tank and closes his eyes to sleep. Tank curls into a ball and also closes his eyes. I remember his hand on my leg in the middle of the night and wonder if it was all a dream.

After we drive a bit, I ask Justin, "Are you and Cal in love?"

"Nah." Justin stretches himself out. "Cal's into girls. We get horny sometimes, you know?"

"Right." Except I don't know. Unless I do.

"I guess you've never been in love?" he asks me.

"I was."

"Yeah? Cool." He raises an eyebrow. "You break their heart? Or they break yours?"

"He broke mine."

And then I realize — broken hearts are just part of the whole thing. A thing I am part of. And hearts change. Like everything else.

A few minutes later, we're at the train yard.

※

The train yard is busy with rail lines and cabooses and engines. Tank names off the different freight shapes: tank car, flatcar, hopper car, gondola, boxcar — which, he says, is the best ride for me.

We sneak along the edges of the yard, hiding among trees. Workers busy themselves about the tracks, but they're focused only on the business of trains.

Tank points to the southwest corner. "The 406 is making up its train." I notice the spine of connected cars chugging slowly forward and backward. He explains that the crew is adding cars to the end. It already looks impossibly long.

Chisel scopes out which car I should take. "When the train stops moving, that means they're getting clearance from the dispatcher to head to Saint John, and we've got about five easy minutes to hop on."

Cal smacks his arm. "*We?*"

Chisel shrugs. "I gotta head out, Cal. The rush of the rails is calling me."

"You can't leave us, Chisel. It's too sad."

They make faces at each other until Calcutta gives up and agrees. Chisel turns to me. "Don't expect private security detail, Twelve. I'm only seeing you as far as Island Yard, then I'm gonna head over to Ponderosa Yard and catch out to Montreal. Or maybe go out west. I'll see how far I can make it this time."

I'm happy for his company, but also glad he's not coming all the way. There's something solemn about going to Beachport that makes me want to concentrate on the journey.

We wait another twenty minutes, then the train stops shuffling back and forth. Calcutta makes me pee in the woods so I won't have to go during the ride. "Once you're on the train, there's only two options," she says. "In a bottle, and good luck with that, or over the edge, and good luck with that." I laugh and head to a private spot.

When I get back, Chisel takes a big breath and says very loudly, "Okay, this is it." Everyone but Alana throws arms around each other. Mo and Calcutta wipe tears from their eyes. "Don't wail, girls,"

Chisel laughs. "You know I'm gonna land on your grimy doorstep again."

"Counting on it," says Cal.

Each of them hugs me hard too and ruffles my hair. Then Chisel grabs my hand and we're bounding past stilled cars and over steel rails, past the line of train that snakes further than my eyes can see, until we get to the boxcar Chisel has picked out for us.

We hop on, and I shrink into the darkest corner, praying no one will come and bust us. But Chisel looks calm now. Like he's found his oasis and is drinking up the most delicious water imaginable.

After five minutes, the train starts to pull out of the yard. Never before have I seen a train in real life, never have I been close enough to smell one, never felt it under my feet, never hopped into one I wasn't supposed to be in. It feels better than any adventure I ever conjured in my mind.

The motion lurches me this way and that, then settles into a soothing rhythm. The wheels and cars clang together and the sound of it rings in my ears. It makes me want to sing. It makes me believe that if I do sing, my notes will come out like Mo's, sweet and clear and true.

The wind comes through the open door and brings with it dust and grit that scratches my eyes and makes me cough. Chisel sits cross-legged right at the opening and stares out, mesmerized. Many times I fight an unfamiliar urge to fling myself through the doorway. I plant myself far from it so my body can't conduct its own experiment.

The landscape slips by steadily, and it is so beautiful. So beautiful and perfect I can't imagine anyone designing it.

I think we might go on like this all the way — miles and miles of perfect silence — but after an hour of riding, when we're passing through a stand of thick woods, Chisel stands up. Very slowly, he turns and faces me.

His eyes narrow like a wary dog. His top lip flexes up to show a sharp line of teeth. I remember Biscuit defending his hole, how he raged at Marlie.

At first I think Chisel is trying to be funny and I laugh. When he doesn't laugh back, my heart starts pounding. Last night Tank lay himself next to me and put his hand on my body. What can I do to stop a person from doing what they want with me? Sweat pops out all over my head and back.

Chisel's small bony shape gets bigger. His skin shines black. His eyes are weapons. He looks dangerous.

"What's up, Chisel?" I say in a small voice, trying to remind him that I'm just a kid and no match for him.

"What's up, Chisel?" he says in a menacing, disbelieving voice. "What's up, Chisel?!" He yells it so loudly I have to clap my hands over my ears.

He yells again, "That all you got, Twelve?!" Then he makes fun of my voice, makes it squeaky and stupid. "*What's up, Chisel?*"

Tears sting the corners of my eyes, but still I keep looking up at him. I try to calculate my options.

There is only the empty train car around us and the open door to certain death.

"I could kill you! That's what's up!" Chisel yells, glowering.

No options available, I cower into a ball.

Chisel struts and taunts me with his hands. "I could take your pathetic little neck and snap it with my fingers. Without even breaking a sweat. That's what's up!"

Too scared to even cry, I huddle my neck into my chest. "Please, no," I say, my voice nothing more than a whimper.

Chisel yells, "I could — " But he stops mid-sentence and buckles his knees into a slump in front of me. "I'm sorry, Twelve. Don't be scared." His change is so abrupt, I wonder if I willed it with my mind.

He takes my hands in his, and I realize mine are shaking. "I'm trying to make a point. See?" He extends a hand toward the car door, his voice gentle again. "In two hours, you're going out there. No Chisel to watch your back, no train cars or hobo-dumps to hide in. You're putting your fate in the hands of whoever is out there. See what I mean?" I try to nod, but tears are on the edge of falling. "I coulda been a psycho, I coulda had it in for you, and you were all 'What's up, Chisel.' Not good, Twelve. Don't trust anybody. You see someone coming at you, you gotta stand up, stand firm, be ready to fight. Understand?" He lets go of my hands, and I wipe an arm across my face. "C'mon, show me. Get up, stand firm." He stands up and beckons me. I stand myself up.

He steps toward me and says, "Okay, give me permission to show you this move and you'll have one weapon at your disposal. But I need to come close. Do I have your permission?"

"Is this a trick?"

Chisel laughs, and I relax. "Like if you give me permission, I shout at you that you let your guard down?" I nod, but also laugh. "No, Twelve. I just want you to know I'm gonna come close and you don't have anything to fear. Okay?"

"Okay."

And he steps close enough for me to feel the warmth of his skin. "If I'm a bad guy who's gonna grab you," and he circles his arms around my upper body but doesn't make contact with me, "all you have to do is crouch down — Are you standing firm, Twelve?"

I look down at my feet. They're splayed all wonky and don't look at all serious. I straighten them and lock my knees. Firm as can be.

But Chisel shakes his head. "No, no. *Firm.*" And he steps back to show me. He stands his legs apart, but he shows how his knees can still flex. He squats and straightens them to show me. I copy him and, satisfied, he steps close again and floats his arms in the air around me again. "Now, bend your knees." I do. "And when you press your legs up, you push the palm of your hand to my chin with all your force." I pretend to do it. "Exactly." I do it again a few times, bending my legs and powering up, feeling the force in my arm and hand as they push up and pretend to hit Chisel in the chin. "Two reasons that's gonna work. One: element of surprise. They're not gonna expect the little girl to fight back. Two: the leverage in your legs will generate enough force to make a serious blow. Got that?"

I smile.

"Good. Second trick is in your legs again. You kick whenever you can. Whatever you can. If he's got you on the ground, you kick. Eyes, balls, eyes, balls. Balls, balls, balls." I start to laugh. "I'm serious, Twelve. No more vulnerable spot on a guy. Turns us weak. Okay?"

"Okay."

"Third trick: you scream. Scream something people will alert to. Like 'Fire.' But scream your fucking lungs out. No cute little warbles. Loud, fucking, crazy-ass screams. *Capisce?*"

"Whatever you say, Chisel."

He grins and throws his arms around me properly and hugs me close. "You do," he says in my ear, "*whatever* you gotta do."

"To survive. I get it." I hug him back, relief inside me, but not certainty.

❧

As the train slows to a stop, Chisel gets up and hangs off the boxcar door, looking out. I follow him. "This is literally gonna be door-to-door service," he says. Even though no one is around and the train is still clanging and chugging, he lowers his voice to a whisper. "You're gonna want to scope out those diners and gas stations." He points, and I see we're heading into a small train yard, much smaller than the one in Moncton, and that it's only a few meters away from a wide, busy road with a row of buildings that back onto the tracks. I know those must be the gas stations and shops Chisel mentioned, where he thought I might find another car or truck to hide in and travel.

"Find a donut shop," Chisel says. "Order something to eat and drink, sit yourself at the window — they're not gonna care if you sit there all day — and watch for your truck. Remember to wait for one that's heading west with American plates, preferably Maine plates — because that's where you wanna go. When they order their double-double coffee and chocolate donut, you listen to their voice, okay? Because a voice tells a lot about a person. You want a friendly voice. When they go to the back to take a leak — because they always do — you very casually wander over to their truck, make sure no one is watching, and hop into the bed. Just like you did before, okay?" He shows me with his own body how I should hide. "You curl yourself into the farthest corner and you pray to fucking God no one stops you at the border. Got that?"

I nod, but don't tell him I've never prayed to fucking God.

30

Chisel and I hop out of the boxcar and run like hell down the tracks. When we get to some bushes behind a gas station, Chisel pushes me down.

"Okay, Twelve, this is where we part ways. It's been a blast. You are a scrappy beast. You'll be fine. Okay?"

"Okay."

We hug one last time, and just like that Chisel is on his way and I'm in a bush by myself.

I get up, brush myself off, and rub my hands through my hair. I know it's important that no one notices me, and for that to happen, I need to be neither too one thing nor too another. I head around the building to the roadside and suss out the coffee shops. It's just after 2:00 p.m.

I pick a large, clean-looking donut shop. It has a lot of vehicles parked in the lot, but no trucks yet with covered beds and American plates. I head over to it and open the shop door. It smells heavenly inside, like warm sugar on sugar. It makes me remember Marlie and her story about the donuts. It's too hard to think of her still being on the island, so I shake it off.

A large, bored girl asks me what I want.

"Double-double coffee," I say, so calm, so regular. "And a chocolate donut."

She asks for money, which I pull from my knapsack and give her.

Then she hands me a tray with a giant donut on a napkin and a paper cup full of steaming coffee. I thank her and bring my treasures to a seat by the front window. Staring out, it almost feels like I'm in Peg's Diner all over again. Except without the beloved colors and beautiful view.

I sit there for a long, long time. I eat my donut and drink my coffee as slowly as it's possible for a human to do — taking the tiniest bites and sipping only every five minutes. I add more and more packets of sugar to the coffee to make time go faster and the coffee taste better.

Pretty soon the sugar starts to go to my head and sitting still becomes harder and harder. I long for a chance to race around outside, to explore the ugly buildings full of mysterious goods. But I can't lose track of what I'm here to do. I force all my unspent energy into my leg, where it jiggles and jiggles with longing — frantic enough to make me want to break it off.

So many cars and trucks come and go. But none from the States, or if they are, not westbound, or if they are, not trucks with a bed I can climb into. I use the ladies' room a couple of times and also wash my face and check my reflection.

My face looks tired and sad. And even though I keep washing it, it still looks dirty. I decide I'll have to work on that before I get to the house in Beachport. I don't want to arrive looking like a sad, dirty gutter-punk.

After sitting there for two hours, I become embarrassed to go back to my seat by the window, and so decide to wait outside for a bit. It's warm and dry, and I figure from outside I can still check the trucks and listen for kindness in people's voices. I spend another hour or so behind the coffee shop, walking lines and throwing stones and even singing quietly under my breath, all while checking every car and truck that comes or goes.

And then the perfect vehicle drives up.

Something about it makes me freeze and push myself back against the brick wall. I don't recognize it right away because it's so strange to see it where it doesn't belong.

The van door opens and Jonah climbs out.

A shock that turns me into a storm. If my heart ever pounded hard before, it's nothing compared to how much harder and louder it's pounding now. I run behind the shop and bend over a bush, sickened enough to puke but forcing my body to hold it in.

I creep back along the side of the building to check on him. Through the glass doors of the coffee shop, I can see the girl who served me handing Jonah a cup, then turning back to the counter to package a sandwich. Jonah waits like a rock. When she hands him the bag, he reaches into his pocket and pulls out Marlie's phone. I'm confused. Then I realize he's showing the girl a photo on Marlie's phone: a picture of me that Marlie took just a few days ago.

The girl nods at him and points to the seat I sat in for two hours, then she points out the door and kind of waggles her fingers. Jonah puts a friendly smile on his face and seems to thank her. I can't move, not sure if I should flee or hide.

If Jonah is three hours away from the mainland dock and all the way here in Saint John, if he's looking for me, then he must have read my letter. He knows I'm trying to get back to my family, and even if he doesn't know exactly how I'm going to manage it, he wants to stop me badly enough to come all this way.

A picture of enraged Jonah eclipses my vision, and I see myself underneath his smashing, bloodied hands.

But a remarkable thought occurs to me: if Jonah is going to end up in Beachport to stop me from getting to my family, then I could end up in Beachport as well. Without even trying, I could end up right at the front door of the only house I want to see.

Jonah takes his sandwich and coffee and eats and drinks without sitting, like a predator surveying the land through the front window.

My eyes never leave his scheming face as the prospect of going with him takes terrible, inevitable shape.

Just like Chisel predicted, before Jonah continues on his way, he goes to the men's room to take a leak. Two seconds after he disappears through the door, I'm creeping into the parking lot and between parked cars all the way to the back of his van. Acting completely sure and innocent, I unlatch the back doors like I've done a million times before and let myself into the junk-filled storage space.

Suffocated by the dust and dampness of the back of the van, I want to scream with rage and fear. A picture of a baby twin blinds me. Paralyzes every muscle in my body. *What's the worst that Jonah has done? What's the worst he can do?* But if I'm to get to Beachport, only Jonah is guaranteed to get me there.

There are cardboard boxes piled in the back, and I quickly empty a 5-cube of its coils of ropes and plastic tarps. I set those among the heaped piles of engine parts, towels, oil-covered tools, and bits and pieces left over from so many tasks either long ago finished or never started. I arrange the box close enough to the front that I have some kind of sightline through the windshield, but where Jonah can't see me through the rearview mirror. Survival rates are higher if the prey has a vantage point to its predator.

I step inside the box. Then I pull my knapsack from my back and set it under me like a cushion. I angle one of the greasy towels over the box, pull the flaps closed over me, and maneuver the towel over the break in the flaps. This way I can breathe, I can be hidden, and — if I peer carefully through the break in the flaps and under the slightly lifted edge of the towel — I have a view of the driver's seat and the road ahead.

I've barely finished settling myself when I hear the rattle of the driver's door swinging open. I don't dare look out, but huddle in the dark cubby of the box and hold my breath. The van heaves and rocks with the weight of Jonah climbing into the seat. He starts up the van and I feel it steer back and forth until it slowly navigates out of the parking lot and onto the road. That's when I let the smallest breath in. And that's how I breathe for so many minutes: tiny sips of breath in and tiny bubbles of breath out.

Words from Jonah's experiment journals flash into my mind. Scribbled notes that I couldn't help reading when I was in the lighthouse cavern, descriptions of how he brought two babies from Beachport and drove them to Canada sixteen years ago.

Under cardboard boxes. The words repeat as I jostle in the van amid the cramped, silent mess of Jonah's stuff. *Boxes punctured with holes for air.*

31

I move my knees about until I find a position that's somewhat comfortable and allows me to change shapes every now and then so my legs don't fall asleep. After Saint John, the road becomes straight and smooth and Jonah is able to drive fast all the way to St. Stephen.

He doesn't drive directly to the border, but parks the van in the small town near it and gets out. I stretch my head right out of the box so I can follow his movements, him checking up and down the sidewalk then walking into a chocolate shop. Through the window, I see him showing the workers Marlie's phone. The workers shake their heads and say a few words that make Jonah nod.

He goes in and out of stores all along the street, obviously to no avail. When he's checked with each one, he looks for a long time at the line of cars waiting to cross the border. He seems to come to a decision because he heads back to the van, and I quickly arrange myself so he won't see me.

He climbs back inside, panting softly like he's arrived after a long run. He rifles through the glove box and pulls out a small black booklet. A Canadian passport. *Illegally acquired. A new name.* He starts the engine, then drives out of the parking spot and to the line at the border. As he slows and brakes and waits for the cars ahead of him to go through, I can feel him trying to compose himself. He takes deep breaths and shakes his shoulders. He opens the passport and checks it intently. I hear him whisper, "Easy. Easy."

I don't know anything about what to expect when you cross a border, except what people sometimes say about the long waits and not being allowed to bring citrus fruit. The cars ahead of us go through one by one until it's Jonah's turn. He coasts to the small building and rolls down his window.

I can't see the border guard, but I can hear his voice. It's not friendly. "Citizenship?"

Jonah hands the man his passport. "Canadian." He sounds nervous. "From Founder's Island. Small place up in New Brunswick. On the northeast side. An hour or so from Moncton. Possible you haven't heard of it, but then again —" he tries a jolly laugh, but the guard interrupts him.

"What's the purpose of your trip?"

"Oh, well, that's an interesting story. I operate a ferry — the *Founder's Spirit* — from mainland New Brunswick to the island, and she broke down yesterday. It's been a disaster, really, the whole area depending on us the way they do. And we've had just the darnedest time —"

"The point of your trip, Mr. Hubb?"

"Fuel lines. Couldn't get them in Canada. Picking them up in Portland. Coming back tomorrow."

"You bringing anything in?"

"Just myself and my gear."

There's a long silence. Jonah coughs and massages the back of his neck.

"Okay, sir, is the back unlocked?"

I catch my breath. Jonah answers obediently, "Yes, sir."

"Please wait here while I take a look."

"Certainly."

I huddle into the smallest ball I can, pulling myself away from the sides of the box so not even a thread or hair will rub against the cardboard. I hear the man come around to the back and pull open the doors. I imagine him looking at everything, seeing the greasy tools and parts, the cardboard boxes that hold unimportant things.

Jonah gives an artificial laugh. "I'm sorry, sir. It's a mess, I know. I didn't plan on this emergency run. Didn't think to leave that stuff at the docks."

It's silent as the man inspects. I don't breathe. Then he says in a voice grave with disapproval, "I suggest the next time you cross, sir, anything unnecessary to your trip is cleared out."

"Yes, of course."

The doors slam closed. I wait, sipping breath, until I hear the man say from the front again, "Thank you." Jonah doesn't say anything but rolls the van slowly forward. As he gains speed, I feel him relax. It should be clear sailing all the way to Beachport.

≫

The road winds through woods, through small towns, past ocean views — familiar enough to make me believe I might fit in one day.

Jonah doesn't put on music, doesn't speak to himself, doesn't hum an unnatural tune. The persistent silence forces a hand over my mouth, tight enough to almost suffocate me.

≫

The minutes beat like a finger tapping my wrist: *you're not there yet, you're not there.*

I'm tired enough to sleep but know I can't lose myself to it. Thirsty and hungry with no food or drink. My bladder is full.

Just as I think I'm about to burst, Jonah slows down and pulls the van into a parking lot. He steps out and slams the door, and I watch him go inside a small restaurant. There are no windows facing the lot, so when I count enough minutes to confirm he must be eating dinner inside, I take a chance and sneak out of the van and run to the treed lot behind the restaurant to pee.

On my way back to the van, I notice an overflowing garbage can and, balanced on top, a plastic bottle half full of water. I quickly steal it and run with it back to the van. I settle myself inside the box and am able to drink my thirst away. I don't think about germs or dirtiness, but just gulp the warm water down and feel a bit better.

❧

We travel on and on, and I have to fight seasickness as I crouch in the dark, sometimes resting my head on my hands, sometimes poking it up to look out the front. Fixing my gaze ahead helps with the queasiness, and eventually that's all I can do not to throw up.

We're driving through a thick pine forest with nothing around for miles when I see a man walking backwards on the side of the road. He jabs out his thumb and hails Jonah with a begging smile. He looks a bit like a bear with his long beard, grinning teeth, and tall, stout shape. But Jonah keeps driving, and the man switches his thumb for his middle finger.

A minute later, there's a terrific crack and the floor bounces and slumps under me. I feel the slam of the brakes as Jonah slows down and coasts to a stop. He hits the steering wheel with his hand. Then hits it again and again. I wonder if his eyes have gone black, if he'll keep smashing his hand until he draws blood.

He opens the door and jumps out, slamming the door behind him with enough force to jar me. Next I feel the saw and sway of the back of the van getting roughed up, and I realize he's taking the spare tire off its rack on the rear door. I secure myself inside the box, knowing what will happen next. Jonah must open the back to get the necessary tools to change the tire. I'm a hidden gravestone when he does. Granite and moss.

He pushes junk around the back and quickly finds what he needs. I can hear the metallic thump of the chosen items. Soon, I feel a mechanical grinding as Jonah jacks the car and removes the flat. Then the side of the van closest to me thumps very loudly and thumps again. Jonah punching the panel. He growls and groans and swears without words. Anger rising and spilling.

The same anger simmers in me. I want to scream at him to hurry. Already it feels too long, too slow. Unreasonable worries ping in: *we're going to miss them, my mother, my father, they've decided to leave, they're moving away right now, I'm missing them by moments as they lock up their house and drive away ahead of us, never to return, never to look back or wonder.*

A deep voice startles me: "Need a hand, bud?"

My body jerks reflexively. I feel an instant impulse to dart out. Like a trapped animal, running could be my only option.

Jonah's voice. "Thanks, I'm good."

"Broken axle?"

"No. Leaf springs. U-bolt is shot. Thanks, I've got it covered." The sound and movement of Jonah getting back to work.

Because Jonah left the back doors open, I take a chance and very slowly rotate my body inside the box so I can sneak a look.

It's Bear Man.

He watches Jonah, who's working on the rear passenger wheel out of my field of vision. He stares hard at Jonah like he's making calculations. Black long-sleeved T-shirt, black baggy pants, long black hair and beard, yeasty skin. Everything scruffy and soiled. Not much different from my friends in Moncton, except for everything about him.

"If you're gonna call for a tow," he says, "mind if I bum a ride?"

"I'm sorry, I'm not calling for a tow."

My anger at Jonah flurries back. He's going to tinker until he solves it.

Jonah says, "Have a nice day." Curt. Indifferent.

Bear Man shakes himself and seems to puff up — his thick arms spreading out as if they no longer fit his body. Agonistic behavior. When an animal displays to compete for something it wants.

If this is what it is — a competition — then the Bear will surely win.

Maybe everything ends right here. Maybe the Bear rips Jonah to shreds and leaves him on the side of the road. Food for the turkey vultures. I'm ashamed at how badly I want it.

Jonah appears suddenly at the back of the van, and I suppress a gasp. But he doesn't look my way, only rifles among his millions of gadgets and parts, checking and tossing pieces. I shrink down until he finds what he needs and moves away again.

"I see what you're doing," Bear says. "Jerry-rigging the bolt. Clever. But you can't install it yourself. That jack isn't strong enough. You're gonna kill yourself."

Jonah grunts and maneuvers and jostles the van.

Now Bear leans in and peers into the back of the van, and again I crouch down until I hear him turn away and speak. When I look up, he's holding a crowbar over Jonah. Wielding it like a weapon.

I take my wish back. I don't want it to end like this.

"You wanna use the weight of the vehicle," Bear says, "to push the springs into place. When it's compressed, I can wedge this in and hold it while you get the bolt on."

Still Jonah grunts and toils. As Bear watches him, he starts to smile. A slow, calculating smile. A grin. "It's the only way, bud," Bear says.

Grunting, toiling, then quiet. Jonah says, "All right. Appreciate it."

Bear lowers the crowbar as if to hand it to Jonah, then jerks it back into the air. "But you gotta give me a ride." His grin is a slash on his face.

Jonah doesn't answer right away. I don't know if he's scared of Bear Man or if he's not interested in getting help from anyone. He doesn't sigh, but I hear it in his voice. "All right."

And they work for ages getting the bolt into place and the spare tire on. I pretend I can't feel impatient tears press at my eyes.

⌇

Bear Man is close enough in front of me that I could reach out my hand and touch him. His hair hangs dirty and matted over the back of the passenger seat. Beside him, Jonah's shoulders and neck betray his fury. His face — what I can see of it — is set in stone.

"Yeah, I'm on my way to see my woman down in Portland," Bear says. "That's why the rush. Can't walk the whole way, man. You hear me? Not when you've got the love of your life to get to."

"I'm not going as far as Portland." Jonah's teeth are gritted.

"That's okay. Whatever you got on offer, I'll take. Where you headed?"

"Beachport." It surprises me that Jonah tells him the truth.

"Beachport … Beachport…. Oh, right. Little town on the coast. Yeah, I heard of it. You have family there?"

"I grew up there, yes."

"Lotta money in those parts."

"My father was a tug operator. Might still be. I don't know."

"So, the other side of the tracks. Gotcha." Bear chuckles. It's not a joyful sound.

"He was a good, salt-of-the-earth kind of fellow."

"A good, salt-of-the-earth kind of fellow?" He makes fun of it. "I get it. I had one of those. His idea of justice was a fist across the face. Am I right?"

"Yes."

"So you going back to take your revenge?"

"I'm going to see my woman. She still lives there."

"Get outta here! Both of us going to our women." Bear turns to look at Jonah. He grins, but this time his expression is easy.

Jonah catches Bear's grin and wears it. His mood seems to lighten. "Yup." The grin takes over his face, and Bear watches, curious. "Believe it or not," Jonah says, "I've known her my whole life. We grew up across the street from each other. Now, hers *was* the moneyed side, so you're right about that." Bear gives the kind of shrug that says, *Of course I'm right.* "Her dad was so rich," Jonah seems to drift to another world, "he gave her the family home as a wedding present. Bought himself a new estate."

"No shit."

"I used to watch her from my bedroom when I was a kid. She was something else."

"I hear you." Bear jerks his fist aggressively up and down. "We're all watching somebody."

"It wasn't like that." Jonah gets instantly serious, and Bear grins at him.

"I'm guessing it didn't last," Bear says. "She got the family estate and you, you got run outta town. That explains the shitty van and Canadian plates."

Jonah stares at the road.

"You trying to get her back?" Bear nods knowingly. "Or is *she* the one who's got it coming?"

"No." I can barely hear Jonah. "Everything I've ever done is for her."

"I heard that one before."

"When I was a boy, she was the only person to see … She called me a natural scientist."

"You're a scientist? How much a scientist make these days? One, one-fifty?"

"I'm still developing my hypothesis. No money in that." Bear cocks an eyebrow like he doesn't believe him. "The critical attachment theory," Jonah says to impress him. "Remember those words. One day I'll be famous for it. She'll come around then."

"Yeah, chicks dig famous men. Hot for money and power."

"Darwin said success for a man of science comes down to this: the patience to reflect, dedication to fact, common sense, and innovation. It's the same for experimental evolution. Even science has to evolve."

"I heard that whole evolution shtick is bullshit."

Jonah flinches. "It is not."

"That's what I read." Bear bends over and seems to rifle through something at his feet.

Jonah says, "Our daughter ran away."

"Huh," Bear says. Something rustles in his hands.

"I have to find her. Bring her home."

"Fucking kids."

"Maybe you could help me keep an eye out. She's sixteen, fair, about five foot two — "

Bear sits up. "DeNitia Jewelers?"

"Hey — " Jonah snaps his head to look.

Bear is holding a small, shiny bag with soft ribbon loops and silver tissue sticking out. I can see it because he raises it to read the silver writing on the side. *Beachport's most exquisite for over fifty years.*

"Put that down." Jonah's profile tenses with indecision — is he going to be angry or placating?

Bear reaches into the bag, past the tissue, and pulls out a small red velvet case.

"That's not yours to look at." The van swerves as Jonah eyes Bear.

Bear opens the lid. A gold ring sticks out of a thin slot, its band dotted with tiny sparkling bits. "Gotta say, man, not overly impressive."

The side of Jonah's face twitches. "Leave that."

Bear pulls out a receipt and examines it. "This is almost twenty years old. How old were you when you wanted to tie the knot? Were you even legal?"

"I was twenty. She was twenty-four. It was perfectly decent. Please don't touch that."

"So, wait, you knocked her up, bought her a ring and never gave it to her, and her old man still gave you the family home as a *wedding* present?"

"Not that it's any of your business, but there were extenuating circumstances."

"Extenuating circumstances." Bear mocks his words. "So this ring has been sitting in your van for eighteen years?"

"No. It's going to someone else now, so please put it down."

Someone else. I think of Marlie and shudder. I picture her delicate face the last time I saw her. The way she said, "Love is something I make up to feel better."

"You giving this to someone else? I mean, why not? Why let a cheap, piece of shit ring go to waste?"

"That's enough." Jonah's hands grip the wheel. Bear is too big a man to care about Jonah's beating fists, but he drops the bag. I hear it land with a soft thud.

There's a brief teetering quiet, then Bear barks out, "The twins!"

I freeze, and Jonah does too. "What?" he says, his voice instantly smaller.

Bear jabs his finger at Jonah. "That's why I heard of Beachport. It's where they took those twins from." Jonah shakes his head, but Bear looks triumphant. "Yeah, it was almost sixteen years ago. I remember because it was the fall I was looking for my first job. Tried up and down the coast. It was all anyone was talking about."

Jonah says, calm and condescending, "I don't think so."

"Yeah, yeah, it was all over the news. Some nut-job stole them right outta their home. Middle of the night. You come from there — you don't remember?"

I can feel Jonah letting off the gas. "I've been gone a long time. News didn't make it to Canada, I guess."

"They never found the dude who did it. Gotta be a cold case."

Jonah steers the van to the side of the road. We're still in the woods, far from anything. "Okay," he says as he eases to a stop. "This is as far as I can take you."

Bear looks startled for the first time. "That wasn't the deal, man. You gotta take me as far as you're going."

"I'm stopping here." He talks to Bear like he's a very young, very stupid child. "I've been driving five straight hours. I want to eat my dinner in peace and get some sleep. Beachport can wait till the morning."

"Fair enough," Bear says. "I'll hang with you. Could use some shut-eye myself."

"Good. I appreciate the company. Let's pitch camp here." Jonah opens his door, and so does Bear. Bear climbs out and slams the door and stands on the graveled edge. The thick pines are a fitting backdrop for his hulking, animal shape.

Jonah slams his door too, but he's still inside the van. A tremendous force yanks me back as Jonah accelerates and takes off down the road. I have only a moment to register Bear's astounded face before he's gone from my sight.

32

We travel for another hour or two. Then the van slows and I can feel something different about the way Jonah drives. As if the car is going in circles. I take a chance and peer out.

We're in the middle of a town. I recognize it immediately from the newscast on the video. I remember the announcer's monotonous voice: "The small, close-knit community of Beachport is on high alert." The road sign: *Beachport, Maine, Where the sea takes your breath away.*

There are many impressive buildings, obviously built a long time ago: a city hall, a library, a post office, a bank. There's a large park with benches here and there and a fountain. Smiling mothers push babies in strollers and small kids skip along beside them. The trees have leafed out, some blooming with white or pink flowers.

Jonah looks around too, like he's maybe remembering how he used to skip in that park with his mother or how he explored that library to find another science textbook.

After we circle the town a bit, Jonah drives toward the sea. He stops on top of a hill and parks the van. A huge harbor spreads out below, and I recognize it too. The colorful mishmash of steel and masts. Hulls of every shape and size. Ocean breezes playing with flags and sails. People wandering the docks. I wonder if this is where Jonah's father used to work on the tugs, the *good, salt-of-the-earth kind of fellow.*

Nerves swell up inside me. I don't know yet how I'll get away from Jonah and to my family. Will he drive to the house and then I'll sneak out of the van? Or will I learn where they live, then sneak out later and find my way back to them? Another answer I want to know is if my parents can help me help the ones I left behind.

Marlie. A violent storm of guilt overtakes me. Would Marlie stay with him? Would she accept his ring and invent their love to make herself feel better? She doesn't know anything about experiments, about stolen babies.

The sun starts to set behind us, dipping into the horizon, and the sky flushes pink then mauve. Jonah starts up the van and pulls away from the curb.

He circles back until we get to a beautiful neighborhood, full of grand houses and extravagant gardens. Slowly, he navigates turns and angles his head this way and that. Probably looking for me.

He drives to a winding street that curves like a wave up and down a hill. Along one side, the houses are huge and sit on wide lawns that are guarded behind stone or brick or iron gates.

My body starts to shiver. I see it, the house from the video. *Kevin and Shannon Birkshire's home.* A large house with an iron gate and a long driveway. Painted shutters around every window. No lights on inside. No car in the driveway.

Jonah pulls the van over and turns his head to look at the other side of the street, the side where the houses are simple and small. *We grew up across the street from each other*, he said to Bear. He checks out a brick and shingle house with broken steps leading to a forsaken porch. *I used to watch her from my bedroom when I was a kid.*

Jonah cranes his head about, casting for me in the shadows. When he doesn't see me, he settles in to watch the house on the other side of the street. The Birkshires' house. *My house.*

I can't leave the van until I see them, until they can gather me up and protect me.

I hold my breath and count seconds and shove my hands in my pockets and clench and unclench my fingers.

A dangerous excitement builds inside me. One that risks making me do something that will ruin everything.

⤰

When the daylight in the van dulls like smoke and is extinguished, Jonah starts up in his seat, then hunkers down again and watches through the spokes of the steering wheel. I lift my head high against the lid of the box so I can see what he sees.

There's a blur of movement at the house across the street. The front gates at the end of the driveway swing open. A long, beige car is waiting to go in. There's a woman in the driver's seat and she skims in and out of view, flashed by lights in the yard, as she pulls in and parks the car.

She gets out and closes the door, then leans her back against it and blows out her breath. She seems to whisper something to herself. Her forehead furrows. I am already memorizing every bit of her.

Her face is almost unrecognizable, but it's definitely the woman from the videotape. *Shannon Birkshire.* She looks old now, soft skin drooping her face into mournfulness.

The passenger door opens and a man gets out. *Dr. Kevin Birkshire.* He looks older too. He opens the back door of the car, reaches in, and straightens up again. After a minute or so, a little boy, about five or six, jumps out. He's bawling so loudly I can hear him. His shoulders jerk in a hiccup, and this seems to make him angrier.

My mother says something to the little boy, but I can't hear it. She walks to the house. Screaming, the boy follows her. Behind them, my father locks the car and follows too.

The front door of the house is open now and an overhead light glows from the hallway. Every little inch inside looks warm and comforting.

My mother says a few more things as my father and the screaming boy go past her into the house. As she steps into the hall, the light shines on her like a spotlight announcing her arrival. The boy blocks her way into the rest of the house by stomping his feet and crying, and my mother looks down at him, then reaches to lift him into her arms. As she turns, I notice a weariness in her face, a pained surrender I've never seen on another person.

The little boy is so angry that at first he punches his fists at her and flails away. But my mother's head nuzzles in, her cheek caresses his, and just like that, he calms. His whole body settles against her, his head burrows into her shoulder, his hands that were fists relax and circle her, the little fingers flicker up and down her arms.

Something melts inside me too, turning me into a small child. One small enough to be bundled in her arms, to be rocked and shushed and caressed. Moments I never had, but might have had, appear out of empty air: me as a child in this house, running through the grass, laughing, being caught by this mother, me happy and she free of painful weariness, me walking home from school with this mother and telling her the stories of my day, this mother stroking the back of my head. This mother will scoop me up. She will let me erase my anger and fear, let me rub it out on the skin of her neck.

I prepare myself to burst out of the box, to push through the back doors of the van, to run to her, calling and laughing. To scream at her, "I'm here, I'm here!"

I imagine her eyes widening with surprise, then with delight. Her dropping the boy and coming at me with arms flung open. Her laughing too, and crying with happiness. Both of us forgetting the years we missed together as if life were only starting now.

My muscles coil and twitch, begging me to run to her. My heart pounds at my chest — a prisoner caught inside a cell and trying to smash its way to freedom.

But I don't move. Not a muscle, not a hair.

Something stronger has wrapped its dark arms around me. It clamps me down and holds me in my place.

In the hallway of the house, my mother, still holding the boy, steps out of the light and her silhouette moves to shut the door. I picture her hand touching the inner doorknob. The doorknob knowing her touch. Even the doorknob more important. She pushes it away, and the door shuts between us.

In front of me, Jonah sits up and looks intently at the yard. Waiting for me to run out, maybe from the garden, maybe from the street.

But I don't run out. I'm being held inside the cardboard box. I'm being held prisoner by something stronger than me. Because it's too terrible — so unfair, so wrong — my heart, my blood, scream at me. But my body doesn't move. It can't.

My mother and father have a new child.

A son.

A new family.

They are a whole thing without me.

Mo's voice echoes inside my head. "When people move on, they move on."

My heart beats out seconds, then minutes. My body stays rooted. Nothing I say to myself works to get me to open the van door and climb out and run to where I most want to be.

Then the truth rushes at me, clear and cutting: *I'm the mistake.* The wrong one. I always have been. And I won't be able to stop myself from making more mistakes. To helplessly hurt someone I love.

Deep, deep loneliness seeps into me, like storm water welling into a foundation and rising. I need to leave this family in its proper shape. I need to protect them from knowing the truth of me. Because I will only bring more weariness, more pain.

I can't have what I want. That's the problem. That's the truth.

But I can bear to be alone. I know I can. I've done it my whole life.

❧

Fear is supposed to be the worst thing. But it isn't. The worst thing is when hope fills you up and then bleeds away. When hope is gone.

≫

After a long time, I feel Jonah start the van again.

33

I don't watch where we're going. But as we drive, I know I have to get somewhere else.

Leaving that lit-up house is elastic, me pulling myself away, with something equally strong pulling me back. I need to be strong enough to push until the elastic between me and my once-upon-a-time family snaps.

I can go back to Canada and find my train-hopping friends. They know me, they already welcomed me. When Jonah decides to head back to the island, I can ride back with him until we get across the border. Then I can leave him as soon as he stops somewhere and hop on a train back to Moncton. From the train yard, I know exactly how to get to the hobo house. That's a place where I might belong. From the hobo house, maybe I can phone the island and let people know I'm okay. Maybe I can convince them to tell Marlie to leave.

❧

It's after 10:00 p.m. by the time Jonah stops driving again. He picked up some food from the window of a restaurant before we left town and the smell of burger and fries fills the van. My stomach rumbles and I shove my arms into it to muffle the sound.

We're in a parking lot now. Through the back window I see a sign: *Seacoast Motel, Vacancy*. I know this is a place Jonah will want to sleep for the night. I'm relieved. I badly need water and something to eat. I am so so tired.

Jonah takes his bag of food with him when he goes to the motel office. A few minutes later, he comes out with a key that dangles from a wooden cut-out of a leaf. He walks along the front of the motel until he gets to the right room. Then he slips the key into the lock and goes through the door.

It's always a relief when he's gone — my breath works properly again.

I wait for a long time before getting out of the van. When I'm sure he's settled in for the night, I let myself out, as insubstantial as a snail.

Around the motel, it's very still. Only a couple of other cars parked by the rows of doors.

I wander to the road in front of the motel and look both ways. As far as my eye can see, it's only darkness and trees. No little town, no other buildings. No place to buy water or food.

More thirsty, more hungry for knowing there's nothing, I check around for garbage cans overflowing with half-eaten food, but there aren't any.

At the edge of the woods behind the motel, there's a puddle, and I'm so thirsty I consider drinking from it. Instead I suck dew off leaves. Inspecting everywhere, I find no answers to any wishes, and so try to make friends with my loneliness. I imagine we'll be together for a long time.

For the first time since leaving the island, the sky is clear. Somehow the stars in this sky seem brighter than on the island. They seem to wink and blink at me. I find all the constellations I know. Ursa Major, Ursa Minor, Cassiopeia.

"Whatcha looking at?"

His voice makes me jump out of myself. Beside me is a boy about my size. He has very light hair and freckles all over his face. He isn't looking at me, but up into the air, trying to find what's so interesting to me.

"Hercules," I say in a quiet voice.

"Yeah? Like the superhero?"

"No." I want to get away from him, but I know already there's nowhere to go. I notice we're all the way at the end of the motel and that another car has arrived. A young man is walking from it to the same office Jonah used. He looks much like the boy beside me, but a few years older. I hesitate, then answer him. "Hercules, the constellation."

"Oh." The boy looks at me now. He's chewing gum and it cracks between his teeth. "I don't know much about stars. Except the Big Dipper." He points to the big square in the sky. "That's it, yeah?"

I follow his pointing. "Yeah. But it's actually part of Ursa Major. See those stars like a tail and legs around it? That's the same constellation. When you know how to connect the stars with imaginary lines, you start to see it."

"Cool." He smacks his gum. "So where's Hercules?"

I point to a square of stars a little smaller than Ursa Major and a little bigger than Ursa Minor. "That's his head, with his body right underneath. He's supposed to have his leg on his conquest and a raised sword in one hand."

He searches. "Looks like a bunch of stars to me."

I smile to myself. "Hercules was a hero."

"Yeah?"

"When he was a baby, the wife of his father — who wasn't his mom — sent snakes to kill him in his crib. But he strangled them and lived."

"Big deal." The boy puts his hands on his hips. "Thor could crush that easy."

He's talking to me like I'm a regular person from the rest of the world. "Well, he killed a lot of people," I say, playing along. "And he went to the underworld. Which is hell."

The boy eyes me. I like the feel of it. "Go on," he says. He looks mischievous, and I try not to smile with relief.

"He found this old sailor," I say, "who lived on a remote island in the underworld sea. Hercules wanted immortal life and this old guy had the answers. After that, Hercules did all these amazing feats. He conquered a nine-headed snake. He battled the fiercest warrior in the Amazon and took her belt. He wrestled a monster into submission with his bare hands. He amazed everyone because he was always victorious. He only died because his wife accidentally poisoned him."

"That sucks," the boy says.

"The thing is, he *did* get immortal life. See?" I point at the stars. "Because now he's a constellation for all eternity."

He chews his gum for a few minutes, thinking. "Not sure it was worth it."

That makes me want to laugh so hard, I have to cough to hide it. "Maybe not."

But he laughs easily and his freckles get squished and that makes me want to laugh harder.

"What's your name?"

I hesitate. "Twelve."

"Weird name."

I smile at my shoes.

He puts out his hand. "I'm Daniel."

I take his hand and we shake hands very slowly and stare into each other's eyes. I let my smile meet his. It feels so good, as if smiling can pull poison from a heart. I won't be the first to let go.

A voice calls out — it echoes through the silent darkness and I cringe, my eyes going to Jonah's motel room door — "You coming, Danny?"

Daniel drops my hand and looks behind him, then back at me. "My brother," he says, rolling his eyes. His brother is coming out of the motel office with a key. Danny calls back — all of it making me expect the worst — "Yeah, give me a sec, Connor."

He looks at me again. "So whatcha doing out here, anyway?"

I hesitate. I feel awkward suddenly, and shy. The way I always felt on the island with strangers. I try to fight it.

"Come on," he says. "Spill it." He gives my side a poke.

I flinch away.

I want to tell him. I want to be a regular person. But a vision of a family in a house, a mother and child clasping each other in a doorway, comes to me, and I have to shut it out so I can think. So I can speak. "I'm running away."

"Yeah?" I can see the idea excites him. He points to the room his brother went into, which is about four doors down from Jonah's. "Need a place to stay?"

The night hasn't even started and I'm already cold and too thirsty and hungry. But I can't go with him.

He raises his hands. "I'm not going to rape you or anything."

"That's good," I say. Crimes my hobo friends worried about that remind me how little I know the world.

"But I'd be open to some mutual kissing."

"What?"

"With your consent."

"Kissing?"

"You never kissed a guy, right? Could tell a mile away."

I know that breathing into Scotty's ear doesn't count. But I don't say that to him.

"You thirteen … fourteen, what?"

"Sixteen … in a few weeks."

"An older woman, huh? I just turned fifteen."

He also looks and sounds younger than he is. Somehow that makes me feel better.

I examine his freckled, twitching face. A boy my age, or thereabouts. He looks at me too, his eyes glancing around my features.

A whirling starts deep down inside me, familiar because of Scotty and Justin, but also different. I want to kiss Danny very badly. I can almost taste it in my mouth. He must see the hunger in my eyes because he bends in and leans his lips against mine.

At first we're cautious and just rest our lips together. But then our lips get greedy and start to work on their own, one feeding off the other, feeling around, tasting, and then tasting with our tongues too. He smells sweeter than anyone I've ever met. Like soap and something else I can't remember. I feel light and lighter, lifted up by the whirling inside me.

I never knew there were two ways to love a person: through your heart, and through your body.

"Danny!" Danny's brother's voice breaks us apart. My whole body blushes red. Danny looks like he's in a trance. "Get your butt in here, bro!"

Danny gets his normal look back again. His mouth eases into a sloppy grin. He grabs my hand and says, "Come on."

Even though I know I shouldn't go with him, it sounds like the best idea I've ever heard. Blushing fiercely, I let him pull me to his room.

❧

Connor looks at us funny when Danny walks me through the motel door.

Danny puts a hand up. "She's running away from home, Connor. She needs a place to stay."

Connor looks wary. "Sorry, kid," he says to me in the older voice Danny might have one day. "It wouldn't be right, a young girl hanging with guys she doesn't know. I could get arrested."

Emboldened by everything that's happened, I say, "If I could just clean up? Drink some water?" Connor tilts his head, very reluctant. I keep at him — I've watched children beg their parents for things — "And maybe if you have a bit of food? I'm so hungry."

Danny raises both hands. "C'mon, man, she needs help."

Connor looks at me through narrowed eyes. "Yeah, you can

have some food. And use the bathroom. But that's it. You can't stay. If someone calls the cops ..."

Another possibility that means nothing to me. There are no police on the island. No worries about theft or murder. Still, I'm so relieved that Connor will help me, even a little.

He pulls a small cooler from the ground and sets it on the bed. He passes me a bottle of apple juice and a thick sandwich piled with chicken and lettuce and tomatoes and cheese slices. "Our mom made this for the road. You're welcome to it."

I pounce on the sandwich and rip it from the plastic wrap. I can only nod my thanks because the sandwich is inside my mouth before any words come out. My wolfing makes Connor and Danny laugh.

"Okay," Connor says to me, getting serious again. "You go clean up. And Danny? You get ready for bed." Danny scowls, but I don't wait to be asked twice. I finish the last crumbs of the sandwich and drink the juice and run fast to the bathroom to get myself clean.

≫

Hot, soapy shower water runs over my body and takes away all the sweat and dirt and dust from the last two days. It warms me through.

Everything is so different from what it was supposed to be.

I'm too tired to figure out where my place will be in this other world. That's a question I don't want to think about. A question without an answer.

I towel off and change my clothes for fresh ones, choosing my pink hooded sweatshirt to wear, just for now, for Danny.

So many sweet, fresh smells to add to Jonah's van. I guess I really will be a rose in a shit hole.

≫

When I come out, Danny is in his pajamas lying on one bed, and Connor is lying on the other bed reading a comic book.

I can't stop myself from bouncing on the end of Danny's bed. He bounces up and down too, first together with me, then opposite. Connor scolds us and tells us to settle down. He says we'll wake up the neighborhood, which of course I don't want. But a strange delirium powers through me, and it makes me feel more and more crazy. Almost happy.

When Connor goes into the bathroom to shower, Danny teaches me about Spider-Man and Batman and other stories I've never heard before. And I teach Danny the fighting tricks Chisel showed me. And pretty soon we're wrestling on the bed and between the beds, rolling around the floor. It makes us laugh so hard, but in a way where no sound comes out — Danny because he doesn't want to make his brother mad, and me because I know Jonah is only four walls away. We sneak in some kisses while we wrestle, and it goes back and forth like that: playing like kids and kissing like adults.

Connor comes out of the bathroom, which pulls us apart again. He tells us to grow up. Something about that makes us laugh even harder and we try to wrap our legs around each other and flip each other over. Connor wants to ignore us, but he's mad and finally he yells. And just like that, I stop squirming and Danny does too.

"Okay, guys," Connor says. "Twelve has got to get outta here. Now. We need to sleep if we're going to get an early start and make Dad's party on time."

Danny explains that his parents divorced and his mom lives down the coast and his dad lives up it. They're on their way to a family reunion for their dad's birthday, and it's a big deal that their mom let them take the car and travel alone.

When they talk about their parents, a rush of feelings comes over me and again I have to push myself against the memory-door to keep it closed. I have to pretend none of what I saw exists.

Danny says their mom is the best. He says she worried a lot after the marriage ended, and that it was hard on all three of them, but now after many years they've all adjusted and she owns a catering business and is pretty successful. He says they don't spend a lot of time with their dad, but he's pretty cool, even though he's married to someone else and he and Connor aren't a hundred percent certain about her. Even so, they're looking forward to seeing their dad and being part of the family reunion. They're going to see cousins they haven't seen since Danny was little. They say as far as they know their cousins are awesome.

When it's my turn to talk, I make up two parents who are also divorced and a dad who doesn't ever let me see my mom, which made me run away to be with her. I tell them that when I got to my mom's, I found out she married another man and they have all these new kids and they don't want me anymore. I tell them the truth about finding Calcutta and Monique and Justin and Tank and Chisel, especially the part about Chisel and the train hopping, and how I'm running away to be with them in Moncton.

They listen without interrupting much. When I'm done, Connor says I should go back to my dad. So I tell him that my dad is evil and that he hits me. Connor shakes his head. He says he has a friend who gets beat up by his dad and it's a really bad situation. Even the police can't do much about it. Again, I have no idea what police could do about anything.

Then I explain how I'm using my dad to sneak back into Canada, and how he doesn't know that I'm using him. The best part of the plan, I say, is that he isn't supposed to be in the States and won't do anything to let anyone know he's here. He doesn't really care that I'm gone, he just cares that I don't get to my mom. I say the only problem with my plan is that my dad keeps waiting outside my mom's house for me to arrive. For all I know, we might be waiting outside my mom's house for weeks before he finally gives up and goes home.

Connor sits up. "Well, that's an easy fix."

I sit up too, and so does Danny. "How?"

"Okay." Connor gets excited for the first time, like he's playing with us now. "You wait in the back of your dad's van. Give Danny that pink hoodie you're wearing and maybe something else that belongs to you. Danny puts on the hoodie and covers his head — I mean, he's practically your size — and he gets in the car with me in time for your dad to see. So your dad thinks you're traveling with me. See? And he follows us for long enough to know: 'She's not going to her mom's house; she's given it up; I got nothing to worry about.' Either he follows us all the way to the party, where he thinks you've gone to this reunion with, like, a thousand people at it, and I'll tell my dad and his friends to tell your dad to back off — and those guys are *huge*, like, *insane* — so your dad goes, 'Geez, maybe I should head back to good ol' Canada.' But hopefully he sees we're going in the total opposite direction of your mom and he just gives up and goes home. Either way, bam, you're back across the border and, well, you got the rest worked out."

I think about Connor's plan. I truly can't imagine having to spend weeks more in the back of Jonah's van in front of a home I can't claim. Weeks of peeing in woods and scrounging for food and huddling in a cardboard box. Weeks of closeness with the only person I can't bear, and of giving up — day after day — the only people I want to be with. His plan sparks up my old determination.

We go over a whole plan, even getting a bunch of metal spoons from their mother's catering box in the trunk of their car and putting them into a plastic jug. We sneak the jug outside Jonah's door so he'll trip on it when he leaves and we'll hear the clatter and know it's time to fly.

I give Danny my sweatshirt. We make fun of how gorgeous he looks in pink, but with the hood up, he could be me. Danny jokes that he's wearing a superhero cape, and I say it sounds like superheroes spend an awful lot of time interested in fashion. Danny tells me if I have nothing respectful to say about superheroes, I shouldn't say anything at all.

We pass through a covered bridge and I stop myself from imagining trolls and treachery. I notice now that Jonah's anger has begun to color him. The back of his neck is fired up. His breath has started to snort in and out like a running dog. His shoulders are tight, pulling up higher toward his ears. The sound of the windshield wipers scratching the glass — *scritch-scritch, scritch-scritch* — starts to make me sick.

And then Connor's car swerves. Just a small wave on the road, weaving to the left lane and curving back into the right. When Jonah's van hits the same patch, it swerves too, his swerve feeling much wider. More dangerous.

Gravity wants to tip me over, but I tense my muscles to keep myself and the box upright. The car brakes and accelerates and I realize Jonah's confusion prevents him from knowing which to do.

Just as Connor's car is about to cross a narrow bridge, Jonah swerves and brakes and accelerates again. The jolting movement knocks me into the side of the cardboard — this time hard enough to make a sound.

Before I can be afraid of that sound, I feel a punch reverberate through Jonah's van — we've hit Connor's car.

I find the peephole again so I can see what's happening. Jonah's car slides over the glassy road, swerving crazily, away from them, toward them. The van skids forward more quickly than Connor is driving.

Despair burns through me like tinder. How could I have let Connor and Danny help me? How could I have forgotten what happens to every innocent thing that crosses Jonah's path? Like every last one of us, Jonah only wants to survive. Like me, I'm shocked to know, he'll do anything for it.

The bumpers of both vehicles crunch together and apart. Connor's car swerves wider this time and skids too. I bump side to side, and every muscle in my body contracts and tenses to hold me and the box upright.

Then Connor interrupts to ask if I have something Danny can hold that could only be mine. I fumble through my bag, trying not to touch the one thing I have. But the only thing that's perfectly unique is the ratty old mouse that Aidie always kept with her on the pillow in the closet. A stuffed toy that Jonah knows very well.

When I hand it over, Danny can tell right away what it means to me. "I'll take care of it," he says. I can feel a tear coming, but I swallow it back. Danny says gently, "Swear to God, Twelve."

I nod and give the old mouse a last kiss and nuzzle. It even smells like Aidie. "Thank you," I say and let it go into Danny's hand.

Danny stares at me but speaks to Connor. "Can't we take her with us, man? Let's just get her out of here." New hope kindles — because that's what I truly want.

"She crossed the border illegally," Connor says, shaking his head. "They'll arrest her. At least in Canada, they can't touch her."

My hope settles again, and Danny's expression looks settled too. He gets a piece of paper, writes his name and address on it, and passes it to me. I very carefully fold it into my pants pocket. Then he takes my hands and looks deeply into my eyes. "When you're safe, you gotta write me, okay?" I promise him I will.

We don't kiss again because Connor is watching. But we know the possibility is there.

We hug each other so hard it starts another laugh and then we push each other away and then we give each other one last poke in the guts.

I sneak out of their room and creep to the van. Before I climb into the back and into the hole of the cardboard box, I check one last time that the jug of spoons is on the ground by Jonah's door.

The night is clear and fresh. It's cool out, but not so cold I won't be able to catch some sleep in the made-up little cubby in the dark.

34

I wake with a shock. The spoons have fallen.

I peer through the van window and notice two things. One: Jonah is at the door of his room. He's swearing at the incongruity of twenty spoons on the ground. He hesitates, confused and angry. Two: it's pouring rain. I should have known rain was coming. Before I let myself into the van last night, I smelled the dampness and felt that the wind had changed and was stronger. But I didn't want it to rain, so I pretended to myself that it wouldn't.

Jonah steps over the mess of spoons and walks through the drizzle toward the motel office with the wooden-leaf key in his hand. By the time he drops the key into a slot in the door and turns around, Connor and Danny are out of their room.

Danny has the hood of my sweatshirt over his head and the sleeves pulled long over his fingers. He keeps his head angled away from Jonah and holds the old mouse by the tip of its tail so it hangs down from his hand as sad and obvious as a teardrop. He stands by the passenger door of his car with his back to Jonah and waits there — I can sense the energy of his anticipation — while Connor pretends to casually bring out their cooler and pack it into the trunk. Rain pours down on them and they huddle against it.

Danny is my superhero, I think. *And I am his. And I will write Danny when I get to Moncton. And one day we will see each other again.*

Jonah stops. He's spotted the boys. He looks so intently at Danny's back in the pink sweatshirt that I think his eyes will burst seem to notice the rain soaking his own head and dripping face.

When Connor starts to walk toward the office with his leaf key, Jonah hurries to the van and climbs in as quietly as moving carefully not to attract any attention. Connor walks spilled spoons and past Jonah's van — he looks so casual — and his key in the slot of the office door. When Connor passes, crouches behind the wheel and watches Danny's pink huddled ba

Now Connor and Danny climb into their car and slam the do Danny always keeps his head facing away, but somehow also ke showing the mouse in his hand. Either holding it up against a wind or balancing it on the dashboard in front of him. As Connor pu their car out of the lot, Jonah starts the van, and I curl into my usua ball and hold my breath.

The van rocks and jerks around the lot until it's on smooth road again. I peek up now and see that we're following Connor and Danny's car. I'm so excited that our plan is working that I want to whoop out loud. I cuddle myself and push my smile into my arms.

The rain pours down and the van's windshield wipers flip back and forth so fast I think they might break off. We drive for a long time, heading northwest, inland, away from Beachport. I keep waiting for Jonah to give up and turn for the border, but for now he keeps following.

The countryside is beautiful, with lots of lakes and long forests of pine trees. Because of the warm air and rain, everything is freshly green.

Now we drive on smaller roads and the rain shines and polishes them. The cars turn many times here and there, sometimes crossing bridges over rivers and brooks. I wonder if Jonah will follow them all the way to the party, if he'll confront huge men and demand my return. I want to believe it can all be very funny and useless and that he'll leave without trouble.

Connor tries to accelerate his car away. But the nose of Jonah's van is stuck to their bumper. Both cars skid, zigzagging to one side of the road, then the other. The cars are clamped together, a thundering train. It's impossible to tell if Connor's car is pulling the train or if Jonah's is pushing.

Staring hard through the windshield, Jonah grunts and moans. His face and neck burn red. His hands are ice-white, blue veins popping up like sailor's rope tying them to the steering wheel.

I ache to cry out. To warn him. But I also want to hide myself from the next swerve, from the one after that, from the one that finishes us all.

The sound of tires braking on the slippery road is a terrible scream. I tense my whole body, ready to scream too. The cars swerve again, this time off the road and over the gravel on the side. Now the van jitters over each tiny bump, shaking my head, hurting my skin. I try to hold my breath but it puffs from my mouth.

Then, as if it was going there all along, as if it's the only way to stop, Connor's car smashes into a concrete pillar that holds the bridge. The force separates the two vehicles, and Jonah is able to steer his van across the lane. But Connor's car keeps twisting. It bounces off the pillar and veers sideways. It slides and turns toward the embankment. It skids right to the edge of the bridge.

Now the back end dips over the bank and the front end flips up into the air. The car teeters back and forth for so many horrible seconds.

I want to reach out, sure I have the power to pull it back. But that power never comes.

Connor's car teeters one last time, then starts to slide over the embankment under the bridge.

No sound comes out of my mouth.

Jonah hits the brakes, this time hard enough to knock me over.

And everything slows down.

Before I fall I see Connor's car slide backwards down the ditch. I see that it's a long way down and there is a fast river frothing at the bottom.

It's as if I can feel Connor and Danny's unbelieving shock in my own body. I am their terror.

So slow it could be a leaf unfurling, the car slides toward the river. No doors fly open. No windows roll down. No arms of boys come out from the sliding car. No Danny. No Connor. No Danny.

The back end hits the water, the trunk dips into it, broken metal plunges into the furious waves. And that's all I see because my fall is over too. My head hits an old fuel pump and pain echoes through my whole body.

Just before my eyes close, I hear Jonah's voice. "No." A groan. Agony. "No no no no no no." He opens the van door and gets out. My eyes close, my ears close, I am in darkness.

35

When I open my eyes, I don't know where I am. There are voices talking a long way away.

"What was the purpose of your trip, Mr. Hubb?"

"Our ferry to Founder's Island broke down. Lots of people stranded. Had to pick up fuel lines in Portland."

"All right. Have a safe trip."

The sound and feel of the van accelerating.

Between my legs, my pants are soaked. My head aches so much, it feels like it's draining away. My hand goes to it. When I look at my fingers, they're covered with dark, sticky blood. I lie down again and close my eyes. I wait for my body to die.

❧

I'm disappointed when my eyes open again. I don't want to run anymore, don't want anyone to come and save me, don't want to kill Jonah. Just want to sleep and sleep forever.

Every time the van stops, it wakes me up again and disappoints me.

It's very dark around me. Jonah isn't in the van anymore.

The clang and creak of another, bigger engine starts up. There's a drone and rumble of something huge underneath and around us. We're on the move again.

The van sways, and I'm swayed with it. A giant metal cradle. A lullaby of rumbling and groaning. The smell of eggs fried too long — diesel fuel.

The ferry back to the island.

I wonder what Jonah said to the islanders before he left. What lies he'll tell them now. *Gemma ran away. I need to go find her. My beloved daughter is missing. I've done everything I can. She's gone. She's gone.* Everyone mourning for me. *Gemma is gone. We did everything we could to find her. Poor Jonah. Poor, poor Jonah.*

❦

I think about my mother. The lies she was forced to believe. Or forced to make up to accept me being gone. For so many years. *Sixteen.*

How can anyone fix that?

And then I remember: she has a name. *Shannon Birkshire.*

She has a strong face and dark brown hair and gray eyes.

In all the years I imagined her, I never got her right.

And there is a father. A real one. *Kevin.* A doctor. Someone who makes people better.

There is a brother.

Now I know exactly where they are: on a spot on the earth as clear and steady as a compass point.

❦

I feel the ferry bump up against the pier markers in Keele's Landing. I don't know how late it is, but it's very dark out. The sun would have set just before 9:00 p.m. If it's this dark now, it's much later. The time of night when islanders will have been in bed for a long while.

For the first time since I left, I let myself think about Peg. I remember her profile on the stretcher at the hospital. How still she was. The slight tightening of her fingers around the stretcher bars. Her slight fingers touching my wrist and cheek.

I hear Jonah climb back into the van and drive it off. On land, he gets out, closes the ferry gates, and gets back into the van. Even though

I know it's too late, even though I'm too tired to care or wish for it, something in me still waits, waits for people to come running from houses, for them to call after us, calling for me. But the only sound is the crunch of the gravel under the van tires as it winds over the narrow road up to the keeper's house.

The van finally slows to a stop. Still my bloody head rests on the old fuel pump. Still I can't think of moving or of choosing a place to move to. But when Jonah leaves the van and I'm left alone wrapped in the overturned cardboard box, preserved in my own sticky blood and drying pants, as the engine ticks somewhere in the van, ticking down seconds, I know that I need to get up.

My body does the work for me: turning over and reaching up, pressing out of the box, turning the door handle, pushing the door.

By reflex, I breathe in the blissful cool island air. The smells I know so well and love with all my heart. The salt, the trees, the bushes, the dirt. Everything with its own smell, unique and pure.

The house is still repulsive to me, but I draw close to a lighted window, like a dying moth.

Inside, I see Jonah shaking Marlie from sleep on the living room couch. Marlie leans up quickly and rubs her eyes. Then she stands and puts both her hands on Jonah's chest — she's asking him something, begging him. He has a sad frown on his face, and he shakes his head very solemnly. With grave slowness, he pulls her cellphone from his coat pocket and hands it back to her. She doesn't take it but slaps a hand over her mouth, so Jonah puts the phone down on the coffee table. When he straightens and looks at her again, Marlie throws her arms around him and burrows her head in his shoulder.

Am I dead to them, or am I impossible to find?

I can tell from the tremors in Marlie's back that she's crying. Crying as hard as I think I should cry, as hard as I wish I could cry.

From Jonah's coat pocket, left behind when he took out the phone, two ribbon loops stick out — the same loops that decorate the shiny bag from the Beachport jewelers. The old crushed bag with a diamond ring inside.

≽

My body walks me down the path to the lighthouse. It is so dark, but I know every curve of the path. Every turn. Every rock. The closer I get to the cliffs, the more the sea mist thickens.

Once again, fog settles over the woods.

When I arrive at the clearing at the end of the path, the lighthouse gives a bright wave through the darkened clouds. I go toward the light, trying not to think about the hole that Biscuit started and what it covers. Instead, I walk around it and go right to the lighthouse door.

I don't turn on the fluorescents when I'm inside, but close the door tight.

And even though I don't bid it, a sound begins to grow around me like nothing I've ever heard before. An animal roaring and a siren blaring. It echoes all over the tower. Not just me screaming but someone else too.

When nothing is left of the scream but its echo, I make my way to the ladders.

Squares of faded light from the windows guide me up. One rung after another, climbing higher, in and out through shadows.

For the first time I see it is a darkhouse, not a light one.

At the top, I push the door open against the wind and crawl out. I know the view is going to take my breath away; already the breath is leaving my mouth.

Outside, the sun peers over the edge of the horizon and turns the fog around the lighthouse into pink gauze. If ever there's a time to step out on the clouds and walk away, this is it. I won't ever have to see anyone again. Won't have to pretend and make up stories for Peg and Scotty. Won't have to decide what story to tell Marlie. Won't have to pass through air that someone has made poisonous with lies. Won't have to face the keeper.

I climb up onto the rail and swing my feet over the ocean. The wind tugs me this way and that, the fog twists itself around me.

Just one step and I could be on the clouds. One step and I could be standing on fog, light as air, bright as light.

36

ime keeps changing the way everything looks. Aidie's voice sounds so
sweet. I turn, and there she is, sitting beside me on the rail. She's
not at all angry or sad. She's so small.

"Where did you go?"

The rising sun starts to dissolve the fog. A ray of light pierces
through and creates a prism on her luminous skin.

Everything is always changing, she says.

I want to throw my arms around her. "I missed you so much."

Tell me how I got here.

I want to hold her so close that we'll never come apart. "I thought
you were gone forever."

Tell me. How did he do it?

"Let's not talk about it, Aidie. Let's just be together."

You read his journals in the cave.

"I didn't."

You saw the experiment when you were ripping it down.

"I don't remember."

We were four months old.

"Please, Aidie. It's not important."

*He watched her marry someone else, watched their happiness, watched
her get pregnant.*

"She said hello a few times. She smiled at him. She didn't really
know him."

Once, when he was a boy, she called him a natural scientist.

"He invented a singular experiment to impress her."

He left his home in June, right after we were born, so no one would suspect him later. He collected everything he needed to take care of us. He found the island.

"They needed a lightkeeper."

In late October, just before the winter freeze, he went back to Beachport, crept into our house, and stole us from our cribs.

"Stop, Aidie."

He fed us cough syrup to keep us asleep, put us in baby seats, and hid us in the back of his van.

"Under cardboard boxes punctured with holes."

"What were we," he wrote, "but barely developed creatures with flexible behaviors."

"The maternal bond was weak."

We wouldn't miss her.

"We hardly knew her."

The islanders accepted his wish to keep to himself.

"They didn't know. How could they know?"

He spent the winter preparing us.

"We ate together, slept together, grew together."

He taught us to take care of each other. Feed each other. Comfort each other. Reward systems and punishments. Our bond had to be strong. We had to evolve as a pair.

"He was going to take us back when he proved it could work. When our mother would recognize the greatness of his work."

He loved our mother. That might be true.

"But you got sick."

In June, just after their first year, Subject A. expired.

Those were the words he used.

"The birthday he gave me wasn't the day we were born, but the day you died."

Afterward, he told the islanders that he had to rescue his only child. He left with you, hidden, and was gone for a week. Before he came back, he scratched and clawed his own face, and told everyone a crazy woman had done it.

"He wouldn't let Peg dress the wounds."

Everyone was so smitten with you.

A realization settles in. A cloud. "'The other didn't do her part,'" I say. "That's what he wrote in his journal. 'She didn't save her sister.'" I shiver in the cold wind. "I didn't do my part, Aidie. I didn't save you."

Aidie and I look at each other for a long time. I grasp and pull on tears so she won't see them.

Who is Lindsay?

I don't say anything.

Who is Leah?

I shake my head.

Aidie stretches her arms like she's waking from a long, satisfying nap. *He plucked silver birds off ears. Lindsay or Leah whispered to the birds to fly away. Only one silver bird had the courage to leave and it fluttered all the way to the windowsill. Its silver wings were so heavy, it had to throw itself into the mysterious sky. But it only landed in the grass below. And the perilous journey so exhausted it that it couldn't move anymore. So the silver bird hid in the grass until one day it could sparkle up at a tourist who rescued it and gave it back to its rightful owner.* Aidie stands up and balances very carefully on the rail. *And now that the story is over, we get to live happily ever after.*

"You're making that last part up. We never imagine anything right, Aidie, so don't hold your breath."

I am holding my breath. She flaps her arms and pretends she can fly.

"Stop!" I yell. "You'll fall!"

So will you, she says and takes two small steps, one foot balancing in front of the other like a tightrope walker. She whispers something under her breath that I can't hear. When I lean in, she says, *Should*

I do it? She turns to face the ocean and reaches a pointed foot over the rail.

"No, Aidie." Tears muddy my eyes. "Please, don't do it."

Then why else are we here?

The last of the fog clears away and the rising sun shines a spotlight on the ocean. The spotlight ripples toward me. "You'll fall."

Don't worry, I'll be okay.

"I'm sorry, Aidie."

For what?

There are too many feelings and not enough words. "It was my fault."

No.

She flutters her arms and jumps and lands and jumps and lands again on the narrow rail.

"Please don't."

I'm ready to leave.

"No!" I reach for her. "You can't!" I lose my balance and my hands lock onto the rail. Tears keep falling. "Don't go."

Don't worry. I'll be okay, she says. *Don't follow me.*

And before I can say another word, she swings her arms and leaps. Swirling and silvery, she flutters into the sky.

"No!" I reach for her.

Aidie curls and loops into the wind. Already she is smaller. *You can let me go.*

"I can't, Aidie. Please come back."

As delicate as leaves in autumn, or sand dollars, or Peg's white hair, she flutters higher and higher, dwindling into the sky, away and away.

"Help me!" I call after her. She's the only one who can. "I need you."

You don't. I can hardly hear her anymore.

She looks so happy.

"Oh, Aidie." My voice is no louder than a whisper. Like her, I'm fading. "I don't want to forget your face."

I stretch up to see the last bits of her, but she is going then gone. Now I'm all alone in the hush.

Lindsay or Leah is dead. I don't know which.

And Aidie is gone forever.

I creep back to the house. The sun is still new in the sky, and I don't think Jonah will be up yet. I go to his lab and find the key for it in my knapsack. I unlock the door and push through it. The hooks with the garden tools are just inside. I calculate what might be useful and choose the shovel and spade.

Tiny, piercing, urgent calls stop me. The voles inside their enclosures. Generations 54, 55, and 56.

I lean the tools against the wall and go deeper into the lab. As if they've been waiting for me all along, every vole inside every cage is alert on hind legs, whiskers twitching.

"Hello," I say. "I'm back."

Their paws clutch the air, curved around wishes.

I start to pull enclosures off shelves and carry them one by one out into the woods behind the house, setting them on the ground side by side. When each cage is outside, I unlock the miniature doors and fling them open. The voles stand alert in curious groups examining the leaf and needle pulp that makes up the forest ground. I imagine them dazzled by the promise of a new life.

Too dazzled, maybe, because none of them moves.

"Hey," I say, trying to make light, trying to convince them, "at least you have each other."

The first one, alone, sniffs and scurries closer to the opening. Then it sets its front paws on the ground. The others watch, intent, skeptical.

The brave one steps out of its cage and darts a few inches into the woods. It makes some calculations, then darts a bit further. Then, so quickly it takes everyone by surprise — the left-behind voles strain higher on their hind legs — it dives into the brush alone and burrows away.

"Okay," I say to the others, "I have to go. Good luck out there." I turn away from them and head back to the shed. I grab the tools, close the door, and make my way down to Biscuit's hole by the lighthouse.

❧

The sharp edges of the spade cut through the grass roots clumped together under the surface. It's almost too hard for me to dig, until I remember I can stand on the top edge and use my weight to bear down. Pushing down with my body, I slice around the shape I assume the trap door will be, lifting up chunks of grass and dirt and piling them off to one side. I cut all the way around Biscuit's hole, thanking him in my mind for starting this work.

Once, when the sun reaches a specific spot in the sky, I check the ocean, expecting to see it. And, sure enough, the ferry is sailing away from Keele's Landing across the silky gray-green water. The *Spirit* flies toward the mainland, right on schedule, as if nothing is different.

I keep cutting the earth.

When all the grass has been gutted away, I change the spade for the shovel and start to dig, flinging clumps of red dirt and mud off to the side. I dig for hours. For so long, my muscles start to seize and spasm. But I keep digging, stopping only a few times to catch my breath, always digging again. Even when I can barely lift the shovel anymore.

Finally, I hear the shovel hit something hard. The *thunk* and crack of contact is a relief. Now that I know where the trap door is, I can follow the shape of it, noting when my digging goes off course and using the spade again when I need to open up more ground.

Slowly but surely, I excavate the whole shape of the door. I notice that the wood is harder than any wood I've ever seen. It looks like the marbled tombstones down in the island cemetery. I remember reading in one of Jonah's textbooks about forests with petrified trees, and how a lack of oxygen combined with running water full of minerals can change wood into stone.

When I have the dirt mostly cleared from the door, I stop, carefully checking inside the hole. I don't see any hinges on the door and figure they must have rusted away a long time ago. I drop the shovel and pick up the spade again. Now I jam the sharpened edge into all the seams around the door and lift at the same time, trying to loosen it.

After I've cleared enough soil from the edges, I crouch down and use my fingernails to scrape away the dirt around a latch that's carved into the top. I brace myself and pull on the latch, but nothing moves. I get the spade again and jam as hard as I can into the seam of soil beside the latch, then I push with all my strength. The spade enters the soil by millimeters, but finally edges into the seam enough for me to get some leverage. I push and push against it. Sweat runs down my face and into my eyes. The door is heavier than anything I've ever lifted.

Tears start to mix with the sweat. I hear Aidie's voice again and it keeps me going. *Gemma, Gemma.* I can't give up; Aidie is counting on me.

The voice keeps calling, the sound not floating away like Aidie's body but moving in then out, quiet then loud, almost like the sounds from a shortwave radio. Around and around.

Gemma. Gemma.

Except Aidie should know I never want to use that name again.

Gemma. Gemma. Gemma.

It starts to make me angry to hear it. I push my anger into the spade, digging harder and harder.

Gemma. Gemma.

But the door won't budge. It only steals breath from my body. I close my eyes. I want to lie down and give up. Then I realize the calling voice isn't Aidie's, but a different one.

"Gemma! Gemma!"

As soon as I recognize it, I turn to see Marlie running down the path, her hand reaching toward me like it's the most important thing she's ever done. "Gemma! Oh my God, Gemma! Thank God!" I know I want to grab that hand.

She pulls me close and hugs me, kissing my head and saying the wrong name over and over. "Oh, Gemma, I had to keep looking." She bursts into tears. "I thought you'd jumped. I thought I gave you the idea."

Her worry chokes me. I shake my head against her chest.

Marlie keeps sobbing and gathering breath and whimpering into my head. "I thought you wanted to jump. You were so sad." She kisses my hair and whimpers again. "I kept checking the cliffs, praying not to see you in the water. I couldn't tell anyone. Couldn't say the words to any of them. Thank God you're alive. Thank you, thank you for being alive."

My body shivers and trembles and I fight it. I don't have time for tears, not hers, not my own. If I don't tell Marlie the truth, it will disappear under rocks, under dirt, under pretty swaying grasses. It will sink away.

"Jonah took me," I say, looking over her shoulder as she holds me and cries. "He took Aidie. And my real mother and father never knew." My words push past her tears, over the sound of her gasping for air. "I left the island to find my real parents. But I couldn't stay with them. And now the boys are dead." A wave of tears fights to come out of me. It has to be turned into ice and locked in my chest. "They didn't do anything but help me. And now they're dead."

"Oh my God." Marlie pulls her hand back. It's covered with strings of my coagulated blood. "What happened?" She examines the wound on my head. "Oh, Gemma."

"Please don't say that name."

"We looked everywhere." She hugs me again. She doesn't understand. "Jonah went to the police on the mainland in case you'd crossed without us knowing. He looked for you everywhere."

"For the wrong reason."

"He was so worried. He had the police send out a missing persons alert."

"He lied." How can I make her understand?

Marlie leans back to look at me properly. "We were all so worried, Gemma."

"I'm sorry," I say, looking at her properly too. She's very pale. "I should never have left you here. I should have told you. I should have told the police."

"Are you okay?" Marlie checks my forehead for fever.

She doesn't understand. She still doesn't understand. "I have to show you." I back away from her. "I need your help."

"Of course. Anything."

"You have to help me lift the door." I show her the hole in the ground with its huge mound of excavated dirt piled to one side.

Marlie shakes her head, confused. "We should get help. We should wait for Jonah."

"No!" I yell. "We have to do it now, and quickly."

I pick up the spade again and push it into a ridge. Marlie doesn't say another word. She reaches for the shovel and also wedges it under the ridge of the door a foot or two away from my spade. Together we press our bodies against the tools. We grunt and groan together, pressing and pushing. Then the edge gives and heaves up, ever so slightly. We push the tools under the open seam and lift again, jamming the tools in deeper and deeper.

When we get both tools jammed fully underneath the door, I tell Marlie to wait and I run into the woods and find two thin trunks that had split off during the ice storm with wood still dry enough to be strong. I run back to Marlie and shove one trunk under the door edge near her shovel and one under the door near my spade. We push against the posts. We brace ourselves and lean against them with all our strength. Finally the door begins to move. We crank it up like the lid of a casket, angling our bodies underneath to keep it opening. We keep pushing up until the door is fully open, until it's leaning to one side against the pile of shoveled dirt.

For a moment, we need to catch our breath and wipe sweat from our faces. Then I pull myself up and look down into the opening. The smell of must and wet earth scramble out, sticking to our bodies. Marlie stares down at the stone steps disappearing into darkness. "What is that?" she whispers. "A dungeon?"

I pick up my knapsack and lead the way down the stairs. Marlie takes a shaky breath and follows close behind me. Her fingers trace the stones as if measuring how far it's safe to go.

The tunnel and cavern are dark. I remember a bulb breaking and splinters of glass raining down. Determined to show Marlie the truth, I surge ahead and fumble in the shadows for the lantern I brought when I first came. I turn it on, hand it to her, and step back. Confusion furrowing her brow, Marlie shines the greenish light around.

She sees what I saw and the damage I wreaked: dozens of jars filled with preserved voles and torn sheets covered with diagrams and charts lying on the ground like gutted waste. Her expression shows that she's trying to understand what everything is and why it's here. The lantern light swoops around and it lands on the chart that's still tacked to the wall. It has her name on it: *Experiment Marlie Luellen*. Her face hardens when she reads the words, although I can see she still doesn't fully understand.

Now the lantern light finds the box on the ground. As Marlie walks toward it, her hand starts to shake, making the light flit this way and that. The lid is off where I left it, lying to one side. The light puddles over the shapeless bundle inside the box: a small heap of branches in shadow. The beam is a firefly darting over it, trying to land on the tangle but only able to brush past it and back, past it and back.

Marlie slumps down to her knees. Her fingers reach toward the dirty cloth. Her hand lifts the cloth away.

"Lindsay. Or Leah. I don't know which." My voice sounds weak. Marlie looks up at me, her hand resting on the baby's head; under her hand the baby's smile is carved in bone.

I pull a few experiment charts from the ground and lay them out so she can see. *Gemma, Adria, two babies*, a chronicle of their activities. Marlie shines the lantern at the sheets, drawing circles of light over the graphs and charts.

"You have to watch the video," I say. "Then you'll know."

The TV is still on from when I was last here, and so I rewind the VCR to the important part and let it play.

As Marlie watches, she very slowly places the lantern on the ground, as if it's the thing that's too heavy to bear. Her mouth opens, but no words come out. I watch the images too: the worried faces; a mother's and father's eyes, hopeful and then hopelessly staring. And not two unknown parents who are worried, but Lindsay and Leah's mother and father. And then, last of all, the photo of twin baby girls filling the screen, them huddled in matching green frog blankets, pink bows in their hair, silver birds in their earlobes.

"That's where I went." I rewind to show the parents. "To see them." I freeze the image on their worried faces. "But they have a new family now. So I came back."

Marlie reaches her hands up, clawing the air for answers. "What is this?" Panic fills her voice. "*What is this?!*"

"One of the babies is me." I sound so far away.

Behind me, Marlie's voice chokes. "No."

"And the other baby is Aidie."

"No. No."

"But not Gemma and Aidie. They're Lindsay and Leah. I don't know which."

Marlie stumbles to the window. She sticks her head out and gasps for air.

"I came back for you," I say. "I had to tell you."

I look at the box again, the dead baby inside it. I kneel down and unzip my knapsack, then very carefully pick up the bundle cradled inside the frog blanket. I make a nest inside my clothes and gently tuck the skeleton between them. *I also came back for Aidie.*

When I'm sure the bones are safe, I zip up the bag and loop it around my shoulders. I wipe my tears and grab Marlie's hand to pull her away from the window. "We need to hurry."

38

I run up the path from the lighthouse, Marlie right behind me. The weight of my knapsack makes me feel better — the baby is with me.

Marlie and I have to get back to town. If we can get to town, we'll all be safe. I'm starting to believe that people will help me. That they can.

As we head toward the house and then down the road away from it, I notice how it already feels like a place where other people live. It could be a stranger's house whipping past me through the open doors of a train.

Marlie stumbles behind me, slowing us down. She grasps at the air between us. "Gemma, stop." Her voice is cracking. "Stop, please, Gemma, stop."

But all I have in my head is the need to get to town before Jonah comes back. The fact that he hasn't returned to the house yet means the ferry is either grounded again or running late. Is he busy on the mainland trying to find news about my death in a car crash? Is he pretending to the islanders that he's trying to find me? Or worse, is he searching for a place to work, another reliquary of science, another secluded laboratory where he can take Marlie and make babies and start a new experiment — clomiphene in her water, incision in a prophylactic?

Something snags me and jerks me back. My neck hurts from the force.

When I turn to look, Marlie is clutching my knapsack in both hands. Her face is blotched with red, smeared with tears. She can't catch her breath and has to let go of me to heave herself over her bent knees.

I try to pull her forward again. "We have to hurry!"

But her feet are locked to the ground. "Please, Gemma, please." She gasps for air. "Please tell me it's not true."

"We have to hurry. We need to get back to town before he does."

Marlie looks around. She commands the trees, the sky. "It can't be true. Tell me it's not true."

"We have to hurry," I beg her. "If we don't get help, he's going to take you. He wants you to have his babies. He's going to do the same experiment with you. Don't you see? You have to run."

Marlie's breath sputters and gasps. Tears rain down her face. Her own thunderstorm.

Desperation fights inside me and makes me shake her.

Finally she looks at me, and I stop moving. The wildness in her eyes passes, and I watch her breathing even out.

"Yes," she says to me, "I see it now."

She grabs my hand and leads me down the road. Now we run together.

⌁

When we round the bend between East Island and West Island — right where the hedge of bushes opens up to the Roberts' field, right where you can see the whole island laid out in front of you like a map on a table — we see the ferry has arrived back at the dock and that Jonah is driving his van toward the road that leads to us.

We both freeze, skidding to a stop and throwing up gravel.

Behind us is a winding road back to the house that we will have to run faster than we've ever run so we can maybe get to the phone and call for help or maybe get to some kind of protection. The road is edged with bushes so thick you can't see past them, with thorns so sharp they'll tear you to pieces if you try to go through them.

We're already running toward the house before we can plan any strategy. Running the way you run when you face certain death. A vengeful bear in the woods.

The curves of the road buy us time: Jonah has to drive it more slowly than he can any other road, which lets us lead the way to the house. But when we arrive at the end of the drive, the van rounds the corner. Now Jonah knows I'm alive and on the island.

I stumble past the house, suddenly remembering that I cut the wire to the phone. Our only choice is to keep running and hope and wish for a path through the woods that will lead us to safety.

Because it's the first path we come to, we run down the path to the Rock Pit. I listen for the sounds behind us of Jonah running.

I remember there's an old overgrown path along the cliffs that eventually joins the Roberts' field. If Jonah thinks we've hidden in the Rock Pit, inside a crevice or among the jumble of rocks, he might waste time searching it before he heads back to town. On this part of the island, he'll be on foot, just like us. He knows the island well, but maybe not as well as I do.

I grab Marlie's hand and pull her into the woods. We push through the brush toward the coastline.

39

We can hear the quick and violent snap of dead wood. The sound echoes and flourishes over our heads, confusing me. Jonah is somewhere behind us, but where exactly is a question. The sun has begun to favor the far side of the island, and a late afternoon gloom settles over the trees, trapping us in shadows.

I push us deeper through the bramble, and we step carefully, aiming our feet for moss or knurled roots rising up from the ground. Footsteps so quiet they don't signal where we are.

We're almost at the overgrown coastal path when we get hit by a swarm of flies. We start to run through them, but something about it makes me stop. I change course and and follow their trail, aiming for their source. Marlie waves flies away from her mouth and eyes and follows me. The smell hits us, at first masked but then sharpened by the ocean wind.

Even though I have a bad feeling, I keep heading toward the smell. I don't want to see it, but I do: a decomposing body lying in the mush of last year's autumn leaves. Biscuit is dead.

Shock and sadness knocks me over.

Heavy black-red blood is congealed around him. Matted and fly-crusted, there's a deep gash on the top of his head. My own wound throbs then and my hand, unbidden, jerks up to it: a hard, painful lump from the fall in Jonah's van.

I want to comfort Biscuit, to scratch his warm, burred belly, but

Marlie, buckled over, pulls me up and urges me away. She swallows her shock and pushes us on through the woods. I let her take me.

Panting in gasps, Marlie fumbles through her pocket and takes out her cellphone.

"It won't work," I whisper. "We have to run."

But she ignores me and punches buttons and holds the phone to her ear. We plunge through branches, getting closer to the cliff's edge, to the salted air. She hangs up and tries again. Then hangs up and tries again.

We emerge on the coast. The lighthouse is behind us. I take over, leading us away from it, along the coast toward Keele's Landing. Such a long way away.

Marlie's hand squeezes mine. "Oh my God, it's ringing." She stops, astounded. I stop too. She presses her phone to her ear, then shakes her head and hangs up. "It rang, Gemma, I swear. Must be a random signal. Try one of the islanders. Quick, before we lose it." She shoves the phone in my hand.

I take it, my heart crashing in waves. My fingers punch at numbers. Mr. O'Reardon. Scotty. And the phone rings. A trilling cry for help. For hope.

A voice answers, "Hello." A sweet voice, the best I've ever heard.

"Scotty," I say into the receiver: a deep, yearning whisper.

The line cuts out. Pained, I punch in the numbers one more time. Again the line connects, and again Scotty picks up, this time calling into it, "Gemma!"

I don't waste a second. "We're in trouble at the lighthouse!" And the line is dead. Did he hear me; does he know?

Marlie shakes me and points into the woods. We can't see anything through the dense growth, but there's the unmistakable sound of something large crashing through. We have to keep going.

40

Marlie and I struggle to push through the overgrown path along the coast, but the way is so choked that we get torn to shreds. Thin streaks of blood lace Marlie's face; I wipe my cheeks and there are red smears on my fingers. Soon we can't even call the path a path anymore, but only spaces between trees. And not enough spaces.

I start to realize how useless it is, and can tell by her expression that Marlie thinks so too. We signal to each other. We can't make any noise and risk Jonah tracking us, but we know we need another plan. Marlie is the first to react, grabbing my arm and pulling me toward the lighthouse.

When we get there, I can see already how the fatigue is wearing us down. I can hardly move my arms and legs anymore, and Marlie stumbles every few steps. How can we fight Jonah?

Marlie begins to give me cues through her eyes and sign language. She finds the wheelbarrow she stowed behind the lighthouse after she built her sitting circle. I don't question it as she pushes the wheel-barrow to her circle of rocks, tips it to the ground, and pushes and pushes until one of the rocks starts to roll into it.

I run to help her. First one rock, then all four are pushed and rolled into the wheelbarrow. Then we wheel it over to the trap door and behind the mound of dirt dug up to expose it. On the other side of the mound — the side facing the path to the house — the petrified door leans, perched over the entrance to the cave.

There's a gigantic crash deep in the woods. We startle and stop breathing.

Jonah is coming.

I start to tremble. Beside me, Marlie goes rigid.

Then a dreamy, peaceful look comes over her, almost like in paintings of angels.

She pulls me down behind the mound of dirt and shushes me. I meet her gaze and listen. "No matter what happens," she whispers, "push the door closed after him. Understand?"

I nod, under the spell of her serenity.

"It's only leaning, so if you push yourself against it with all your weight, it will fall. Okay?"

I nod again.

"You have to roll the wheelbarrow over it. The weight of the rocks will seal it shut. Then you go get your bike and you ride to town for help."

I close my eyes. There's no more I can do. It's time to give up.

But Marlie takes my face between her hands and urges me fiercely enough to scare me, "No matter what happens."

And now he is here.

From behind the shelter of the mounded dirt and through the dark of the setting sun, we see Jonah. I don't know if it's because of my fear and anger or his, but I don't recognize his face at all.

He marches down the path in our direction, a pitchfork held tightly in his right hand, his teeth bared and biting. The red wave is growing inside him, the rage he has to fight against, that makes him do things he can't control.

He doesn't see us yet, but keeps charging. Then he notices the open door and the stairway going down into the ground and he freezes, his foot stilled in the air as if we've pushed a button to stop him. Now his face becomes the face I know, while slowly, slowly, he lowers his foot.

Marlie pulls me close and holds me tightly for a few seconds. My heart and hers beat against the other. Then she pushes me down really hard and, at the same time, stands up, showing herself to him.

"Jonah," she says, her voice eerily calm. "I have to show you the most wonderful thing. Gemma found it." She points through the opening.

Because I'm hiding behind the mound of dirt, I don't know what Jonah is doing. I listen for his movements, for the sound of him jumping in to attack, for the sound of the pitchfork slicing through the air. But it's quiet for a long time. Until I hear him say a word: "Marlie."

"Come, Jonah," Marlie says. "Let me show you." Above me, Marlie gives an innocent smile. She stretches her shoulders back and sticks out her chin. She takes a step, then another, until she's leading the way down the stairs into the ground. I ready my body to push the door down.

Jonah must hesitate on the path because I don't hear him move. I'm so afraid that he's coming for me that I can't stop myself from peering around the side of the mound.

Jonah is still there, his expression still confused. He stares down into the opening, his mouth working to say something. Marlie's voice echoes from deep inside the cave, "Come, Jonah. It's amazing."

And whether it's Marlie's strange way or her promise that he'll be amazed or his own wrong hope, Jonah loosens his grip on the pitchfork and lets it dangle at his side as he follows her down the stairs into the dark.

And because Marlie asked me to do it, I don't think about what might happen when I throw all my weight against the petrified door and slam it shut over both of them. It makes a tremendous thud as it lands in the dirt. I push the wheelbarrow over the door, making sure it stays closed with him locked inside. I hang myself over the wheelbarrow for added insurance. A cloud of dust spins around me. Gravity rewinding.

There's a loud thump and crash of something trying to get out. Him on the other side.

I throw myself down on the door, laying myself over him.

His voice strains to reach me, "Gemma, let us out." I can't stop myself from listening. "Let us out now." His voice rises higher, booming through the door. "This is very dangerous, Gemma. Open the door."

I press my mouth to the wood. "You took me."

"You don't understand, Gemma. I'll explain it. You'll see, I promise. You'll see." He starts to yell. "Gemma!" His voice is bursting. "Gemma!"

"I'm not Gemma," I say, tears sliding into the dirt and curdling the mud. "And you are nobody."

On the other side of the door, everything goes quiet.

Then I remember Marlie.

Keele's Landing is too far away. I can't leave her behind again.

41

The climbing gear is on the ground by the lighthouse where I left it. It's secured around my body before I even notice I've picked it up. I snap hooks in place and attach the rappel device to the rope, memory working my fingers when all thinking is gone.

I face the edge again, me beside the lighthouse, maybe holding its imaginary hand.

I'm not courageous or fearless, but simply doing everything I know I have to do. Turning, bending, pressing, falling, holding.

I'm almost at the window in the rock when I hear their voices. Jonah's voice sounds very close.

"I was going to destroy it all," he says. "Only two days ago, I brought everything here so I could throw it in the ocean."

"But you couldn't do it." Marlie's voice echoes from deeper within.

"No."

"Because it's too important."

"That's right. It's too important."

"It's your legacy, Jonah."

"I was never going to hurt you."

"I know."

"I care about you. For the first time in years, I know what that means."

"I believe you."

"Everything can be different with you," he says. "Better."

"A better experiment?"

"I knew you'd understand."

"I do."

Does Jonah still have the pitchfork? Or did Marlie manage to grab it? I measure the distance into the window and calculate how quickly I'll have to move to take him by surprise.

"I don't want to hurt you."

"I know, Jonah." Her voice sounds very sure. "Two babies are growing inside me, Jonah. I can feel them."

A pause so electric it burns me in the wind.

"Two babies?" Jonah says, his voice expectant.

"It worked. We can do this together." Marlie's voice is fading, as if she's moving deeper inside the cave, maybe toward the cavern door.

"We can do this together?" Jonah echoes her, his voice also receding into the cave.

I take a chance and rappel through the window, dropping onto the solid floor and slipping out of the harness.

The lantern is still glowing where Marlie left it, and it casts the room in its greenish half-light. The pitchfork is on the ground by my feet. Dropped by someone and not picked up.

Down the tunnel, eyes catch light, almost like wild cats. Marlie is pressed against a wall. Jonah is very close to her, but he's looking back at me. A scientist observing all the evidence. He measures me, measures her, measures the room. Graphs and charts probably ordering themselves in his brain.

"What happened to Adria, Jonah?" I keep my voice calm, but it echoes over the stone and tarp-covered walls. Still surprised to see me, Jonah tilts his head in a question. "How did she die?" I say with more conviction.

Jonah takes a step toward me. He says, not understanding me, "What *happened*?"

A question is a hook in my chest, tearing at it. "You said I killed her."

"You?" Jonah's eyes shift focus, searching for a point to land on. "The experiment died. You were part of that."

A sob overtakes my heart, my breath. The ice in my chest threatens to melt and drown everything.

"What happened, Jonah?" Marlie's voice comes from another world. "Did you get angry?"

Jonah's brow furrows.

An alien's voice. A god's. A goddess. "Did you punish Adria?"

"No," he says. "I went to her crib." He lifts his hands. "She wouldn't let me touch her." His eyes go blank, as if mesh has been pulled down over them. His hands shake and he stares at them like they had motives of their own. "Screaming. That's all she was."

"So you picked her up?"

"She was nothing. Just a sound."

"Did you shake her? Was it an accident?"

"When the sea destroys, we don't call it wrong and punish it for its waves."

The sob clambers over everything inside me, pushing blood and organs out of the way. Dying to come out. "Why didn't you kill me too?"

Jonah looks at nothing. "Kill you?"

"Why didn't you? It would've been over then."

"I don't *kill.*" His eyes find me and lock onto mine. He takes a step. "Don't you see?" he says, "My work is for the betterment of humankind."

I gird myself, ready for anything. The pitchfork is at my feet. "But your science doesn't work."

Jonah's face contorts. "What?"

"It will never work."

The center of Jonah's eyes contract, then expand. "If it can't work …" he says, black holes staring at me, "… why did I do it?"

I shake my head.

"Why did I do it?" he says, more insistently. Blood floods over his neck and face, and his jaw hardens into a vice. His muscles quiver and his hands clench. "*Why?!*"

Before I can answer, he runs at me. He grabs my shoulders and fumbles for my throat. I imagine his fingers squeezing my breath out. Finally doing what he couldn't do back then.

I want to let him do it. I want to let him end it now.

But my body won't allow it. My legs root and bend and launch. My upturned hand drives with monumental force upwards. I push all my pain into him, using all the power and rage inside me. Behind us, Marlie screams and it fires off the walls and binds us together.

Jonah is on the ground, disoriented, holding his face. I jerk my foot back and aim it at his stomach, then kick with all my strength. Jonah twists into himself and groans in agony. "Stop," he says, sorrowful. "Stop."

But I don't want to stop. I keep kicking and hitting and clawing. I want him to lie in pieces at my feet.

"It's over, Gemma," he groans.

It's not over and never will be. I want him to know that. I want him to feel it through the rage of my attack and in the bruises and cuts on his body. To feel it in his blood.

Then I see him: a huddled man.

The urge to finish him evaporates. I bend over, panting and crying and helpless. Jonah must sense I can't do any more, and he rounds over and gets on his knees.

All my anger and hate is gone. I am humiliated. Hurt by my own brutality. Jonah's daughter after all.

And that's when we hear the deep rumble of something moving over the entrance door to the cavern. Voices drift through the opening as the door is moved out of place one last time.

Scotty has found us. And he's brought the islanders with him.

42

Before I can stop him, Jonah bounds to the window. He wraps the climbing rope around one wrist and climbs onto the ledge, pushing himself outside. With a few strong pull-ups, he'll be able to climb to the top and maybe escape.

Marlie runs toward him. "Jonah," she whispers, hardly able to speak. "Just stay here. Please. Stay here and we'll figure out what to do."

Jonah is pitched over the water, hanging off the rope. He turns back and his eyes find mine. He stares down at me, and I stare back to challenge him.

If I have to face what happened, so does he.

Instead of letting out words, I hold my breath. My fist raises between us, but I'm not sure what to do with it.

In his hands:
A fossil
A seedling
An open page with his finger running along the words
A femur bone of a fox
A deck of cards
A glass of milk
A brand new stuffed mouse
And once
         my hand.

Only Jonah was real.

Jonah was always there. He was the one I listened to, who I did my chores for, who I ate dinners with. Who I'd been a baby with, a young child with. Who had done mindful things for me. Who had taken care of me. Or else I would have died.

Somehow, Jonah saved me.

≫

My fist opens and the fingers stretch out. Maybe: *Come back*. Maybe: *Goodbye*.

But Jonah's eyes don't really look at me. They stare in concentration, like he's reading a textbook. Yes, I'm sure he's making something up to see.

His pupils become tight holes, a drain closing off, and he reaches along the rope. All around me there's the roaring sound of a gasp as I pull in my breath. Then Jonah's body arches very far back and I hear myself yelling and he flings his hands out in a line, one of so many lines that he is becoming, arms lined outward, legs lined downward, body lined between, neck line stretching, all lines crisscrossing and spreading and flying backward over the water, and still he looks through me, his face bright and brighter as he falls, his eyes gaping, no sound coming from his mouth, but only my scream filling the hollow of cavern and cliff and ocean around us.

43

Scotty leans his head against the window while he drives. His face is pale, his expression knotted. Marlie is crying, and the car is crunching over years-old gravel. It's a clear night. I can smell spring.

The knapsack with the baby — Aidie, or Lindsay or Leah — is safe, resting on my lap.

A line of cars follows behind us. Headlights dot the bushes that edge the road. Like a star I might grab. The star splits, then multiplies. Now it's a constellation. Now it's a galaxy.

After a long while, Scotty's voice drifts through the cab, thick with tears. "I am so sorry."

I turn to look at him. "We can't know everything."

He will always be my friend.

❧

Because everyone has heard what happened, they leave me to my silence. Doris doesn't force toast and jam on me. She doesn't make me drink the glass of milk. She offers her own bed for me to share, but then shows us to her spare room when I take Marlie's hand and lean my head against her arm.

They tell me that Peg is getting better. That she's in a hospital in Moncton and that she can't wait to see me.

I don't sleep much that night, but watch through the window as the stars wind up. When Cassiopeia is almost out of sight, Marlie's voice whispers in my ear. "Did you say you went to see your family in Beachport?"

I lie with my back to her. Her arm is over me.

"And they didn't take you in? They sent you back here?"

The blanket isn't enough to keep me warm. Neither is Marlie's body curled around me. I don't let myself shiver. The shiver is deep inside me, forced into the bowl of my stomach.

Even though I don't wish it, my mouth opens. All the things that happened to me tumble out. Running, hiding, Jonah's rage, his pursuit. My mother, my family, my abandoned home. Aidie and Adria, two sisters I can't ever keep. Danny and Connor, two brothers drowning in a river for me. My heart breaking over and over, so many times it's just crumbs in my chest.

When the words stop, Marlie lifts herself up and offers quiet, soothing reassurances. Then she says with such tenderness it hurts me to hear it, "If you were stolen from your parents, Gemma, you need to be reunited with them. It will be the most important thing in their lives to find you."

I can't believe her. It's just a crayoned picture of goodness.

"Maybe they had to give up on that possibility. But I promise you, they never wanted to. That's a thing that's forced on people. You never make a better life. You maybe — *maybe* — try to make peace with it."

People move on. They turn into who they need to be.

"Gemma, there are so few things I can say with real certainty, but this is one of them: your parents want — with all their hearts — to know you."

She puts her hand on my arm and holds it. "When we get up tomorrow morning, you have to promise you'll let us tell your real family that you're here."

I just want to sleep forever.

"Promise me. Please."

I stare out the window. *She is right, she is right.* Maybe she is right.

44

The ferry crosses the water fast enough to bundle me in the spring wind. I stand at the bow, wrapped in a quilt Peg told Doris to give me. It's Peg's most special quilt, edged in lace.

Marlie has her arms around me. Behind us, the rest of the islanders accompany us to the mainland. They say they want to be with me as long as possible. Doris has dozens of Thermoses of hot chocolate and coffee and she walks up and down the ferry's hold pouring out steaming cups. Scotty checks with everyone to make sure they're comfortable and secure, every five minutes checking in with me. He told me that Dr. Thomas is driving Peg back from the hospital in Moncton and that she'll meet us on the mainland.

In the vehicles filling the hold, doctors and nurses and police officers and officers from the RCMP and Victim Services watch us but also give me privacy. For almost a week, they came and observed me. They ran tests to make sure I truly belong to the Birkshires. They asked me question after question. They brought news of Connor and Danny — two boys pulled from a car in a river and now recovering in hospital. Something to make a person hopeful.

My real family is waiting three hundred miles away at the border so Immigration can finalize my papers. Until everything is sorted, I'm a "ward of the court," belonging to no one.

Marlie offered to go with me to Beachport and stay until I felt safe. But I said no, and she said she understood.

I slowly untangle myself from her arms and lean against the bow of the ferry. My hands spread along the rail. Peg's yellow quilt spreads with them like wings.

I might never see Scotty or Peg or Doris or Marlie or any of them again. I am never going to drive the road from Keele's Landing again. I am never going to explore the Rock Pit or climb the lighthouse. I am never going home again.

And now I am going home.

I will meet her. My mother. And I will meet my real father. And there's a little brother, Derek, who might even be interested in superheroes.

The man who watched me grow up is gone. And so is Adria. And that can't ever be changed. Aidie is gone, and she is always inside me.

I guess I'll be Leah. In the newspapers, she's the twin on the left.

Acknowledgements

First of all, I acknowledge that there are some areas of poetic license in this story. For example, the viability of certain forged documents and crossing certain borders, etc. I thank you for bearing with me. I thank you for reading.

The poem Tank recites is from Walt Whitman's *Song of Myself*.

A huge thank you to the literary team at The Rights Factory, especially my beloved agent Sam Hiyate and editor-at-large Diane Terrana. Without their astute insight and guidance, fierce dedication, and unflagging support, this book wouldn't be here. Every writer should be so lucky. Thanks to everyone at Cormorant/DCB: Marc Côté for being a publishing lighthouse, Bryan Jay Ibeas for his tireless attention, Tannice Goddard for an interior design that surprised and delighted me, and Andrea Waters for her elegant precision. Special thanks to my publisher Barry Jowett for believing from the start, for his warmth and gentle humor along the way, and for guiding me to bring the story to the next level.

Incredulous gratitude to Stefanie Ayoub for this brilliant, nuanced cover design.

Thanks to my readers for their invaluable feedback (there may be some missing from this list, and I thank you too): Amy Ayoub, John Batchelor, Daniel Clay, Michael Fahey, Angela Gei, Genrys Goodchild, Annemarie Kearney, Sherrie Lally, Lori Landau, Cheryl

MacInnis, Colin Mochrie, and Annette Redican, and for above-and-beyond, Hollye Dexter and Gae Polisner.

To my cherished friends, please know you have been indispensible reinforcements and cheerleaders. Every one of you. Special mention to my BabyFesters, Briar Boake, Kate Ashby and the Broads, and the WBBC.

Immense gratitude for my necessary angels, Alex Appel, Josée Caron, and Lori Landau. And for the most amazing writing partners, readers, and soul sisters a person could ask for, Vickie Lavoie and Deb McGrath.

Thanks for guidance re science, psychology, trains, and rock climbing. Respectively: Rhiannon Batchelor, Ewa and Peter Kasinski, Petra Breiner, Steve Bokyo, and Michèle Duquet. Any mistakes or missteps (intentional/unintentional) are mine.

Thank you to my parents and sisters for reading and offering enthusiastic feedback, and for their unconditional love: Dieter Radecki, Brigitte Radecki, Nicole Radecki, Catrina von Radecki.

Words cannot express my gratitude for the best and truest of friends, Charlotte Sheasby-Coleman. Without her tireless encouragement, endless readings of drafts, inspired comments and advice, and regular porch visits, Gemma would be stuck on some little island in my imagination.

And thank you to my most precious circles of light. Always there, always curious, questioning, striving, celebrating, rejoicing, giving, loving: my husband, my rock, Philippe Ayoub, and my magnificent daughters Stefanie and Michele.

About the Author

Before transitioning to writing, Barbara Radecki was an actor with many film and television credits, including the voice of Sailor Neptune on the iconic Sailor Moon series. She has several screenplays in development. Born in Vancouver and now based in Toronto, *The Darkhouse* is her debut novel.